Jasper R Monroe

Dramas and Miscellaneous Poems

Jasper R Monroe

Dramas and Miscellaneous Poems

ISBN/EAN: 9783337335199

Printed in Europe, USA, Canada, Australia, Japan

Cover: Foto ©Andreas Hilbeck / pixelio.de

More available books at **www.hansebooks.com**

DRAMAS

AND

MISCELLANEOUS POEMS.

By DR. J. R. MONROE.

INCLUDING

WILL COBBETT'S VISION, OR, THE DEVIL AND TOM PAINE;

ARGO AND IRENE; MALACHI AND MIRANDA;

FATE OF FATAH; ETC. ETC.

CHICAGO:
KNIGHT & LEONARD, PRINTERS.
1875.

PREFACE.

More with the view of rescuing, for his own and the satisfaction of a few partial friends, a portion of the writer's scraps from the chaos of publications and manuscripts in which they are scattered, than with any expectation that they will be sought or read, are they embodied in this volume.

CONTENTS.

DRAMAS AND MISCELLANEOUS POEMS.

INTRODUCTORY AND APOLOGETIC.

I'M almost tempted to become a poet,
  Eschewing pills and powders, lint and lotion;
I've store of verse, and straightway would bestow it,
  Where it will do most good — (insane emotion;)
I think I may be mad — I almost know it;
  Unstable is my mind as is the ocean;
Ambitious longings surge my cerebrum,
And here I stand expecting fame to come.

A fellow must be in this sort of fix
  Ere he can vomit forth poetic fires;
And common sense is mighty hard to mix
  With moulten lava that your bard respires;
He builds his castles without stones or bricks;
  With gorgeous battlements and golden spires;
And peoples them with creatures of his mind,
With whom he moves much more than with his kind

He is quite harmless; — worse than he have won
  (With zigzag verses, lain like a worm fence,
Woven on gates and on wheelbarrows spun,
  Creaking and rasping, without mood or tense,)
The world's applause. See what Bret Harte has done,
  With lines six inches long. He can dispense
With all except the yard-stick and italic, —
No rolling eye nor surging encephalic.

And the breech-clouted songster of the ledges,
  The whilom Modoc wanderer of Nevada,
Who made to Indian maidens burning pledges,
  And stood to scores of papooses as "daddy;"
While skulking in the sage brush and the sedges; —
  He too is famous, but so like a foot-pad he
Waylaid the world and gave it such a shock
As fixed its eyeballs on this wild Modoc;

And frightened it into some faint applause
  Of the weird warblings of this wampum bard,
This scalp-dance bigamist of ugly squaws,
  Who wrote sweet verses, but being hugged too hard,
In dusky arms and in the grizzly s paws,
  Vamoosed the ranche, still rhyming by the yard;
We have no gentler Modoc, or squaw-killer,
Nor milder mangler of our tongue than Miller.

And funny writers have we by the hundred;
  Worse too, 'tis feared this tribe's increasing daily;
The public have looked on and wept and wondered
  At the dread jokes of the bombastic Bailey;
O. C. K.'s mackerel troops so bled and blundered,
  That nations roared; poor Artemus joked gaily;
But chief amongst the mirth-provoking train
Stood the stove steamboat stevedore Mark Twain,

Until the mournful hero of Detroit,
  Blown higher than Mark T., struck for the crown;
The steamboats yield both wits, but that exploit —
  Caucasian upward, Ethiopian down —
Pitched Lewis in the arena with the adroit
  And solemn wits — cast suddenly in, chief clown —
Sent upward more absurdly and some quicker
Than was Mark Twain by the Bogardus kicker.

Your wit, unlike your bard, needs common sense,
  Although success is possible without it;
With wit itself some witty men dispense;
  (Read the Danbury Nutmeg if you doubt it;)
I wish the wits would wind up and go hence;
  But then I don't care very much about it;
For laughter lights the heart — care oft hath broke it —
So here's to laughter and whoe'er provoke it.

But for the poets I am here to plead;
  I want the world to note this injured class;
Down at the heel, and always sore in need
  Of everything on earth except 'tis gas;
They've elfins, fairies, and young fawns to feed,
  And wild does grazing on the prairie grass;
And butterflies to chase and doves to yoke;
And some are drunk, or else deadbeats, or broke

And cross'd in love — there never yet was one
  Worth sixty cents until he was thus crossed,
And torn all up with jealousies, or run
  Entirely crazy by some fair one lost;
His young hopes ended just where they begun;
  Like a young bean cut down by cruel frost,
Or like a pig stuck in a garden fence,
That squeals for life till liberated thence.

And half the world can't understand their use,
  The other half think them mere butterflies;
And critics subject them to fierce abuse,
  So no one can get justice till he dies;
And then the world, ere that blind and obtuse,
  Wakes up, like some one taken by surprise,
And straightway falls to worshiping the dead,
And praising madrigals before unread.

The music of the soul is still the same,
  And so is poesy in all the ages;
And genius comes through the baptismal flame
  Flashed forth from heaven. Time hath its stops and stages,

And swoops up generations;—love can claim
  Exemption from his ravages and rages;
Springing from the eternal fount of light,
It is the mainspring of the Almighty's might.

And so it is the dear old music over,
  When the true poet doth the lyre attune,
He strikes the chords struck by the earlier lover;
  He seeks his lady-love midst flowers in June;
He ranges fields gleaned oft by tuneful rover;
  He rides the sunbeams; he explores the moon;
He reads the stars and ranges through the spheres,
Like his ancestors for six thousand years.

And far back in the ages dim, remote,
  The untutored poet, by love's passion fired,
In rude and mystic hieroglyphics wrote
  The same hot story that is now inspired,
When I look in my lady's eyes and gloat
  Upon the precious treasure thus acquired,
And never cease to express my glad surprise
That the world's wealth is garnered in her eyes.

Love hath one language, poetry one tongue,
  And souls are girt with telegraphic wires,
O'er which intelligence is nimbly flung
  Of burning passions, or of fond desires;
And answering messages are quickly brung,
  Eyes being the mediums of transmitted fires;
So love is thus enabled to converse
In its own tongue throughout the universe.

But I am writing to apologize
  For writing what I've written, or may write;
But like a half-tamed bird the subject flies,
  When I reach forth to grasp it. I am quite
Put out by this. I want to state the whys
  And wherefores that I thus, in sorry plight,
Bring to the assayist ore, and would be told
Whether 'tis oroide or really gold.

A lucky miner sometimes in a lode,
  Worked and abandoned by an earlier miner,
Finds glittering treasure in some cranny stowed;
  And so a poet, or a penny-a-liner,
May write a lucky essay or an ode,
  On a worn subject, that, if scarcely finer
Than former pannings out, may be no lesser,
And pass as current as a predecessor.

But here's a thought that very nearly smothers
  My rhyming aspirations altogether;
My poetry perhaps may be another's,
  Found in some volume bound in gilded leather;
These very lines may be some rhyming brother's!
  How in the deuce will I discover whether
They were not written long ere I was born
Thus putting me to trouble and to scorn!

Still I say not what I sat out to say;
　I'm like a palsied man, whose shaky finger
Points all the time in the contrary way
　To that he wills it. That is why I linger,
And eke this Introductory out all day;
　And here my muse flops down, (this rhyme has winged her!)
I wish that Webster had made some provision
To save a run-out rhymster from derision.

But as I said, I'm trying to say — and now
　I think I see a way to bring it out;
My muse reminds me of a breachy cow,
　That leaps in every pasture on her route;
(And here I've lost the thread again somehow;)
　The reader well may ask what I'm about;
I'm trying to tell him why I've written more
On subjects written threadbare heretofore.

The reason is — I really don't know what;
　Indeed I don't believe I have one after all;
And since I come to think of it, I've got
　Just where I think the curtain ought to fall;
But I'll run out this stanza on the spot,
　Or hover o'er old Webster like a pall;
I don't believe I've said what I intended,
But rather think the Introductory ended.

WILL. COBBETT'S VISION;

OR,

THE DEVIL AND TOM PAINE.

[It may be well to state that Cobbett's Vision was written by a boy in his teens. It was composed in Louisville, Ky., at a time when religious discussion ran high in public debates and in leading religious journals. These made an impression upon the mind of the writer that resulted in the composition that follows. Love for the cherished memories and impressions of boyhood's brief spring-time forbids any attempt to improve it, or to apologize for its imperfections.]

THERE is a lake of lurid fire
　Lighted by God's revengeful ire,
Wherein all souls are cast that stray
From virtue during life's brief day.
This lake of fire by God conceived,
Is fixed (or so it is believed)
Far down beneath — so far below
That none except the damned shall know
Its dreadful depth ; nor can the mind,
With fancy's pinion unconfined,
Conceive so deep, so wide a den
As this designed for sinful men.

Mind is immortal — matter dies —
The limbs we have — the face — the eyes —
Must perish, vanish, fail, die, rot;
But we have that which dieth not.
It was in the Creator's plan
To put one particle in man —
One attribute derived from Him —
That death cannot despoil nor dim.
And though some three-score years and ten
The mortal part of mortal men
May own — may hold this quenchless spark,
In some so bright, in some so dark —
Soul — intellect — thought — reason — mind —
Immured in matter — not confined;
Something that, when the brain is gone
Which it did animate, lives on.
This is the immortal part of man,
And let him value it who can;
Because on this side of the tomb
Is fixed its everlasting doom;
As evil and good — inviting dishes —
Are open, and each takes which he wishes.
You choose the good — then to the skies
Your soul goes when your body dies·
But if you make rash choice of evil,
Down goes your soul straight to the Devil—
The Devil, the sooty fiend that rules
The lake of flame that never cools.
But even the existence of this pit
Some folks deny, and so 'tis fit
To give what proof we have of it.
So, reader, let me lead you through
    The lake where howling devils dwell,
Unfolding scenes as strange as true,
    That happened some years ago in hell.
This tale, confided to my care,
I ought to keep, but it is fair
To think the millions now alive,
    Who hold through tickets to that den,
Would like to hear how that hot hive
    Of devils do who once were men,
And it may help confound the few
    Who swear there is no future pain.
Rash skeptics! in this vision view
    The horrors which you spurn in vain!
And then this vision may assist
    The honest, earnest partialist;
His creed may find, by quoting it,
Strong proofs not found in Holy Writ;
For when hell's actual scenes we view,
Who can dispute or doubt them? — you?
There seems a deal of revelry,
Of frantic mirth and fiendish glee,
In this hot and sulphurous place,
When any soul which, lost to grace,
Makes its arrival at the gates,
And cowers before its future mates.

That misery seeks to be allied
To misery scarcely is denied;
And hence there is a grand revival
In hell on every fresh arrival.
And these are constant — every minute
The gates swing open — crowds rush in it.
Pell-mell they come — a ghastly crew,
Looking like politicians do,
Who, after the election's carried,
    Rush to the capital with woeful faces,
Lest their petitions will be parried,
    And others get the spoils and places.
But they who throng the Devil's gate,
    Unlike the politicians here,
Find that they never come too late
    To gain the administration's ear.
If Cobbett's vision should be true,
    It proves that God, provoked to wrath,
Made man and put him here, yet knew
    He would pursue a certain path —
A path that leads him without fail
Where devils gnash the teeth and wail.
This path God aimed that man should tread
    For when he formed the human heart,
He formed it so it could be led
    From love and holiness apart.
God doubtless did possess the might
    To form his creatures to rebel.
Who made the heavens, the day and night,
    Had he not power to make a hell?
Some (whose belief's of little worth)
Hold still that hell is in the earth,
And that, though wickedness is rife,
'Tis mostly punished in this life;
A burning hell doth ever rest
In every erring mortal's breast.
Without our knowledge, God doth give
A soul that must forever live.
We find this never-dying breath
    Inhabiting a house of clay;
'Tis not for us to say when death
    Will come and call the soul away.
Our souls were made to follow sin,
A hell made to torment us in,
Unless, 'tis said, we do atone.
    What is atonement? — who can tell?
Is it the hypocrite's deep groan,
    Prompted by craven fears of hell?
Think God did foreordain at first,
That certain souls should be accursed,
While certain others should be blest,
And leave our doom to chance at best?
Thou fond young wife, think thou couldst be
Happy in heaven if thou couldst see
Thy partner dear in pain below? —
Thou tender mother, couldst thou go
And dwell in glory in the skies
While thou couldst hear the wailing cries

Of husband, daughter, and of son?—
Wouldst thou be happy?—or undone?
This hell-fire creed is held full dear—
This faith that worships God through fear;
And proof of it would glad the mind
    Of him who shouts in solemn glee
That all the sinful of mankind
    Will writhe in hell eternally.
                For hell is waiting
                (So they are stating)
                And God is fating
                    Poor souls below;
                So all the evil
                In hell shall revel.
                They seem to know,
                As death does mow,
                Three fourths do go
                    Down to the Devil
                And endless woe!
                    But to relieve us
                They kindly say,
                    God will receive us
                If we will pray—
                Spend night and day
                In sad beseeching—
                In screams and screeching
                (Such is their teaching)
                While here we dwell;
                    Still time is winging,
                    And hourly bringing
                Sad tales that tell
                Some sinner's fell;
                His funeral knell
                    In earth is ringing
                While he's in hell!
                Thus God doth make us
                But to forsake us—
                Lets Satan take us.
                Still they rely
                    Upon a treasure
                    That God doth measure
                To some who die;
                'Tis said they fly
                Straight to the sky,
                    To bask in pleasure
                    With God on high.
But these bad rhymes will scarce convince
The man who reading them doth wince.
The man who knows that you are wrong,
Will not be satisfied with song;
Although you rhyme till doom shall crack,
He'll have at you, and argue back.
Hence it is futile for the muse
To praise one creed—one to abuse;
Though creeds are bad and men are worse,
Neither is vanquished by bad verse.
Who could dig out, with pick or pen,
The absurdities sealed up in men?

Therefore my muse, berhyming many,
Is not the advocate of any;
Speaks not in spirit of derision,
But comes to chronicle a vision.
This much is merely prefatory,
So now have done, and to my story.

A THUNDER-STORM — A BIG SPREE.

It was a sultry summer day,
The sun had shed his latest ray,
Which hung upon the western sky,
As if unwilling yet to die,
But smiled at twilight's mystic frown,
Till darkness flung her mantle down,
And nature for a moment seemed
To lie like one who sweetly dreamed —
In that half state 'twixt sleep and wake,
Whence dreams their gorgeous liveries take,
And fancy decks a little sphere,   .
With beings indistinct though dear.
Just as the twilight closed its eyes,
    While stillness walked upon the air,
Some threatening clouds began to rise,
    Like robbers from a hidden lair.
Above the horizon they crept
    In black and terrible array,
To fright the earth, that sweetly slept,
    With battle's uproar and dismay.
The storm-fiend quickly massed his force:
The winds came forth — the thunders hoarse,
With lightning's quick, terrific flash
To add more horrors to each crash.
Then all the elements together,
That go to make outrageous weather,
United their malignant powers
To make the worst of thunder-showers.
The night from dark to blackness grew;
The winds with all their fury blew;
While sheets of mingled rain and hail
    In torrents from the clouds were poured.
Still fiercer grew the furious gale,
    And louder still the thunders roared,
It was upon this luckless night
    That Cobbett, from his home belated,
Refused to wait for morning's light
    Or till the furious storm abated.
He, with some precious friends, had been
    The whole of the preceding day
Carousing at a country inn,
    And now a jovial set were they.
But Will., resolving to retire,
Could not be baulked by flood nor fire;
And though the storm was waxing stronger,
His friends could not detain him longer;
So with a last regretful glass,
They stood aside to let him pass.

Emerging from his cozy inn,
One minute wet him to the skin;
Nor was he two yards from the door,
Till he was crawling on all-four!
But rising midst the pelting rain,
He onward trudged, with heated brain;
Caring no more for slush and mud
Than surgeons care for flesh and blood.
Already had he got as wet
As it was possible to get.
With hailstones bouncing from his pate,
And swearing like a reprobate,
He tugged ahead, but inly swore
He wished he had not left the door.
And ere he was ten minutes out,
He half resolved to face about.
But now our hero did not know
Which way he came, nor which to go.
Still on he groped, but vainly groped,
And hoped, and just as vainly hoped,
To find some hut or humble shed,
To shield him till the storm had fled,
Pelted with rain — wet through and through —
Deafened with thunder — blinded, too,
With lightning's fitful, forked flashes,
Singeing, he thought, his very lashes!
Blown up and down and round about,
He felt his courage oozing out.
At length it left him, like his hat:
The winds had rushed away with that.
Still on our hero madly strode,
To find a shelter or a road,
Cutting more antics than a clown
In scrambling up and tumbling down;
'Twas wormwood in his bitter cup,
This tumbling down and scrambling up.
At length he stumbled in a road
  He thought he had not trod before:
Here, too, must be some one's abode;
  He groped and found an open door.
He gladly entered in, although
  He thought 'twas but a cattle shed,
By whom possessed he did not know,
  And did not care: his giddy head
Was in a whirl of thick confusion;
  And as he stumbled in the sty,
A flock of sheep at this intrusion,
  Went scampering out with bleating cry.
The first merino, as it passed,
  Upset our hero in its flight;
A hundred more rushed out so fast,
  That he was trampled breathless quite.
He roared with pain, while every sheep,
  As it went bleating, bounding out,
Contrived to take a flying leap
  From prostrate Cobbett's bleeding snout.
Poor Cobbett thought the dreadful hour
  Of death and doom was close at hand;

But cursed the sheep while he had power,
　　And words and breath at his command.
The sheep were gone — the last one's feet
Had rasped our hero's face complete.
His senses, like the sheep had fled,
And there, clear drunk, and worse than dead,
With many a deep and bleeding wound,
He lay upon the chilly ground.
There let him rest while we repair
　　Unto his comrades in the hall —
Wine, songs and jests were passing there.
　　While Will. was quite forgot by all.

THE THIEF.

Mine host was in his chair asleep,
　　When suddenly a crash without,
Caused him to start —"My sheep! my sheep!
　　Some thieves are stealing them no doubt!
There cannot pass a night like this,
　　No matter be it hot or cold,
But in the morning I must miss
　　A good fat wether from my fold.
Come, boys, let us surround the pen,
And if we take those odious men,
You shall have drink and lodging free,
　　And aught beside that you demand;
I'd give one hundred pounds to see
　　Those villains on the scaffold stand."
As quick as thought away they flew,
　　Though still the rain in torrents fell —
The night still dark and dismal too,
　　As a convicted murderer's cell.
The wind in fitful gusts did blow.
　　Now shrieking shrilly in the trees,
Now o'er the chimneys moaning low,
　　Now wailing o'er the distant seas.
Our friends advanced with cautious tread,
And softly crept about the shed.
But save the wind's inclement sigh,
　　No sound fell on the listening ear;
No object met the straining eye.
　　"If robbers caused the rumpus here,
They with their booty must have fled;
Or are they lurking in the shed?
Those rogues are very sly and bold."
Our host resolved to search the fold,
And as he groped to find the door,
　　He pitched headforemost o'er the sill—
One low, deep-muttered curse — no more—
　　Was uttered by our hero *Will.*
Now if our worthy host had fell
　　Upon a tigress in her cave,
He'd not have given a wilder yell,
　　Nor fiercer bound than now he gave.
He started like a frightened deer,
　　Though he was an unwieldy sot—

"Murder! — O, murder! — murder! — here!"
He suddenly thought a fearful plot
Was laid to take his precious life;
He almost felt the assassin's knife
Between his ribs.—He flew about —
"O Lord! if he were only out!"
He had received a nameless note,
Some time before, which said his throat
Should soon be cut from ear to ear —
He knew 'twas the assassin here
He felt that he deserved the blow:
For he had sold the fiery waters
Which caused the bitter tears to flow
From suffering mothers, sons and daughters.
Yes, he had lived and thrived for years
Upon the want, disgrace and tears
Of many a family, that would be
Better and happier far than he,
Were it not for the accursed cup
That swallowed all their substance up.
Reflecting thus he ceased to bawl,
But softly crept around the wall,
Hoping that if the door were found
Ere he received the fatal wound,
He yet might, by a desperate run,
Escape a death by gash or gun.
His friends, he felt, had, in affright,
Sought safety in ignoble flight.
But little had those revelers thought
To leave their host and run away;
They had with desperate valor sought
To gain admittance to the fray.
One of the braves had wisely been
Dispatched to bring a lantern out.
The cry of murder ceased within —
Their hairs stood up with dread and doubt —
When suddenly a flying form
Went rushing past.—"Was it the thief?"
His tramp was heard above the storm —
The chase was sudden, bold and brief.
The fugitive was quickly nabbed,
For he was anything but fleet,
And three or four stout fellows grabbed
And dragged the villain through the street.
While he was mute from fright or pain,
They dragged him roughly through the rain.
His nose was sliding o'er the mud,
And tinging it with valiant blood.
They quickly dragged him to the house
Where they had held their late carouse.
But when they brought him to the light,
Why start they back with dumb affright?—
If each had seen his mother's ghost,
He'd not have shrunk in more dismay
Than each man did to see his *host*
Quite lifeless on the hearth-rug lay.
Here was, indeed, a pretty fix!
The maids went off in hysterics —

The hostess in a double swoon —
" If we do not relieve them soon,
The ladies will have ceased to kick.
Bring water — camphor — hartshorn — quick! "
A quart of water suddenly thrown
    On each, for better or for worse,
Brought forth from each a shriek, a groan,
    A kick, a half-suppressed curse.
Their mouths were then filled full of salt,
    Which had a wonderful effect —
It caused them suddenly to vault
    Upon their feet, and to eject
The offensive dose with sputtering spits;
When each fair one was cured of fits.
Meantime our host had come around,
And finding he was safe and sound —
O'erjoyed at his escape from danger —
From brutal murder and the manger —
Fancied, with undisguised delight,
Himself the hero of the night;
And though as stingy as a flint,
He sat out liquor without stint;
And seated with his friends at table,
    Taking a glass of brandy first,
His fearful battle in the stable,
    With full particulars, he rehearsed.

THE LANDLORD'S BATTLE.

He said that there were half a dozen or more,
Who grappled with him at the sheep-fold door,
He struck out at random — though often he missed,
Yet he had knocked some of them down with his fist.
At last he was seized by the hair of the head,
And dragged by these murderers into the shed;
And here he was buffeted round in the straw
Till he got a fair lick at a daring outlaw.
The shock of the blow sent them both to the ground —
One fell by the blow — one by its rebound.
A half-muttered curse at his horrible luck,
Was all that he heard from the one that he struck.
In short, he encountered the villains no more;
But as he retired by the sheep-fold door,
He pitched over one of the rogues as he lay
Where he was knocked down in the open door-way.
He thought that the blow must have killed him outright;
That his comrades in terror had taken to flight.
Such is the account of the battle as told
To his horror-struck friends by their landlord bold.

THE MISTAKE.

Meantime the bottle flew about,
    Re-animating every one,
Till they resolved to sally out
    And see what mischief had been done.

Guns, pistols, axes, hoes and spades
  Were quickly mustered for the fray;
The hostess, with her waiting maids,
  With torch and lantern led the way.
Just as they issued forth the blast;
  As armies on the battle-field,
Sum all their fury for a last
  Terrific charge before they yield;
Even thus the warring elements
  Did in a brief, concluding shower;
Terrific, fearful and intense;
  Concentrate their remaining power.
'Twas past: The moon with silvery ray,
  Looked softly down on hill and vale,
Where late the pall of darkness lay,
  And roared the wild and furious gale;
Like rays of sunshine suddenly sent
  Upon the reeking, smoking plain,
Where the fierce war-god just has spent
  His strength in dealing death and pain;
Just as the last fierce charge is o'er,
  And silent is the cannon's roar,
And all is dark and doubt beneath
  The smoke that rising, doth reveal
The carnage and the work of death
  Wrought by the foemen's shot and steel,
No cloud could now be seen above,
  In all the arched and pure expanse;
And all was placid as the love
  For which the mateless turtle pants;
While many a bright and glittering star
Was twinkling softly from afar,
The nightingale's delicious note
Was ringing in the woods remote:
And merrily on yonder hill
Broke forth the noisy whippowil,
Our friends led by the petticoats,
  Approached the scene of recent strife,
But cautiously, for fear their throats
  Might suddenly feel the assassin's knife.
They halted opposite the door,
  And raised their torches in the air;
When, sure enough, one man or more
  Was stretched apparently lifeless there.
What should they do? — could he be dead?—
Were others lurking in the shed?
He was not dead — the hostess swore
She heard the monstrous villain snore!
He was prepared for bloody work —
Our host could plainly see a dirk
Held in his fist with savage clutch —
The women plainly saw as much.
'Twas now resolved to fire at him,
  For sorely was our host afraid
There was on foot some stratagem
  To draw them into ambuscade.
The law would justify the act —
No mortal could dispute the fact.

"Now," said our host, "let every one,
Who has a pistol or a gun,
Fire, and together, at the foe,
And then with axe and spade and hoe,
Rush on and break the murderer's head,
And beat him till we're sure he's dead!"
After this brief and bold address,
Each aimed as well as he could guess;
A pause ensued — each heart beat quick —
"Fire!" cried our host — click — click — tchu — click!
None killed — they had not touched the man.
One had no priming in the pan;
Another one had lost the flint —
Besides there was no powder in't —
'Twas loaded only with a ball —
One musket was not charged at all;
Some had been primed, but there had been
Nor shot nor powder put within.
"Charge!" cried our host, "with pick and spade!
Charge on the villains! — who's afraid!
We're not the men to turn our backs!" —
Commanding thus he seized an axe —
"We may be killed, but damn the odds!" —
    They charged with firm resolve to kill —
The axe was raised — "Hold! — by the gods,
    'Tis our convenient comrade *Will !*
He's crawled in here to take a nap,
Thus nearly causing a mishap."
            "His eyes are dim;
            You've murdered him,
        You vender of bad wine!
            You rogue, 'tis clear
            That many a year
        In prison you must pine!"
            "O," cried our host,
            "Though I did boast,
        I swear most solemnly
            'Twas all in fun,
            I struck no one,
        And no one struck at me.
            I think that it
            Must be a fit,
        Most likely epilepsy,
            Brought on perhaps,
            By thunder claps,
        And being wet and tipsy."
            "He's wet and muddy,
            His face is bloody;
        Yet still he moves, he lives —
            Jim! Jack! and Dick!
            Run boys! — be quick!
        And bring restoratives."
            A glass of gin
            Turned suddenly in
        His stomach by a waiter,
            Quick brought him to
            So that he knew
        And struck the perpetrator.

Our hero was borne by his friends from the shed;
  They examined his bruises, and dressed every wound;
And soon he was snugly reposing in bed,
  His nose giving notice of slumbers profound.

THE VISION — THE ANGEL.

As soon as sleep had closed our hero's eyes
He heard a voice commanding him to rise.
The voice was strange — unearthly — with affright
He started up, when lo! a dazzling light,
Shone through his room —'twas not the light of day —
Daylight were darkness to its vivid ray.
Our hero gazed around with timid eye,
But not a human form could he descry.
Close by his bed the voice appeared to be: —
"Arise! thou skeptic! rise and follow me!
I am commanded to conduct thee hence —
A righteous judgment on thy past offense.
I am an angel from the realms on high,
And long, though viewless to thine earthly eye,
Have I watched o'er thy guilty, erring head,
And marked with weeping eye thy downward tread.
Thy days are numbered in this sinful world;
Soon thou wilt soar above or else be hurled
Down to that hell where torments never end,—
Down to that hell which thou durst to contend
Hath no existence. It remains to see,
After the horrors I disclose to thee,
And thou returnest to thine house of clay,
If thou wilt by repentance wash away
Thy many sins; or if thou still wilt run
Thy race of wickedness long since begun.
Since time began there never yet hath been
A mortal taken from this world of sin,
And shown the mysteries beyond the grave,
And then sent back to warn mankind to save
Their souls from hell; and further to remain
A living witness of eternal pain.
Such is thy lot — it is ordained that thou
Shalt see this lake of fire, and then avow
The fearful fact unto thy fellow-men,
When thou return'st unto the earth again.
Thou shalt return, and though thy days are few,
Life will be spared until thou makest a true
And faithful record of what thou shalt see,
And seek'st for mercy if't seem meet to thee."
Our hero felt a pang shoot through his heart,
As if his soul were struggling to depart;
A sense of suffocation in his throat,
While indistinctly objects seemed to float
In the dark distance — yet a struggle more —
'Twas past — the soul was free, and hovering o'er
The silent breast where it had long been pent;
The pulseless, lifeless corse which just was rent
By many a pang, ere it would yield the breath
Which was its life, but died not with its death.

With snowy robes and wings like angels wear,
Our hero's spirit floated in the air;
The holy angel hovering near was seen,
Fair as a lovely virgin of sixteen.
In fact, it was a young and lovely girl,
With soft blue eyes and many a wavy curl
Divinely floating o'er her cheek of rose—
Her flushing lips but faintly did disclose
The pearly teeth that filled her dewy mouth—
Her breath was sweet as incense from the south.
Now did this lovely angel mount the sky,
Commanding Will. to follow her on high.
Away they soared above on heavenly wings,
Leaving the earth with all its earthly things.
Nothing was hid from Will.'s unfettered soul;
The heavens, the earth, the oceans—all—the whole
Of vast creation opened to the view,
As they were soaring through the ethereal blue.
But now their course was downward, downward still,
Much to the horror of our hero Will.
The climate, too, was getting rather hot;
He groaned in terror, fearing 'twas his lot
To be cast in the pit of endless woe—
A smell of sulphur issued from below.
But now behold, by cords swung in the air,
A writing table and an easy chair.
The angel said with firm, but pitying tone,
"Be seated in the chair—reporter's throne—
Write what thou seest with true and faithful pen,
And print a book upon the Devil's den.
Here, take this pen and ink, and paper too."
These words she spake, and vanished from the view;
And more than this, our hero's wings were gone,
With the white robes which he so late put on.

HELL, AS SEEN BY COBBETT.

Half dead with fright and prompted by despair,
Will. grabbled firmly to his swinging chair;
For look beneath him! what a fearful sight!
There he beheld the realms of endless night,
There hell's hot flames in seething volumes rolled,
Most positively frightful to behold.
As far as Will. could see on every side,
The roaring flames formed a resistless tide,
And horrors on black horrors heap up higher!
Will. saw dark beings walking in the fire!
He thought 'twould take ten thousand men a year
To count the damned ones he saw roasting here.
And he could hear the groans of those beneath,
The weeping, wailing—gnashing of the teeth;
The cries for water for the parched tongue;
The imprecations on the fates which flung
Temptations in the way—and then, for crime,
Doomed souls to roast in fire throughout all time.
Will. clutched his chair and pen with nervous grip;
He feared a slip of pen, but more a slip

From his big chair, whose consequence most dire
Would be a leaden plunge plump in the fire.
With glaring eye-balls and with shaky hand,
He spread his paper on his writing stand.
His knees smote other till the bores did rattle;
And like the bristles on the boar in battle,
His hair stood up;—his teeth had rattled loose;
What wit he had was not for present use;
The blood was boiling that was in his brains,
While all the rest was frozen in his veins;
His joints were locked, his sinews stiff as boards;
His dead tongue as incapable of words
As so much beef; nor liver, melt and gall
Could muster one idea 'mongst them all;
Perhaps no author e'er essayed to write
With worse surroundings or in poorer plight.

THE DEVIL, AS SEEN BY COBBETT.

Amidst the flames Will. saw the Devil stand,
With a red poker in his iron hand,
With which he now and then stirred up the coals
To benefit some late-arrived souls
Will. recognized him by his cloven foot.
Which never could be hid in shoe nor boot;
But saving this he was surprised to see
How plain a monster Satan seemed to be.
But be it known to every Christian nation
That Satan has great powers of imitation,
And can at pleasure put on any shape —
The form of man — of woman — serpent - ape —
Or aught besides that suits his aim or whim;
But his cleft foot is a fixed part of him.
He can take off his horn, his tail, his ears —
Come as a youth, or as if weighed with years;
But his cleft hoof betrays his presence still;
He never hid it, and he never will.
Short, thick and heavy-set he now appeared;
Cross-eyed, humpbacked, bow-legged and lop-eared.
His skin was rough, his great eyes fiery red;
He had a tail like to a quadruped.
A horn like a rhinoceros, and great claws
Like a fell dragon, as he is, and was.
He now stood still, and seemed lost in reflection,
Like candidates just beaten at election.
Thus Cobbett, as it were, saw face to face
The ancient enemy of Adam's race —
The Christian's foe — the father of all lies —
And heard the monster thus soliloquize:

THE DEVIL'S SOLILOQUY,

AS RECORDED ON THE SPOT BY COBBETT.

And now there fell on Cobbett's ear
  A shrill, prolonged, terrific shout;
The poor man started in his chair —
  In fact he almost tumbled out.

This was the Devil in his glee
Arousing from his reverie,
Then did this horrid monster cry,
"Hurra for hell! I do defy —
Almost defy — the power of God:
The best of men my paths have trod;
At least for me they were the best.
Tut! I care nothing for the rest,
So that my followers do contrive,
    While living in the sinful world,
To keep the current crimes alive,
  . And when they die to hell be hurled.
With God for ages did I dwell;
But some of us dared to rebel;
And then he hurled us in the dark.
But we possessed the electric spark: —
Though from his presence we were fated,
We could not be annihilated.
We fallen angels wandered round;
Nor light nor resting-place was found;
Water was all that we could find;
    We flitted on with weary wing;
Damp clouds ahead, and fogs behind,
    And conscience stabbing with its sting.
At last the rest resolved to cry
To our offended God on high;
But I was rash — I would not bow,
Nor ask for mercy even now.
At this the Lord was so displeased
His wrath can never be appeased;
This lake of fire for mine and me
Will burn to all eternity.
But God, in fact, could not revoke
The dread anathema he spoke
When he in fury cast us out,
Although he wished us back, no doubt —
That is, there is no doubt that he
Desired to pardon all but me.
But he could not receive us now —
    The eternal laws of heaven were broken,
And God had registered his vow —
    The dreadful mandate had been spoken.
And yet we wept to see our woe —
Our wandering in the void below.
At last he summoned us on high;
We flew to meet him in the sky.
When, frowning on us, thus he spake:
'I would, but yet I cannot take
You back to heaven — but yet you may
Return, though in a tortuous way.
I'm going to put you in the earth —
To give you a material birth;
And I will fill the world with light,
And if while there you do aright,
Then will I take you to me here,
Though you must suffer many a year.
The clayey temple each will fill,
    Will last you but a little time;

When 'tis worn out you either will
  Return to this unclouded clime,
Or enter in another one,
According to the deeds you've done;
So on till time shall pass away,
You'll pass from house to house of clay,
In case you dare to disobey.
I first shall try but one of you,
And when I see what he will do,
More clayey temples shall be formed,
And by your souls be moved and warmed.
This is the way you must alone —
In this way, and in this alone,
Can you find favor in my sight,
And be restored to realms of light.
While in your tenements of clay,
You will be tempted many a way;
Be watchful and resist it all —
One slip entails an age of thrall.
Error and Truth will each engage,
And struggle for your patronage;
Now you'll love virtue, and now vice —
Each will attend — each will entice;
And you may think them near allied,
Still you will want no law nor guide
To point out as you pass along,
The line dividing right and wrong;
For in each bosom there shall be
An umpire, sleepless as the sea:
Do you a right or a wrong act,
That instant you shall feel the fact.
The body I shall put you in
  Will have strong passions, fierce desires —
Will be disposed to follow sin —
  Will heat you with the hottest fires.
Yield if you please — joy will attend;
And if you like it yield, and spend
The remnant of your time below.
  You have some attributes of mine,
Therefore (I grieve to see you go)
  Do what you may I will combine
With earth's infirmities and care
Some bliss as sweet as angels share.
I hope to see you all return,"
He said, and then addressing me,—
"But you, black Lucifer! I spurn!—
Be gone!—and cursed forever be!"
I felt his words in all their weight,
And shuddered at my fixed fate.
But I have been avenged for all,—
I planned our own and Adam's fall.
So now to carry out the plan
  Which the Almighty had in view
He made a creature — named it MAN —
  Made it in his own image, too.
The plan, as it would seem, was this:
  The earth to be a bower of love;
The fallen here to dwell in bliss,
  Such as they had enjoyed above;

While serving their probation here,
 The penance to be void of pain —
Joy, joy for them in either sphere —
 Joy to return — joy to remain.
For even if they should transgress,
The bliss would be but little less;
At most 'twould but prolong their stay —
They would be happy either way.
I was the only soul alive
With whom the Almighty seemed to strive.
Even in their banishment he blest,
And sought to reinstate the rest.
All that could captivate the eye —
 All sounds that could delight the ear —
Were formed for man by the Most High;
 And then he placed a WOMAN here.
The fallen soul in Adam thought,
 When first he saw this charming flower,
That the relenting gods had brought
 One of the angels to his bower.
Though she was nude, yet still he did
See nothing that he wished were hid;
And loved her not a whit the less
Because she was devoid of dress.
O what a lovely girl was Eve,
 As thus I saw her long ago,
And sought her only to deceive,
 And fit her for her life of woe!
In rapture Adam viewed her charms,
And longed to clasp her in his arms;
But dumb with awe, love and respect,
He could not speak to her direct.
But still he gazed with glad surprise,
While downward turned her timid eyes.
Poor Eve could not hold up her head,
While thus the Lord to Adam said:

THE FORBIDDEN FRUIT.

"This woman is to be your bride;
She'll walk and slumber by your side,
Feast on her beauties with your SIGHT,
But do not touch her day nor night.
Should you so much as touch her hand,
'Twould chain your spirit to this land.
Let her be sacred in your eyes;
Look, love, long, languish — yet be wise.
If you give way to passion's power,
And touch or taste this fragile flower,
You will prolong your sojourn here
For many and many a weary year.
She will be with you night and day,
Till you wear out this frame of clay;
And if you do resist her till
Your body dies, why then you will,
(Your penance paid,) pure and forgiven,
Return at once to me in heaven.

But if you should be led astray,
  Soon as your present body dies,
You'll go in a new house of clay,
  Instead of going to the skies."

THE TEMPTATION — THE FALL,

AS GIVEN BY THE DEVIL HIMSELF.

Straightway I went and tempted Eve,
I found her willing to believe,—
It was not very long, I guess,
Till eager Adam did transgress!
God cursed the earth and all in it,
For Adam's promptness to commit
This horrid sin. Thus was I pleased,
Thus my starved vengeance was appeased;
And thus I saw God's plans frustrated:
Millions of souls were soon created;
But God made this eternal hell
The very hour that Adam fell;
And Prince of Darkness, with dread power
Was I ordained that very hour.
Because his love was turned to wrath,
  In consequence of Adam's fall,
Who failed to tread the narrow path,
  And was so prompt to sin, withal.
The other fallen spirits were
  Called back to heaven without delay,
Because the Almighty did not dare
  Put them in tenements of clay;
For men had sprung so fast from one,
He saw no end to what he'd done.
He wished he had not tried the plan —
Wished he had not created man;
It grieved him very much indeed;
But now he could not well recede.
He made their lives a brief career,
And then confined their spirits here.
It gave him pleasure to condemn,
And damn each sinful rogue of them.
Since Adam's fall not one in ten
Has missed the torments of this den.
God gave me power in hell and earth
To torment all that should have birth.
This dreadful power thus given to me
  I've exercised throughout all time —
I've used all kinds of subtlety
  To fill the earth with fraud and crime.
How many a war have I created,
  Merely to see the warriors slain,
Knowing that most of them were fated,
  To this black pit of brimstone bane!
Oft have I walked the battle-field,
  And urged the insane combatants on
My agency so well concealed,
  That each believed his weapon drawn

For God, for justice and for right;
While, I, sole causer of the fight,
Have laughed to see the red blood spout
From fools who'd naught to fight about.
And when the murderous work was o'er,
And heaps lay smoking in their gore,
Then have I scampered back to hell,
   To welcome the unfettered souls,
And have the villains toasted well
   On beds of seven times heated coals.
Thus far I've kept God's fools at strife —
Forced one to take another's life —
Caused some to gamble — some to steal —
The strong to make the feeble feel
Oppression's rod. How many a maid,
In truth and innocence arrayed,
Whose young and gentle heart ne'er beat
To aught except emotions sweet,
Till some fair-spoken villain came,
With hungry but inconstant flame,
And in a dark unguarded hour,
   In his false and seductive arms
Has lost her all — her heavenly dower —
   Her peace of mind — her charm of charms —
And from a bright and gladsome girl
   Fell to a shunned and loathsome thing;
Her future life a giddy whirl
   Of shame and sin, and sorrowing!
What power impelled him to destroy
   Such treasure for such transient joy?
'Twas I who urged him to the act —
'Twas I! — I glory in the fact!
Millions who own the name of God,
   Join church — profess to tread the path
That Christ and the apostles trod,
   Have felt, or yet will feel, the wrath
Of a just God, who will not let
   One sinner miss this pit of pain,
Nor pardon the base hypocrite
   Who takes his holy name in vain.
And in the pale and pews of churches
Is where hypocrisy most perches.
I always heap the hottest embers
Upon those hypocritic members.
All worship of the Lord I hate,
And so I've managed to create
Endless disputes among the fools
Who toil for God, yet are my tools.
I glory in sectarian fights
And controversies about rites
And ceremonies, and so forth,
(Which altogether are not worth
One sinner's soul,) for ites and isms —
Burning at stakes, church wars, wide schisms
Grow out of these — these I promote.
I also cause each sect to quote
The scripture, amply to attest,
That loving it, God hates the rest.

The path of righteousness is plain,
  The scripture's easily understood;
But I distract each teacher's brain,
  So none interpret as they should.
I am the patron of discord
Among the churches of the Lord.
I sow the seeds of fell dissension
Among all Christians worth attention.
I think perhaps I've made a sect
  For every chapter in the book;
And some, I do admit, reflect
  Small credit anywhere. They look
As if they had no instigator —
Redeemer, country nor Creator.
I do despise ridiculous fools,
Who hope by rigmaroles and rules,
Wan visages and dress fantastic,
Loud bellowing and feats gymnastic,
To make a little noise and show! —
Such nonsense does provoke me so!
I always help to multiply
Sects and absurdities; but I
Am forced to blush, though that seems odd,
At certain worshipers of God.
Another animal I hate —
The creature who sits down to wait
For what may come — is this nor that —
Nor "man nor mouse, nor long-tailed rat" — .
Will take no side in controversy —
He is not worth a single curse — he
Has nothing positive about him;
I want him not, and God must doubt him; —
Too bad for God — too good for me —
I don't know what his fate should be.
There ought to be some place between
For those who're neither good nor mean —
For those who walk through life so level,
Trimming between God and the Devil.
I like a downright reprobate,
Or one who walks into me straight;
The former is always fit for use;
The latter I may perhaps seduce.
But I despise your neuter gender —
Your faint defamer — faint defender —
Indifferent about salvation —
Too indolent to earn damnation.
Such mortals are of small account —
No matter if they descend or mount.
They have no influence in the earth —
Unfit for heaven, and yet not worth
The fire and brimstone that would burn 'em
Therefore I'll none of them — I spurn 'em.
And if the Almighty spurns them, too,
I don't see what they're going to do.
The Pope has, in the basement story
Of heaven, a place called purgatory; —
A place for Catholics, temporary —
A very clever notion — very —

Whence they're redeemed by dint of masses,
(Bought by the humbler, meeker masses,)
And then sent upward, purified
From the small sins in which they died.
But these nobodies are, I hope,
Held in such odor by the Pope,
That one dares not intrude his face
In this Catholic half-way place.
I like divines who go in strong—
Who swear all but themselves are wrong;
I like intolerance—it tends
To forward and promote my ends.
However preachers disagree,
They're one as to their hate of me.
I am the monster horned ox
'Gainst whom the congregated flocks
Make common war, but mostly get,
I think, somewhat the worst of it.
They've force sufficient, I am sure,
But then their strategy is poor;
They seem to have no general plan
Against the enemy of man.
Their leaders are not well selected;
Their flanks are oft-times unprotected;
They fight in companies and squads,
And mostly where I have the odds.
But for the way I keep them scattered,
I should be most severely battered.
They've pluck, and zeal, and vengeful ire;
But cannot concentrate their fire;
They cannot concentrate—they scatter:
I think that's chiefly what's the matter.
Yet preachers will pursue the project:
And with bad grammar and worse logic
I'm still assailed; at times, I trust,
To well-bred people's slight disgust.
But I can bear to take abuse
From men I put to so good use.
And frequently, as I infer,
Men of quite moderate caliber
Are urgently impelled to preach—
Knowing nothing makes them want to teach,
Learning and brains are not required
By men miraculously inspired.
Let these their native tongues still mangle—
(Poor bait with which the Lord doth angle
For a few sinners, but he catches
Only some poor and ignorant wretches).
There are divines of heavier mettle
That I make use of to unsettle
The Christian world, and tear in tatters
Theology and such like matters.
Oft do I set two such debating
On scripture points, while I am waiting
To snatch their souls, not caring which
Leads the most followers in the ditch.
While each to yield his point is loth,
I laugh, for I am sure of both.

With satisfaction I review
The old devices and the new
By which I've made the world a hell,
Almost as hot as where I dwell.
I think the cleverest trick of mine
Was teaching men the use of wine.
I found man much too cold — too tame,
And made him wine to heat — to inflame.
I think I can effect with liquor
More crime and misery — do it quicker
Than with all other means together;
And I have sometimes doubted whether,
Without its use — without the bowl,
I'd long have kingdom or control!
And hence, though scorning to imbibe,
I'm friendly to the liquor tribe —
To all the venders and distillers —
To all the tipplers and the swillers;
I'm for its general use, that's flat,
For hell were empty but for that."
He paused, then suddenly gave a shout,
  A fierce, prolonged and frightful yell,
Which split the ears, Will. had no doubt,
  Of even the deafest imps in hell.
By this the damned were notified
  To rally round their chieftain grim;
And instantly, from every side,
  Came millions crowding unto him.
From every course and quarter round,
  Through the hot sea of seething flame,
With flagging feet or furious bound,
  The fire-doomed legions quickly came.
Then Satan gestured with his paw,
When down went all the imps in awe;
And thus in thundering tones he spoke,
While from his mouth came fire and smoke.

THE DEVIL'S SPEECH,

AS TAKEN IN SHORT-HAND BY COBBETT.

"Give ear, you prostrate imps of hell,
To what I say, and mark me well.
Since my own fall I have not slept;
Since Adam's fall I have not wept.
My mission it has ever been
To overwhelm the world with sin;
And to scorch, roast and torture you;
Which I have loved — still love to do.
Your Maker and yourselves I hate,
Yet I feel called upon to state,
While love and mercy I discard,
I think your punishment too hard.
It is unjust that you should be
Tormented here eternally —
Burnt ever, yet still left entire.
I do approve the use of fire,

And burning you is my delight,
Yet I would burn you up outright,
And feed the whirlwinds with what cheat
The greedy flames refused to eat.
But it is God's benevolent will,
. So you must burn, you devils, still.
But I am going to set you free
For a brief season, so that ye
May have some rest while I repose;
For I am now resolved to close
My weary eyes and take a nap;
But to provide against mishap,
Here's Cromwell, who will take command;
His will is law; but understand,
Unless you do something that's right
   He has no power to punish you;
Your torment ceases from to-night.
   Till I have slept a month or two
This fire that has been burning here
For many and many a hundred year,
Shall now be quenched, and you shall revel,
From fainting fiend to fearless devil,
In rivers of the purest water —
   Which I shall presently cause to flow,—
Sire, son, and mother, sister, daughter,
   Shall have a short respite from woe.
No fire shall burn in my domain
Save in yon pit prepared for Paine.
Poor Thomas Paine! — the wrath of heaven
   Will soon be hurled upon his head,
Because he's so perversely striven
   A little common sense to spread.
There is no reason in the masses —
   Poor Paine will find, perhaps to-morrow,
That he's been preaching unto asses,
   And that to his eternal sorrow.
In some dispatches from on high,
   Which I received some days ago,
I learn that Paine is soon to die,
   And come to me, of course, you know.
And it is God's express desire
That I shall light the hottest fire
That it is possible to light,
   For Paine's especial benefit;
'Tis done, and should he come to-night,
   You'll plunge him headlong into it.
But first, you'll drench him well with lead,
   And mind that it is boiling hot;
And heap live coals upon his head.
   He'll beg, of course, but mind it not.
Remind him of the books he wrote;
Then ram a reptile down his throat;
And hurl him headlong in the pit,
And throw more brimstone into it;
And then throw in some snakes and toads;
We've plenty here in my abodes.
Thus, should he come while I'm asleep,
   Enjoy his torture and your glee;

But mind, so quiet you must keep
　　That your mad orgies wake not me.
The heavenly powers must wreak their wrath
　　On this rebellious worm of theirs,
Because for many years he hath
　　Taught mortals anything but prayers.
He has denied that I exist,
　　But he will presently change his mind,
Especially when he feels my fist!
　　For I intend to beat him blind!
Because I urged him to deny
The existence of a God on high;
And though he's labored hard to show
That there is not a hell below,
And thus far has subserved me well,
By helping people into hell;
Yet still I urged him to proclaim
　　That men and brutes are on a level —
That their hereafter is the same —
　　That there is neither God nor Devil.
Without regarding hints of mine
He looked around and saw DESIGN;
And from observing Nature's Laws,
Inferred and argued a FIRST CAUSE.
And this first cause, he understood,
Was great and wise and therefore good,
And merciful, and just and pure —
A pretty doctrine, to be sure!
And to be set up by my *friend!*
Why even the Christians don't defend
God's character — their doctrines go
To prove, in fact they clearly show,
That God is a revengeful God,
　　Who glories in your torture here;
And they urge men to shun the rod
　　By rousing that base feeling, *fear.*
For this I'll have a lick at Paine;
　　I'll teach the rascal to rebel!
But now we'll have a little rain,
　　Where never yet a drop has fell."

INHABITANTS OF THE MOON — THE ANGELS AND THE LORD — A
SHOWER — THE DEVIL ASLEEP.

Will. cast his eyes about with some concern,
But not a sign of rain could he discern;
Which pleased him much, for the forgetful fellow,
Had come away without his silk umbrella.
The stars were twinkling and the sky was clear;
And the great moon hung high above his chair.
In looking up he casually perceived
What he supposed would hardly be believed.
He had long wondered who lived in the moon,
Not dreaming he should ascertain so soon;
But gazing now, his admiration rose,
To see great flocks of women without clothes,

Mingling with men whose robes were snowy white,
Walking 'mid flowers and bathed in golden light.
Such women, too! — the plainest would make mad
The whole wide world, if it such beauty had!
No old ones there — they all were young and gay;
So were the men, and smiling as sweet May.
And in the groves and arbors and sweet bowers,
Were crowds of smaller creatures gathering flowers.
If this were heaven, it would seem a truth
That there the aged are restored to youth;
And that the little children there appear
In the sweet innocence we so love here.
Great was Will.'s joy as he could now discern
That little children were not doomed to burn.
He dashed the words so the whole world might know,
He saw great crowds above but none below.
As from a picture the prolonged gaze
Still brings new charms and wonders to amaze —
Brings charms and wonders that ne'er meet the eye
Of slight observer, or of passer-by;
So the fixed look of Cobbett brought to light
What had at first escaped his ravished sight;
He saw what man ne'er saw and never will —
He saw his God, and then his eye stood still!
Fixed was he in his seat as sculptured stone,
At sight of God and his bedazzling throne.
Great was his stature, but his beauty rare —
A woman's softness with man's sterner air
Was sweetly blended; but our hero's sight
Was blasted with intensity of light;
And this is all that he could e'er record
About the moon, the angels and the Lord —
Except when one day some one wanted proof
As to his hanging in a chair aloof,
And wondered how a chair or a balloon
Could hang all night on nothing 'neath the moon,
He said the cords that held his chair forlorn
Were tied securely to that planet's horn.
But suddenly a strange and rushing sound —
A hissing, roaring, loud enough to drown
The uproar of a thousand surging seas,
With all the cataracts combined with these,
Fell on his ear, and looking down below,
He found that it was raining, pouring so
That in an instant all the fires were out,
And the hot regions lay in smoke and doubt.
Poor Cobbett had seen many a heavy shower,
But till this rather inauspicious hour,
He found he'd not the least idea at all
How fast the rain could in some countries fall.
Compared to this he thought that Noah's flood
Was but a little puddle in the mud;
For as the smoke went floating from below,
He saw lakes sleeping and great rivers flow,
Where late quick flames were banqueting on souls,
And nimble fiends cut capers in the coals.
The rain was over — it did not extend
To the observatory of our friend;

Still was he dry without and parched within;
Indeed he felt like swallowing wine or gin,
Brandy, or even whisky, if 'twere good,
After the frights and troubles he'd withstood.
All round below as far as he could see,
Black devils dived and swam triumphantly;
While it amused, it did astonish him
To see the thirsty devils drink and swim.
No sign of fire could now be seen below
Save in one pit, whose red and sullen glow
Caused Will. to shudder, for indeed 'twas plain
This was the furnace for his friend Tom Paine.
And this huge furnace with its frightful glare,
Was right beneath our hero's swinging chair.
He grabbled to it with convulsive grip
Fearing he might incontinently slip,
And land in hell by a mere accident,
Before being properly consigned and sent.
This was indeed a very fearful pit,
With massive iron walls surrounding it.
In looking down Will. saw what would appall
The stoutest heart — he saw huge reptiles crawl
In the hot fire — writhing and hissing in it!
And knew that if he fell, in half a minute
They'd pick his bones. But look! there fast asleep
Lay the Arch Fiend, while frantic imps did leap
With very joy; with Cromwell on his hump,
The fiend was getting many a kick and thump;
But he it seemed was very hard to wake;
For neither kick, nor thump nor savage shake
Did he regard, and so with good intent,
The kicks and thumps between his ribs were sent.
Though Satan felt nor heeded not, yet still
Each devil needs must kick him, and poor Will.,
As the mad furies kicked with all their might,
Was pleased so that at last he laughed outright.
Now Cromwell, rising, uttered a wild yell,
Which quickly brought the myrmidons of hell
About their master, who remarked: " At last
Old Nick's asleep; and now let's chain him fast;
Which we may do though I have doubts of it;
Then lower him gently in the Tom Paine pit,
Which we will arch, and raise on top of that
A mountain higher than Mount Ararat.
If we succeed, farewell to fire and woe;
Then these bright waters shall forever flow —
Instead of burning we shall drink and swim,
If we succeed in getting rid of him.
Our cause is desperate, our condition bad;
This is the first chance we have ever had
To free ourselves from hell and Satan's power,
Which I propose to do this very hour.
Of our success, I have indeed some doubt;
Though I believe Old Nick cannot dig out,
If we pile up the mountain I propose,
Before his heavy eyelids do unclose.
And mewed up safely from the atmosphere,
Why, even the Devil can't live a half a year.

There's chance of failure, but at any rate
We can't intensify the Devil's hate,
Nor bring more grief upon us at the worst,
For we've had torture's acme from the first.
Rebellion adds not strength to tyrant's chain,
And but by it do slaves their freedom gain:
Reforms are half way carried when begun ;
And without venture there is nothing won.
. On earth I stooped not to establish laws,
And by bold venture was I what I was."

THE DEVIL IN CHAINS.

FRENCH METHOD OF FINISHING INCONVENIENT INDIVIDUALS.

These brief remarks elicited loud cheers,
Which luckily reached not the Devil's ears:
And every one expressed his eagerness
To do his utmost in a cause like this.
Deceitful as he was, 'twas ascertained
His sleep was real, and not merely feigned.
The heaving belly and the heavy breath,
Bespoke a stupor near allied to death.
His limbs were loaded in a trice with chains,
And hooped with bands of steel with careful pains,
Just as they were prepared to put him in,
The Frenchman who contrived the guillotine,
So that machinery might facilitate
French leave and severance from the cares of state,
And then received his country's gratitude,
Which gave his neck to the machine for food,
Proposed that he should be decapitated ;
" Because," as he with force and reason stated,
" No tyrant ever — (some might doubt and scoff) —
Gave further trouble when his head was off."
His doubt alludes to the belief, thought sound,
That martyred blood cries ever from the ground ;
In France they've laws prohibiting this cry,
For there no man dares with his head on die ;
He is responsible, alive or dead,
Until the basket has received his head.
Cromwell, who was not favorably impressed
With these French notions, still believed it best
To trim his sails to suit the popular breeze ;
He could not lead such furious hordes as these,
Except by following (when they took the bit),
And giving rein without their knowing it.
In this he did like politicians here,
Who, while behind and lagging in the rear,
Affect to lead the masses, but are led,
And led the more the more they seem ahead.
The Frenchman seized his sharp and heavy axe,
And gave the Devil's throat a dozen thwacks.
But this fierce chopping of the Devil's neck
Harmed it much less than the woodpecker's peck
Harms the tough oak.   The axe's edge
Was battered duller than an iron wedge ;

But the hard neck received no scratch nor scar,
At which the Frenchman foamed and swore by gar,
That any fiend was but a natural fool
Who thought, by axe, or saw, or other tool,
To make a mark upon such hide as *that ;*
And gave it as his own opinion flat,
That if the Devil ever really died,
It would not be by puncture through the hide.
A life protected by malignant charm,
A hide invulnerable to any harm,
His thronging subjects eyed him as he lay,
With looks of slaughter, but no power to slay.
While thus the nonplused legions stood amazed,
The usual uproar at the gate was raised
That did occur whene'er a soul had quitted
The world in sin, and came to be admitted;
When instantly the blackened fiends did break
To greet the new arrival, and to make
The salutations and the shouts and jeers
That always deafened a new-comer's ears.
The Devil was abandoned as a bore,
And thoughts of freedom troubled them no more.
Thus crowds of men on deep affairs intent,
Oft, at some casual shout or incident,
Resolve into a mob, and then enact
What none of them approve in point of fact.

ARRIVAL OF TOM PAINE.

Scarce had the crowd collected when the gates
Swung open by the order of the Fates;
And frantic was the fiendish joy to find
That Thomas Paine had left the world behind;
Had done his little work in his small way,
And come to his employer for his pay.
Here, with a holy angel by his side,
He stood half trembling, yet with conscious pride,
"Where is your savage chief?" inquired the sprite;
"This reprobate was smitten down to night;
And I had orders to conduct him here;
His punishment cannot be too severe."
And with these words the angel of the Lord
Dissolved from view, while, with their own accord,
The heavy gates of hell together swung,
Leaving the doubting Thomas Paine among
The hideous, uncouth, but delighted crew,
Many of whom, somehow, he thought he knew.

SUSPICION — CONVICTION — TRANSFORMATION.

Said he at last: "Is this the Spirit Land?
I cannot comprehend nor understand,
As everything seems indistinct and gloomy,
Exactly what it is that's happened to me.
If this is hell, then I suppose I'm gone.
But where's the fire that preachers harp so on?
Where are the brimstone flames and the black smoke,
Of which, 'tis said, the old apostles spoke?"

And then addressing Cromwell, Thomas said,
"Where is that roaring fiend of whom I've read? —
That lowing bull — insatiate Beelzebub?
Are you the Devil's self, sir, or his cub?
I scarce can see, my sight is growing dim;
But you, I take it, are a monster grim;
And yet you do deport yourself so civil
I cannot think you really are the Devil.
But you're, in fact, a frightful looking crew.
I'd hate indeed to be like one of you;
I'd hate to be like one of these or those,
And have a tail and tusks and iron toes!
The Bible mentions that you weep and wail,
But does not speak, I think, about a tail.
You've rivers here — the banks are broad and green,
And brighter waters I have never seen;
But your black looks and this sulphurous smell
Force me to think that you are imps of hell; —
Confirm me in the view I'm forced to take,
That this is hell itself, and no mistake.
And much I fear I'm doomed to dwell with you,
And have a tail and tusks and talons, too.
Suppose you have no fire — there's none I see —
Still here is deep, excessive agony.
To dwell in this dark and sulphurous region! —
And revel with this horrid, horrid legion!
Alas! alas! it is too late! — too late!
I see, I feel, I realize my fate!
Hark! — O, it is the angels I hear sing
Triumphant anthems to their glorious king.
Alas, if I were in that heavenly throng;
If I could join them in that joyous song;
If I could now fall at the Saviour's feet;
If I could promenade the gold-paved street;
If I could wear a garment snowy white;
If I could range the green fields of delight!
But no, this cannot be! — O, never, never! —
I'm banished, doomed, and damned, — forever — ever!
How many a weary day and night I've spent,
Swift on my own and others' ruin bent,
In writing that erroneous 'Age of Reason,'
A shallow effort at the vilest treason
Against the just and fixed laws of heaven.
Alas, I cannot, cannot be forgiven!
Alas, it is too late, too late for me!
I enter here on hell.—Eternity!
Appalling word! — O, thought of dreadful weight!
O, heavy, heavy, heavy, heavy fate!
But gods, stand by me! — See I've lost my shape! —
I've got a tail, a tail, like to an ape!
And horns — look at my horns! you devils look?
Are you not apprehensive I may hook?
I'm half a bull — were I town bull of hell,
I think I should become the station well.
And see! I've got great tusks and fearful claws —
Think what I am — what might have been — what was!"
Thus Cobbett saw the friend he held so dear
Changed to a fright — half varmint and half steer!

PAINE IN THE PIT — THE DEVIL'S FALL.

And now poor puzzled Paine was roughly caught.
The boiling, bubbling lead was quickly brought,
"Remember, Thomas Paine the books you wrote!"
And the hot lead went hissing down his throat.
A horned snake, with many heads, was then
Forced in his mouth, and reached his vitals, when
He seized it by the tail with savage claws,
And bit with all the vengeance of his jaws;
But could not stop the snake, nor draw it back;
When he grew faint and sick, his hold did slack;
The reptile crawled about his melt and liver;
His head grew dizzy and his limbs did shiver,
And in this state they dragged him to the pit,
But at the first glimpse which he got of it,
He swooned outright — his sense and feeling fled;
And the fiends cried, "He is deceased — he's dead;
But 'tis no matter — pitch him o'er the grate;
He shall burn in hell's fire, at any rate.
There, Paine, receive the wages of your sin!"
Thus saying, Tom was rudely tumbled in.
But coming to, he roared with lusty shout,
"O, you black devils, take me, take me out!"
These urgent cries were seasoning to their mirth.
They twitted him of deeds done in the earth.
"O, Tom, my boy, you doubtless now forget
The soul-destroying volumes that you writ!
Look upward, sir! — ten thousand here have read
Your wicked books, and by them were misled.
Your artful pen, you howling rogue, you know
Has sent its tens of thousands down below."
"Be damned to you!" roared Paine, "and damn the books,
Since they beget such grimaces and looks.
Begone, you swine! and leave me to my fate;
You have no love, and I despise your hate!
I wish I could get up just now at you —
I'd thrash the whole accursed and grinning crew.
But these hot flames make me so sick and dizzy,
And these infernal snakes keep me so busy
In dodging round this hell-invented pit,
To keep myself from getting badly bit,
That I have not a minute's time to spare
On you, you greenhorns, grinning at me there."
Meantime, poor Paine was streaking it around
His amphitheatre, at every bound
Crushing the toads — the snakes in hot pursuit —
Greeted with deafening cheers and yells to boot.
And Cobbett, though half dead, laughed out to see
His whilom friend rush round so furiously.
At last the snakes with generalship profound,
Left a small force to race the rascal round,
While the main body ambushed on the track
That he must travel on his mad way back.
Poor Tom did not perceive this stratagem
Till coming round he ran straight into them.

At this the devils raised the wildest yell
That till this moment had been heard in hell.
'Twas loud enough to jar the Devil's brains,
So that he woke and found himself in chains.
But to snap these required not half a minute;
And rising, he rushed to the pit, and in it
Beheld his victim; and as thus he stood,
He cried, "Aha! my Thomas Paine!—that's good!
Like you the snakes with which you writhe and twist!
O, how I'd like to beat you with my fist!
If I were in the pit, you rogue, with you,
I'd maul you till even hell itself were blue!"
While thus old Satan o'er the wall was bent,
Some devil with the very best intent,
Tripped up his heels; and then as quick as thought,
The Devil's claws sprang out and clutched at naught;
And thus midst yells and hoarse demoniac peals,
In went the indignant Devil, neck and heels!

BATTLE BETWEEN THE DEVIL AND TOM PAINE.

FROM AN EYE-WITNESS.

As Satan fell he raised a vigorous shout;
Roared he, "Tom Paine, now you may well look out!
Because for this absurd and cruel fall,
I'll murder you, snakes, toads, and devils—all!"
Paine could but smile, but 'twas a sickly grin,
When Satan tumbled thus abruptly in.
'Twas hard for him with the small snakes to fight,
While a huge one was swallowing him outright.
He felt himself drawn backward, and still going
Down the snake's throat and where there was no knowing.
While the small snakes and toads he so much feared,
Ate him by inches as he disappeared.
No wonder then, his smile was but a grin
When Satan fell, and stove his head fast in
A lucky crevice in the floor of rock;
And though right smartly worsted by the shock,
Was more enraged, and bellowed, roared and bawled,
So that the snakes and toads slunk off appalled;
And the big one that had half swallowed Paine,
Reversed his throat and threw him up again.
Now Paine, though once a brave and gallant man,
On being puked up, incontinently ran;
But seeing Satan still fast sticking there,
And knowing well that on a footing fair,
With his Herculean foe he could not cope;
And further, feeling he had naught to hope,
Thought it was best for him to take the start,
And so he charged on Satan's hinder part
With all his force, and rushing in pell-mell,
He did maltreat and thump the Devil well.
At this assault, so suddenly, fiercely made,
The devils cheered and yelled, "Be not afraid!
Go for him, Tom!" they whooped with wildest joy,
"If you can kill or cripple the 'Old Boy,'

You shall succeed that moment to his throne,
And call his kingdom and the earth your own."
When Tom's quick ear these welcome words had caught,
With furious energy he fiercely fought,
And Satan roared and did his uttermost
To injure and demoralize this ghost.
At last the Devil's head came from the crack,
But from a surge that threw him on his back;
When in an instant Paine lit on his chest,
And then each monster did his worst and best,
With fist, and claw, and tooth, and tail, and toe
Each devil dived and digged into his foe.
The big snakes blowed, and the flat toads did blink,
While small snakes hissed, but knew not what to think.
The mad spectators cheered with deafening cheers,
While Cobbett wiped away the sweat and tears,
And hoped and prayed that Tom would win the fight,
While devils shouted with their utmost might —
"Another blow like that! — Hurra for Paine! —
O, that is beautiful! — Hit him again! —
He has no friends! — He has no friends down here! —
Hurra for Tom! — Ten thousand on the steer! —
Gouge Tom! — Tom kick! — Tom choke! — Tom hook! — Tom bite! —
Gouge out his eyes! — Tom, hold his weasand tight! —
Knock out his shoulder! — There! — Unhinge the other! —
He's breathing thick! — By all the gods, he'll smother! —
Be active, Tom! — Mash his potato trap! —
Hurra! — By Jupiter, that brings the sap! —
Cave in his head! — Carve up his ugly mug! —
Why Tom's a skilled, a scientific plug! —
He staggers! — See! — He's sick! — The Devil is sick! —
Now Tom's you time! — Be cautious! — Tom, be quick! —
Now smash his smeller! — Flat his big red snout! —
Hurra! — Well done! — Hurra — His eye is out! —
Gouge out the other! — There! — Hang to him yet! —
Now Tom! — Now Tom! — Hurra! — That's it! — That's it! —
'Tis out! — Both eyes are out! — He cannot see! —
Bully for Paine! — Whoop! — Whoop! — We're free! — We're free! —
Three cheers for Paine!" — "*Three cheers!*" Will. Cobbett cried,.
But at that very instant he espied
The heavenly angel hovering near his head;
She merely touched the cords, and then like lead
Poor Will. went down — down — down — the cords were broke —
And with a bound, a shriek, a yell, he woke.

ARGO AND IRENE.

PERSONS REPRESENTED.

ARGO, *a Poet and Author.*	IRENE.
MAGOON, *an old man of low habits, but very rich, and without heirs.*	*Mother to Irene.*
	SAM, *servant to Irene (Colored).*
A Publisher.	DR. SLASH.
A Literary Critic.	DR. SPANKER.
A Lawyer.	DR. SMICK.
Two Old Ladies.	DR. SLABBS.
A Farmer.	DR. ABRAM TURNER (*Colored*).
TUBBS.	*Friends and Attendants.*

ACT I.

SCENE I.—*A lady's room.* IRENE *seated at a table. Enter* SAM, *with letters.*

Sam. I hab youh letters, Miss Irene. You gets a heap ob lub letters, but you is a lubly young lady. You is de lubliest ob de lubly and de sweetest ob de sweetly.

Irene. Why, what insolence!

Sam. Insolence?

Irene. Yes, insolence, you black scamp!

Sam. Black scamp? Look a heah, miss; Ize a gemman, if I is culled!

Irene. You a gentleman! Ain't you a nigger?

Sam. Niggah! niggah, miss! dar be no niggahs now. True nuff, Ize culled, but Ize no niggah. Ize a gemman od cullah. Massa Linkum wiped out de stigma ob niggah. Ize de ekal ob de white man in 'spectability and 'telligence.

Irene. Yes?

Sam. Yes, miss, I is; de law gibs me ekality before it and behind it, and Ize gwine to hab my rights. I admires youh beauty, bad as you treats me, and I hab a right to 'spress my feelins if I is culled and is youh servant. Niggah, to be shuah!

Irene. Well, well, Sam, I'm not going to fall out with you. See if my mother doesn't want you below.

Sam. All right, miss; Ize not mad. I jes wanted to show you dat I hab de spirit ob a man, if I is culled, and dat I is a warm 'mirer ob de female sec, ob whom you is de perfection dareof.   [*Exit.*

Irene. Alas, what have we come to in this country,
     When all the servants think themselves the equals
     Of those whom they do serve. Can we raise them
     To our refinement and intelligence?
     Or will we rather, by the force of habits,
     Through constant commerce with the serving class,
     Sink to their level? But this sooty fellow
     Admires my beauty; in his amorous eye
                [*Looks in a glass*]
     There lives a critic who doth say: She's pretty;
     And compliments unto a woman's beauty
     Are sweet to the possessor of that beauty
     Nor can she wholly hate the man who pays them,
     Though he were seven times black.
                [*Opens a letter and reads.*]

TO MY HEART'S IDOL.

How slight a circumstance may blast
  The blossoms the young heart puts forth,
And tender buds of hope—how fast
  They fall in frosts of frigid north.

This morn our wishes are in flower,
  Amid the golden harvest sheaves,
But ere the noon come blight and shower,
  And we have but the wilted leaves.

O, heart of lover, doubting still,
  And never peaceful and at rest,
But ever wooing omens ill
  To weigh upon the weary breast.

O, there are moments when the heart,
  The lover's quick barometer,
Doth feel the death ere yet the dart
  Hath left the string whence it doth whir.

ARGO.

Alack, what means this riddle? how is this?
Doth he spy out the evils that await him?
By intuition hath his fruitful mind
Some dread forebodement. O, there is a sadness—
An air of plaintive wailing in his song
That falls like funeral dirge. It breaks my heart.
I who do love him, but must still betray him,
Do feel the force of his great spirit more,
The farther I go from him.

[Opens another letter and reads.]

DEAR DUCK: I have just returned from Europe, and shall call upon
you to-day. I am glad you have kept the affair between us so quiet
that the quid-nuncs haven't got wind of it. Have a kiss of welcome for
me, love.

Have a kiss for me,
Have one, two, three;
I have scores for thee,
And will spend them as free
As the waters that run.

There, Duck, that is the first poetry I ever put upon paper, and here
I am fifty-nine years of age last Wednesday.
Thine eternally,
M. MAGOON, Major.

[Throws all the letters pettishly aside.]

But fifty-nine on Wednesday. O, how sad
To see the old man fighting off his years,
And faded dames in the decline of life,
With artificial teeth and withered limbs,
In gay attire and sallow cheek in paint,
Still aping youth and keeping time at bay,
Forswearing half the years that speak against them,
And yielding, when compelled to, without grace,
To the behests of age! O, this is pitiable!
But still poor human nature may be pardoned,
For lovely is our youth, our age decrepit;
And not till youth hath slipped away and left us,
And age, with ache and blindness and white hairs,

Doth creep upon us, do we value youth.
No wonder then that the old man should strive
To keep away the years, and sweat and tug
With every faculty that flags or fails him,
To worry or to woo it to performance,
As in the flower of youth.

Enter MOTHER.

Mother. I have good news, daughter. A note from Major Magoon
informs me of his safe return from abroad, and that he will presently
call upon us.

Irene. I have his autograph; he tells me here
That he will call and claim me for his wife;
And he hath written me a pretty song;
For loving me hath made him court the muses;
And I intend to set the song to music
And play it to the fiddle at the wedding,
And by the murmuring brook beneath the willows.

Mother. Now, Irene, I would! But I am glad to see you are recon-
ciled to the match. Give me the Major's song. [*Reads it.*] A pretty
song, I do declare. It is quite equal to any of the mad poet's produc-
tions. When you are Mrs. Magoon we shall be enabled to regain our
lost position in society. It will be a splendid match. You will be envied
by the entire tribe of marriageable ladies in the city. The Major's great
wealth will put us in a position to return with interest the many slights
that have been shown us since your father's bankruptcy and death. He
is really a good-hearted, jolly old gentleman, and will keep you from
despondency; and then if you should lose him in a few years, you will
have his wealth. He has no heirs, and proposes to will all to you before
the marriage.

Irene. But, mother, bears he not a naughty name?
They say he is the patron of light women,
And thinks the best of us but little better
Than those with whom he herds. Hath he not mistresses?

Mother. Well, what of that! He is not worse than most men on that
score.

Irene. I've seen tobacco juice upon his beard;
He tipples and he smokes incessantly;
Some say he snores that sleepers wake in fright,
Thinking the roof being from the rafters ripped;
And that he tugs with nightmares in his sleep,
Gurgling and groaning in the dead of night,
That passing strangers beat upon his doors,
In horrid apprehension that within
Red murder hath some victim on the rack;
He's great of entrails, and is gluttonous;
His walk's a waddle as you are aware;
He's old, and peevish with the aches of age;
Bootmakers, tailors, hatters, barbers fail
To trim four hundred pounds of pork like this,
So it pass current for a gentleman:
He is all animal; his appetites
Are gross and sensual: O, how can I wive
With such a man as he!

Mother. Nonsense, daughter! Do not think of these things. You
can conquer his appetites. He is but mortal man. Refuse him if you
will, but only your marriage with him will save us from beggary. I
wish myself there were some other deliverance for us, but there is none.
O, what is to become of us!

Irene. Do not despair, dear mother; now suppose
    I sell myself to this old man? — what then?
    What will become of Argo and of you?
    Argo will suicide, and can you hope
    As mother-in-law to lead a happy life
    With such a son-in-law? Will not his wassail —
    His retinue of riotous old men, with daily feast
    And nightly drinking bout, make you distract,
    Even if he give you shelter?
Mother. Not so fast, girl. The Major agrees to make a settlement
upon me before the marriage. I shall have a home and be independent.
As for Argo, the young man is muddled in his wits, and is so regarded;
and his prospects are so poor that it matters little what he does or thinks.
    Irene. But, mother, he has genius; it will tell;
        Like murder, it will out; it will be heard from.
Mother. It will out at the elbows; and be heard from the poorhouse,
the madhouse and the pauper's grave. Genius, my dear, is of mighty
little account in this matter-of-fact age. There was excuse for genius in
the days of Shakespeare and Byron; not that even they made anybody
better or happier; but people were not then totally absorbed in the routine
of fashion and money-making; and the poets served to amuse the wealthy
and indolent classes. We have had quite enough of genius. It brings
no advantages to its possessor, and very little to the world; and, as a
rule, it is so provokingly allied to poverty that sensible folks generally
shun people of genius as they do a pestilence. There is nothing, my
dear, that can bring us true happiness but wealth and social position;
and wealth is the only sure passport to social position.
    Irene. Well, mother, have your way; I am resigned;
    You shall not live in poverty and want
    While I have wares for sale. But my poor heart
    Is with the spring time buds, not with the leaves
    Of sere and bleak November. O, farewell
    To the sweet dreams of girlhood's guileless hours!
    I yield to fate which no one may defy;
    Come any fortune; see! I am as wax;
    The merest child can mould me.
Mother. Really, child, I see nothing to invite despondency. The cards
of fortune are running in your favor.
    Irene. I will lend you my fortune, mother; if
    You'll take the fat man with his money bags,
    I tender them to you.
Mother. He is an epicure, my child. He will diet upon spring chick-
ens. But I must away and put the house in order for his reception.
                                    [*Exit* MOTHER.
    Irene. And this it is to be a woman; this
    Is money's power to purchase; I am sold;
    Sold to the highest bidder, like a slave,
    For uses worser and more loathed to me,
    Than e'er were stripes and drudgery to the slave
    In any age or clime. Not so with boys:
    I never knew one bartered off, or bought
    For a bed-fellow to a dame of eighty.
    O, curse of sex! why were not I a boy,
    That I might tease the pretty girls nor mate
    With rheumatis and wrinkles, gout and age,
    Due at the graveyard any day in the week!
    My sexuality is merchandise; 'tis stock,
    Quotable on 'change; it hath its fluctuations —

Its rises and its falls in open market;
Depending on the greeds or whims of men,
And their ability to buy and carry
The coveted commodity: O, yes!
And it is ratable like grain or pork:
As this is prime; this number one; this family,
Or common merely; she will make a wife,
A fine machine to manufacture children,
And be a patient drudge till old and ugly,
And then be ousted from the family hearth,
Because, forsooth, her owner sees in market
A fresher piece of goods. There goes another,
With furbelow and filigree and floss;
With jaunty hat, and haughty eye and air:
She is in market for the highest figure,
And straight the bulls and bears are in commotion.
Her price is fixed; she rates with Flora Temple,
Or any other fine two-fifteen nag:
While here another in plain gait and gown,
May own a gentler heart and finer form,
And not fetch fifteen cents. Such is the power
Of tress and trapping, wriggling gait and giggle,
To whet the appetite and warp the judgment
Of our pursuers; whom if we deceive,
(And to deceive them is the chiefest pleasure
Of more than half our sex,) it is not worse
Than they deserve, nor worse than they do us.
Like many others, I'm so poor and starved
That I must force my goods upon the market,
And sell them in a private shameful way,
Or in an open way almost as shameful,
Which has the sanction of society.
I would sell cheap if I might choose the buyer,
And be his slave while he enjoyed the purchase.
But how I prattle, knowing I am sold
By my good mother for the ready money,
And that I love and pity her so much
That I shall ratify the sale to-morrow.
And gossips will declare I've brought enough;
O, there is not a tongue in all the land,
But it will wag and say: she sold herself:
She is well sold: he is too good for her;
It was his money, not himself she married;
If he should cut her off without a cent
He'd serve her right, the proud and heartless flirt,
Who by her arts won the poor, weak old man!
Thus will they scan me. But this is a play,
Myself am the chief actor; we shall see
The end when it arrives; chance will work out
What destiny has fixed. My mother says,
In course of nature the old man must die;
But he may hold out longer yet than I;
She further hints if I can understand,
That certain goods sell well at second hand.
Would Argo deck his boudoir with a flower,
Whose sweets had wasted in another's bower?

Enter SAM.

Sam. De crazy young man dat rolls his eye at de moon and talks to hisself desires to see de angelic young lady ob de house, as he 'spresses it. Lod! I wish I was dat young man, crazy as he is!

Irene. Show him up, Sam, but bid him wait a little;
I must have leisure to compose myself.

Sam. Thank you, Miss Irene. I will retard him till you exposes youhself. I will entertain de young gemman wid some new heretical theories on particular 'conomy. Dey rignated in dis brain, which is de fust culled brain dat ebber abfluscated a highlysophical 'say on a absurd science.

Irene. O, he will be delighted with you, no doubt. [*Exit* SAM.
     Ye ministers of evil that diffuse
     Your poisonous breath in mortal atmospheres,
     And you fell powers that prompt unhallowed purpose,
     And brew injustice, cruelty and wrong,
     If in your sightless substances you see me,
     And hear my invocation, come to me,
     And fill me quickly to the finger tips
     With your malevolent and baleful natures.
     Suppress and sear emotion, and seal up
     The sources of love, pity, shame, remorse,
     And fill me with hypocrisy to the toes,
     So I may look and act and seem the saint,
     And be the devil I am. My woman's bosom
     Fill full to bursting with abhorred deceit,
     So I acquit me in the cruel role
     Which my fell spirit has resolved to act,
     Being tortured to extreme. That man who smiles
     And stabs you while he shakes your friendly hand,
     Is as a cherubim compared to me,
     Who must strike down the man I idolize,
     Nor give him reasons, nor a chance to plead.
     Ay, there's the point; if he knew all, saw all,
     If I could tell him half he might excuse me,
     Or hate me something less. But no, no, no!
     The raven's creaking voice must croak no warning
     Until the lightning shivers down his castles,
     And he is whelmed in ruin! Here he comes.

Enter ARGO.

Argo. The spirits that inhabit peaceful homes
     Rest in this house! How fares my love to-day?
Irene. I am well and yet am ill. How is't with you?
Argo. Quite well in body, but depressed in mind.
     I have not found a market for my wares,
     And now begin to think them valueless;
     My tales and poems sleep in manuscript,
     For lack of name to give them currency,
     Or gold to buy the critics. Art thou ill?
Irene. I was; but now that you are here with me,
     There's healing in the air and I am well;
     I wish you could remain a hundred years.
Argo. I wish I could, and when I win a name,
     Or any little fortune, I will bring it
     And give it all thee.
Irene.   Live coals of fire! [*Aside.*]
     These words are cruel, Argo, and denote

4

The presence of the mystic messenger,
That sometimes gives the soul presentiment
Of viewless evils hedging it about.
The mewling calf from teeming udder torn
Uplifts its frighted voice as if it saw
In vacant air the gleaming butcher knives
Whet thin and sharp to shed its little blood.

Argo. I could not say a cruel word to thee.

Irene. And yet the words of kindness are more cruel,
To him whose heart doth harbor cruelty,
Than bitter words of hate. The helpless babe,
Lain by the cruel hand of hapless mother
Upon the stranger's sill, that smiling sleeps,
As she abandons it, doth reach her bosom,
By its confiding trust, and touch and wring it
When struggle and acclaim would fail to move
Her cruel heart to pity. Dagger points
Ride on your loving words, and find a lodgment,
Each dagger in my bosom, although invisible
And all unknown to you.

Argo.   Then let me know—make me to see them, lady,
That I may turn their points upon myself.
If I unwittingly have given thee pain,
The spacious globe cannot afford a pleasure,
Till I atone for it. Some heavy cloud
Hath cast its shadow o'er my lady's brow,
For her fair features wear a somber hue,
Like nature's in a summer sun's eclipse;
And gloomy resolution seems to settle
Upon her lips where smiles were wont to play;
Her voice is solemn, as in benediction,
And speaks in similes that breathe of sorrow.
If thy young life is bowed with any trouble,
Not known to me, that knowing I may cure,
O, speak and let me know it, that as swift
As turtle's wing, or message over wire,
Or woman's prayer to ascend, my willing soul
May speed to thy relief.

Irene.   I nurse a trouble,
Which but for sickly troubles not my own,
Would vanish like a nightmare at the touch
Of friendly finger on the imprisoned brow:
By nursing one I kept a score at bay,
That howl like hungry wolves, and threaten points
That I, for weighty reasons, must defend.
Duty, when it o'ermastereth desire,
Leaves quiet conscience in the aching heart,
And angel wings to fan the saddened brow
That sorrows o'er the death of tender hopes.
'Tis better to endure than to inflict,
When duty makes endurance laudable.
I am a novice, yet cast for a part
Almost too heavy for a veteran actor;
A part as far from my true nature as
Great Mars is from the earth.

Argo. My lady speaks in riddles that confound;
I have no clue nor key to her enigmas.

Irene. All things are riddles—all the world's a riddle,
And all the people in it mere enigmas:
Existence in its various forms and phases,
From microscopic midge to mastodon—
From minnows to the monsters of the deep—
From burrowing moles to eagles in the clouds,
Through all the range of being—all is riddle:
Even thought, perception, memory, are enigmas—
The globe itself and all the whirling planets—
The mighty sun—the merest drop of water—
Are mysteries—puzzles that confound the sense
And mock the understanding. All we know—
All we can comprehend of anything,
Is that we cannot comprehend it, and
That all is mystery, puzzle, doubt, enigma.
The powers that shape events do write in riddles,
And signal us in omens and in dreams,
And say in circumstance thought accidental
A sermon every hour. Our minds are woven
From threads pervading space in all directions,
And interlaced, like webs of curious spiders,
With every substance having shape or motion;
So any danger or disturbing force
That moves toward us agitates the mesh,
And sends us trills of warning, could we read them.
Do you believe in dreams?

Argo.   I hardly know.
There are a kind of dreams that puzzle me:
In that condition known as sleep, wherein
The brain recruits its nourishment for the soul,
The soul itself seems free to wander off
To other realms, retaining still by threads
As frail as gossamer, connection with the brain,
And spanning the bounds of temporal and eternal,
The mysteries of both unveiled, it reads the future,
And sees as clearly, haps to come to-morrow,
As we can see them after they arrive.
But there is an entanglement attending
Conveyance of this knowledge to our senses.
After the soul returns and we awake,
It gives us glimmerings—whisperings of its walks;
Fragmentary pictures of dissolving scenes;
Of gala days and ravishing delights;
Of fame, of triumph, glittering wealth achieved,
Or of reverses, pains, imprisonment;
Failure, misfortune, loss of home and friends:
But the recital is befogged and clouded;
Confused, perplexed—although at times so vivid,
That we are shaken with presentiment,
And quake with mortal fear. Either the soul lacks power,
Or else it is forbidden to impress
Upon the brain, distinct to wakened memory,
Retainable and readable, the revelations,
The secrets and the mysteries unveiled to it
While it is roving in the spirit realm
And we lie dead in sleep; hence dreams are shadows,
Whose substances elude and mock our senses.
Sleep! mystery indefinable! Curious dreams!

Tangled and inexplicable webs connecting
Our mortal with the immortal. There be dreams
That bode like howling dogs or crowing hens:
To dream of fire — to dream of skulking naked; —
Of eggs, of meats, of fish, of silver coins;
Of sailing ships or coasting on the waters;
Are bodements of confusion, like the croaking
Of rookery kites and night crows on the coming
Of crashing storm and tempest.

Irene. From misty ages, sayings, signs and omens,
Come down to us, clad in antiquity;
Our great grand dams, and theirs, and theirs, and theirs,
Put faith in them, and conned them like their beads.
Do you regard these signs?

Argo.   Well, no; and yes;
Involuntarily I always turn
To greet the new moon over my right shoulder;
Begun in jest it has become a custom,
So apt are jests at times to end in earnest: —
Yet I am joking; still I am imbued
With apprehensions if it happens that
The paley planet peeps at me through brush,
Or greets me over the left, on re-appearing,
To run her monthly cycle round the earth.
Last night while strolling in the cemetery,
And holding converse with the eloquent dead,
I paused beneath an ancient willow tree,
That drooped in mourning o'er a new-made grave;
And there by accident I caught a glimpse
Of gentle Luna's silvery crescent, through
The somber foliage of this solemn willow,
On which in her faint light the dewdrops glistened
Like tears on cheeks of matrons clad in mourning,
And mutely weeping some great mutual sorrow.
Pray do not smile, but this slight circumstance
Doth weigh upon me like an incubus,
Filling me with forebodings of some trouble
Of more than common blight.

Irene. Then you will not be taken by surprise,
Though shots may come from quarters least suspect
Of harboring hidden foes. Had I the right
I would be with you and shield you from danger
In these my loving arms. Pride makes us slaves,
And drives us from the fruits and flowers of summer,
To starve in deserts and in discontent.

Argo. Thou art a woman — say what we should do;
A woman's instinct is worth more than proofs,
Though sworn in open court.

Irene.   Some would have married
And sought their fortunes after.

Argo.   Not so I:
Though thou art precious as the sense of sight,
I will prepare a cage to hold my bird
Before I trap the bird. And more than this:
There is no person worthy such a being;
Thou art so delicate in all thy tastes;
So pure of thought, so winning in thy ways;
So strangely fascinating are thy smiles;

And so bewildering are thy many beauties,
That tongue cannot describe, that it were sin
To blast thy bloom with marital debauch.
'Tis not that I would marry thee, Irene;
I would not smelt the coarse refuse that forms
This uncouth, graceless piece of mechanism,
With the fine essences that enter in
The precious compound of thy perfect person.
O, no, I would not join this frame of mine,
Composed of boils, carbuncles and corruption,
To the fine, incorruptible qualities,
That form the person of my sweet Irene.
I'm but a man — thou art an angel pure,
Bright as the stars, fair as a May-day morn —
Canst thou be mortal? — thou must hail from heaven,
For every element combined in thee
Is the quintessence of divinity.
Hence it were incongruity too gross
For us to wed.

Irene.   O, Argo, you are mad.
I fear you deem us but as butterflies,
And love us mostly for our pretty wings,
That please your eager sight. Know, gentle youth,
That our exterior charms hide imperfections,
Which like the butterfly's ephemeral wings,
Expire with the brief summer of our youth,
And leave exposed the loathed worm beneath,
Whose sight doth sicken till men turn away
And wonder why they loved.

Argo.   I wonder why
Men sometimes doubt that woman is perfection:
I'd rather perish than think her imperfect;
And if the angels have some shape not hers,
Heaven will lack charms for me: In her unite
All beauties found in nature: hath she faults
They're stamped on her by man. I am not mad,
Or if I be it is so sweet a madness,
This darling estimate I have of woman,
That I will nurse it to my dying day.

Irene. This sacred reverence for the weaker sex
If it were general would ennoble man,
And stimulate poor woman to deserve
The homage tendered her, whose elevation
Is the advance of all: Man's noblest work
Is to ennoble woman.

Argo.   So I think;
And as a wanderer in some floral hall,
Who loves the floral kingdom as a whole,
May yet select some special, perfumed flower,
To concentrate his loving wonder on:
So I who worship each, all, every woman,
Do yet select thee from the gorgeous throng,
For my particular tulip, rosebud, lily,
To wear within my bosom: or, like one
Who, gazing in heaven's star-bejeweled vault,
Selects some special twinkler to affix
His wondering eyes on more particularly,
While charmed with the bright galaxy in general;

So choose I thee, and while admiring all,
My love for thee is speciality;
It is my trade — my occupation — aim —
I have no other business.

Irene. But is this love not tempered with hot blood?
Wilt thou still love me when my personal charms,
Like blasted rose-leaves, fall off one by one,
And wither in the winters of my age?

Argo. Not with so wild a love. Love in our youth
Is a delicious madness; but in age
It is a reasoning, reverential love;
And graces of the mind rise up to smooth
The wrinkles of old age: thus love in age
Makes up in purity and holiness
What it may lack in heat. O, I shall love thee
Away to dateless death; and I will wed thee
And keep thee but to look at, deeming thee
A piece of ware too fine for mortal use,
Or vulgar eyes to look on; I could stand
And guard thy untouched innocence through life;
Such is my love. O, could I lure thee off
To some lone island in the trackless sea,
Securely hidden in some southern clime,
Where eye of man could never spy us out;
Where summer blooms eternal, and where flowers
And gaudy birds make glad the orange groves,
Where ripening fruits and rippling waters tempt
The eye and appetite — such wilderness,
With thee, were wealth enough.
No, no, I would not wed thee, gentle girl!
And doom thee to a life that, stripped of gloss,
Ideal freedom, feigned supremacy,
High-sounding title and most flimsy tinsel,
That hide the chafing fetters underneath,
Is but captivity and servitude,
Wherein the wife buys with her toil and care
The coldest corner on the family hearth.
Why, the black wench, doomed to the cotton fields,
Dared to deny the lustful overseer
Possession of her body: Your supervisor
Will not be put off thus; he has the law;
And his perquisites and prerogatives
You may not safely question. What but pain,
Wasting disease, wan cheeks and spirits broken,
Are the attendants on the average wife?
Who midst child-bearing — rearing — making — mending;
Administering to her husband's needs or whims,
Plods onward hourly, daily, monthly, yearly,
With scarce a moment that makes no demand
Upon her failing strength; — plods onward thus
Toward death's dismal vault: in which at last,
Bowed down and wrinkled — worn to the very bones,
The poor remains of one erewhile quite lovely,
Are laid away to rest. No, no, my girl,
Though youth's hot blood run riot in my veins,
And passion's appetites gnaw at my nerves,
Would I, not even in wedlock, which invites
And makes respectable the shameful practice,

Assuage those hungry heats and appetites,
By feeding them on otto of the roses,—
Whence spring the chief infirmities that wait
On gentle woman's life: I nurse a holier
And more exalted love;—a love that falls
As softly as the welcome rains of April
Upon the early flowers;—falls thus as gently
Upon the object loved;—awakening its sweets,
And not with rudeness robbing it of odor.

Irene. Then would you have me as a spirit-bride?
Coming as man to one endowed as woman,
Would you ignore our earthly attributes,
And with our spirits still materialized,
But having affinities that find their likes
As lightning its conductors, set up here
A heaven of our own?

Argo.   Such is my hope.
But we must marry as the custom is;
For custom hath its laws and usages,
Whereby two fools are kneaded into one—
Beaten and brayed in matrimonial mortar,
Without regard to incompatibles,
That mix as mincingly as oil and water,
Or tastes as sundered as the antipodes,—
Most holy marriage!—oftentimes mis-matching,
But still infallible as fate in filling
Our towns, our poorhouses, our prisons,
With misbegotten simpletons and knaves.
O, we will marry, but not as many do:
Not with the appetites that whet their loves;
The spur that goads the common herd to marriage,
Will we commingle in connubial life;
But with a chasteness delicate and pretty
As cooing courtship of contented doves:
Our chaste desires, like harp-strings sweetly tuned,
Whose every tone melts softly into others,
And these in others, swelling in grand accord,
And ravishing the ear with heavenly sounds,
Of soulful symphony:—so shall our loves—
So shall our tastes, attuned in sweet accord,
On contact coalesce, like globes of mercury,
And make of many one.

Irene. This is too flowery, Argo; it were like
The amours of the angels; we are here
Upon a lower plane, and must play out
Life's drama after nature. I do fear
That your sensations and fine sentiments
Rise yet in youthful blood. I am but woman;
And you are ravished with my woman's charms;
'Tis not the spirit in mine eyes you love,
But the soft eyes themselves.

Argo. What are those eyes but windows for thy soul?
And pretty shutters are those lily lids?
Whose severed fringes send the spirit forth
To set its charms upon the countenance,
That men who see it playing in the features,
Fall sick of love and dizzy with desire.
O, woman's face is a sweet piece of music;—
'Tis heaven's own viol, daintily attuned,

On which the immortal soul within her plays
Its ravishing endearments, to bewilder
And wonder-strike the world. I am enamored
Less with thy manifold and matchless beauties,
Than with the soul that lurketh in those beauties,
And gives me earnest of its attributes,
By the delectable and dainty colors
It paints upon thy cheeks.

Irene. Whate'er you love me for I know you love me,
And I love you for loving me so well;—
For reasons, too, as plentiful and pretty
As summer birds that fill the groves with song,
Which while it charms defies analysis.
And love like ours, once rooted in the soul,
Lives like the ivy, though the tree may die
Round which it twines its tendrils; storm and frost
May sere its leaflets, but its lease of life
Extends beyond the winter of our years
Into the spring and summer time of heaven:
Hearts thus united are not lightly severed:
Detraction, clamor, disappointment — doubt —
Delay, estrangement, nor divergent paths
Can shake the trust of the true heart that loves:
The pilgrim's eye, bent on its holy shrine,
Dwells not more fixedly and firmly there
Than true love dwells upon its own beloved,—
In sleeping, waking, resting, or at labor;
Or sundered as the east is from the west;
Or wrapped in storm and fog, like ships at sea;
True love, like the true needle's point, will veer,
And trembling, turn to its attracting star,
The haven of its hope.

Argo. My love is fired with charming inspiration;
She doth forestall and rob me of expression;
She paints my very thoughts in brilliant colors,
And sets my sentiments in similes
That grace them as do golden picture frames
The mellow tints of pictures.

Irene. Death in its visitations culls the best;
The gentlest, fairest, truest, earliest fall;
And so the gods upon the tenderest loves
Affix the earliest blight. Blind disappointments
Swarm in the heart-cells with the holiest love,
Like bats in caves where precious ore is hid,
Unmindful of its presence.

Argo. More enigmas.
What would my lady have me understand
By these abrupt allusions?

Irene. That our love,
Having demands so greatly in excess
Of our poor possibilities to answer,
May meet with crushing crosses, and that we
Must be prepared to meet them.

Argo. All will go well
If we wait patiently the happy hour
When we may prudently unite our fortunes.

Irene. Then till that happy, happy hour arrives,
You still will be my something more than friend,
No matter what may happen?

Argo. Ay, more than friend — some fifteen times thy lover,
Nor less than husband in all gracious office.
I will be multiplied by forty thousand,
And troop about thee like a veteran army
About a conquering general. Doubt me not:
When I prove laggard in my fond attentions,
Then look for general famine and disaster:
And when thou find'st me false, look for eclipses,
For stars to strike and craters to break forth,
And bellowing thunders underneath the globe;
And for the moon to draw the ocean up,
That dry land disappear! O, never doubt me, .
For I am thine clear through, and filled to the brim,
With love that eats all other passions in me,
As acidi nitrici eats up brass,
And leaves pure gold untouched.
Irene. Then should my honor ever be assailed,
As if the gossips should say: She is proud;
Or she is fickle: she is false at heart;
You would defend me, Argo?
Argo.   I! — would I!
Why, I would fight for thee on fifty streets;
I would rush naked-handed on a thousand,
If one in that whole thousand gave a thousandth —
Ay, one ten-thousandth part of an allusion
To possible fault or fickleness in thee!
Let any slander come within my gripe! —
Him I'll eviscerate — hogs will I feed
Upon the offal of that man on sight,
While he looks on and howls.
Irene. Then make your name and fortune in a hurry:
And when you bring them with your mind unchanged,
I will accept them and we then will wed.
Argo. And not till then. Farewell; the word is said. [*Exit* ARGO.
Irene. O, woe is me! O earth, fly from your orbit,
And fail away some billion miles to the north,
Out of the range of heat and light and air;
And be like me, a dead and frozen star,
Lost in perpetual night; or open wide,
And make a yawning chasm, deep as hell,
And topple me down from the frightful brink,
Clear to the inky bottom, where are brewed
The sulphur fumes that suffocate the damned!
Then close the crevice that there be no trace
Of the huge gap that swallowed me alive.
And then, O earth, that opes my way to death:
Bear not upon thy bosom any mark
Or footprint made by me; let blind oblivion
And blank forgetfulness suppress the name
Of one erewhile so wretched;— forced, as 'twere,
To play at treason;—and yet tied to the track
Almost by my own hands, the thundering train
Just rounding yonder curve: still there is time;
And I may yet unloose the cords and live.
But that were playing treason north by east,
And I am bound to play it west by south.
I am resolved. What kind of person am I?
Methinks I must be some rare sort of villain,

And not the hapless maiden, whelmed in woe:
Else why not true to nature and to love?
Ay, there's the question:— I am true to both,
And yet am false to each. My loves run counter —
They clash, and one must die, or I must die,
And thus end all with benefit to none.
I must be villain to myself and lover,
Or else crush out the life that gave me life,
And with it peace! O, dread alternative!
My lover is no ordinary being;
He is an emperor in mien and manner;
He hath the several graces of the gods,
And intellectually he is a giant
Amongst his fellow men. The proudest empress
Might be too proud of him. And I must lose him!
And in his place must take a ton of tallow;
A tierce of lard, a washtub full of offal;
With pipes, tobacco, whisky!—all topped off
With some two million dollars! Still I ask
What sort of girl am I? I have suspicion
That I was cut out for a cautious rogue,
And not much spoilt in making. Mean I well?
This is a question for my heart to answer,
And half of it says, no! My lover's thoughts
Go forth for virtues as the honey bees
Go forth for early flowers; while mine, I fear,
Take more delight in fishing down in hell
For treason, falsehood and black-faced deceit.   [*Exit.*

SCENE II.—*A room. Enter* MOTHER.

Mother.   Close me these doors. Let me commune alone.
Soul must not know the secrets of this heart:
If they were hissed in any ears but Satan's
Those ears would burst like goblets suddenly heated.
The cautious have no confidants; none know
The secret workings of the prudent mind.
They say that women cannot keep a secret,
And that foul murder cannot be concealed;
But secrets that concern the woman keeper
Are locked as safely in her bosom as
The secrets of the earth are locked down in
The center of the globe; and many a murder
Lies hid and will until the crack of doom.
Speak I of murder?—a church-going saint —
Noted for piety — with heart as tender
As those of nursing lambs, or turtle-doves —
Much given to prayer—to visiting the sick —
To giving alms! Ay, ay! but I can murder!
I can imbrue my hands in blood as coolly
As any pirate! Ay, I know it, feel it.
And my religious life affords a cloak,
Concealed in which I may securely strike,
Nor draw suspicion after If I fail
It is but ignominy and death, less dreadful
Than living poverty. But I'll not fail;
And so I strike; so clutch the glittering prize.
I have read deep in poisons; three small grains,
Inodorous, tasteless, potent little grains,

Placed in his posset when far gone in drink,
Will entertain his stomach with such pangs,
As shall divert the lechery from his liver.
O, he shall have my child, but never, never,
Shall he lie down with her; the man she loves
Shall have her as she is, if the hot fool
Does not go crazy and destroy himself;
And he will not, for I observe that ranters
Rarely go to extremes except in ranting.
There is more danger in that rash, mad girl,
But I will watch her. Little dreams she now
That I am planning to risk soul and body
To give her to her lover, while I seem
To force her to the arms of one she loathes.
The sweets of my first love are well remembered,
And I can feel for the poor child's distress;
He wants my child who could have had me, when
I was as pretty as my blooming daughter;
He knew it and he cut me openly;
So I can put a spider in his tea
Without a qualm of conscience — thrift and vengeance!
And she is no true mother who would higgle
At drinking blood to make her daughter rich,
And happy for all time. My God, how different
Do I appear to that I truly am!
How poorly can we judge the human heart,
From outward show or movement of the tongue!
O, help me, help me, devils, and I'll send you
The fattest sinner in this hemisphere:
Then for a glorious life. And then! — and then
For the hereafter after life is over!
Ay, there's the dread: to plunge headlong — soaked through,
Dyed, steamed and boiled in blood to the very liver, —
To plunge thus inked, begrimed, incarnadined,
Headlong into the blind unknown hereafter,
With this four hundred weight of bloated carcass
Hung like a ton of lead about my neck —
To plunge thus down to hell — to the very bottom!
But cannot prayer, repentance, charity,
Remove this weight and bleach my soul like snow?
And make it light as down, so it shoot up,
Like steam from the strained engine's throat, to heaven?
I'll risk it, even were hell to yawn next week!
I'll risk my soul's salvation for revenge,
That empties riches in my daughter's lap,
Gives her her lover, and restores to me
The leadership of the proud city dames
That flout me in my fall from affluence!
Down fear! and up ambition!

SCENE III.—*A drawing-room. Enter* IRENE *from one side, and* SAM
from the other.

Sam. O, you is heah, is ye! Dat ole fellah dat owns de bank stock
and de big stomach is down dah at de doah below in de biggest hurry
you eber seed anybody in, and I tries my best to strain him, case I
knows you wants time to take a good cry arter de crazy young fellah
lef. But he says he must see de lubly Miss Irene 'mejitly. Blebe my
soul dat ole coon is in lub, too.

Irene. Sam, go and tell him I am not in.

Sam. But you is; doesn't I see ye?

Irene. Say to him that I am not dressed to receive company. Tell him I am ill—I am in bed—I am dead—anything. Tell him to come to-morrow.

Sam. Look a heah, Miss; I professes to be a gemman of honah, if I is culled. De rules ob good 'siety forbids a gemman to pack a diswonable proposition. Wid all due 'spect toh you as a lady, and my ekal, I declines to convey any communication 'cept it be de truff. 'Scuse me.

Enter MAGOON, *overturning* SAM, *who retires in fright.*

Major. Pardon my abruptness, Miss Irene. Lord bless you, I couldn't endure another moment's suspense. Why, upon my soul, you've grown into a downright beauty. I shall be the happiest man on this globe. I shall be envied by the male population of the entire universe, for I will travel the world over to exhibit you and proclaim my felicity.

Irene. Have you been well, Major?

Major. Never better; I have starved more doctors than any man of my age. Have no faith in them; hence I'm alive and well. Have seen your mother and settled matters. Have made a will; matrimony is risky; all liable to die. You heir my property, with the exception in favor of your mother, if I die while we are amicably together as husband and wife. Here are the papers for safe keeping. This match saves some of the grandest scoundrels from merited vengeance. Was going to will my entire wealth to endow a society for the detection and punishment of the villainous adulterers of liquors, by which so many of us jolly young fellows are cut off in our prime. And now, when shall the wedding take place? I have lived fifty-nine years without a wife. That's long enough.

Irene. Fix the day yourself, Major. I am taking no part in this transaction. I am passive. I am in the hands of Fate. I am as a blasted leaf in spring-time, blown about by whirlwinds. Nothing shall I promote; nothing resist. I shall float with the tide. Love you I do not, Major; respect you I must, for you are good and kind. But I will be dutiful and obedient.

Major. O, you will fall in love with me, pet. Time enough for that. Be cheerful. Don't go to grieving. Can't bear to see you cry. Cheer up, pet, and name the day, and let us be gay. (How this love does run a man's ideas into poetry.)

Irene. I will try to be cheerful; and as to the wedding, to-day, to-morrow, any day, will do.

Major. Bless you, my sweet jewel! It shall be to-morrow, with a grand banquet at night.

Irene. I shall be in readiness. Here comes my mother. I will retire. Perhaps she would like private conference with you.   [*Exit* IRENE.

Enter MOTHER.

Mother. Well, Major, how do you find my daughter disposed toward you? She has been reading poetry and cultivating romantic ideas of late, and I feared the effect upon her mind.

Major. She's all right, Madam. Whole affair arranged. Marry to-morrow. Doesn't love me, but a young girl's love is light as her smiles. Give a young girl plenty of dress and finery, and she will be happy. A fig for love; it can be cultivated at leisure. I can plant it and raise it like a cabbage.

Mother. The disparity in your ages, Major, is great, and the world is accustomed to frown upon marriages of this kind, though I think them eminently proper.

Major. So do I. The world, as it is called, isn't always right.

Wouldn't it be absurd to join two snowballs in the hope of generating heat? Let the icicles of age be thawed in the furnace of youth. What is the use of adding fire to fire? Youth is too hot; age too cold; fuse them and you have a healthful thermometer. Let heat be diffused that coldness may be overcome, and life and pleasure be prolonged. What would two as cold lumps as you and I do together, but freeze?

Mother. Thank you, sir. I am no cold lump. I am as warm as any woman.

Major. O, I think you will make an admirable mother-in-law. Good morning. Push the preparations. [*Exit.*

Mother. The unwieldy old monster! to call me a cold lump. I'll make it hot enough for him! Why, I was offered marriage a week ago by a handsome young man of twenty-four, with a comfortable income. Cold lump, indeed! So soon as it is known that I have a competency in my own right, I will not be regarded as cold and old. I will get a husband that can call him grandfather. Cold lump! [*Exit.*

ACT II.

SCENE I.—*A bedroom.* MAGOON *in bed groaning. Present:* IRENE, MOTHER, *two old women nurses,* SAM *and Friends.*

Enter DR. SPANKER,

(*With surgical instruments and appliances, which he hastily spreads on a table.*)

Dr. Spanker. What's the matter? Who's sick? Male or female? Obstetrics? Hernia?

Irene. O, doctor, what do you want with all those horrid instruments? It is medicine the Major requires.

Doctor. Always go prepared for emergency, Madam. Glad it is no worse. Expected an operation for hernia, or an amputation at the least.

Mother. O, doctor, be quick; the Major has had a fit.

Major. Devil a fit. It is the cramp colic. I had it in London. They injected me with a side break engine. O dear! O dear!

Doctor. (*To himself.*) Depressed pulse; cold skin; abused stomach; too much pudding; too much beer.

Mother. (*Aside.*) That's what I thought.

Doctor. Did he eat a heavy supper?

Mother. I should say he did! Why he has vomited four gallons.

Irene. O, no, mother.

Major. Yes, I have; I'm as empty as the air.

Doctor. (*Writes and hands prescription to Servant.*) Go immediately to the apothecary's with this.

Sam. (*Spelling out the paper, a little way off.*) R-e-c-i-p-e. Dat stands foh recete. What dis? H-y-d-r-a-r-g.: yes, hydrarg., dat's calomel. C-h-l-o-r-i-d. M-i-t.; Chlorid. Mit., grains sixty; dat's calomel, too. O-l-e-u-m, Oleum; dat's oil. T-i-g-l-i-i, tiglii; what de debil can dat be? M-i-n-i-m-s, minims five; dat's five draps. Foah God! dat's crotum oil; dead shuah to kill. Wid de 'dition ob one pint ob terpentine, dis is de 'xact 'scription I used to gib massa's hoss foh de botts.

Irene. Why, Sam! you here yet? Why don't you hurry?

Doctor. What has emancipation brought us to! Such unpardonable indolence!

Sam. It has brought you to de knowledge dat de culled man is competent to rassel wid de great problems ob life. Indolence, to be shuah! Larnin' in de culled man is indolence! Oho, can't cober up youh calomel in latting from de culled man now! [*Exit.*

Doctor. Apply a blister to the nape of the neck and twenty leeches to the pit of the stomach. Close the room and give him rest. I will see him in the morning.   [*Exit.*

SCENE II.— *The same. Present:* IRENE, MOTHER, *old ladies and* SAM.

Irene. Do you feel easier, Major?

Major. Devil a bit. I'm worse; ten times worse. My neck is on fire, and my stomach! Mercy on me! Give me some hot punch. O dear! Hasn't Spanker come? Toddy, toddy!

Mother. No, my dear Major. The poor man is almost without hope.

Major. He is, eh? Send for another doctor; I want no hopeless doctors about me. Toddy, toddy!

Mother. Pray, Major, shall I call my family physician?

Major. Call anybody; a horse farrier can't do worse than Spanker. Give me the toddy!

Mother. (*To* SAM.) Go for Dr. Smick. [*Gives the toddy.*]

Sam. I hab a poah 'pinion ob dis Smick. His pills isn't bigger dan heads ob pins. Dey will neber mobe dat worrum from de Majah, foh it be a zagerated case ob tapeworrum, shuah as Ize culled.

Irene. Never mind, Sam, what it is. Go and bring Dr. Smick.   [*Exit* SAM.

Major. Bring me some more toddy. My bowels are tied in hard knots. Toddy! toddy!

First Old Lady. Have a little of this pepper tea, Major.

Second Old Lady. Major, I have some water and flour teemed together. It never fails to break the colic. If you could only drink a quart of it.

Major. Give them to me. Give me the toddy, the toddy, the toddy, the toddy! [*Drinks.*]

Enter DR. SMICK.

Major. O, doctor, I am about seven-tenths dead.

Doctor. I see. You have had Spanker with his heroic treatment. Well, if people will be killed with blisters and calomel it is their own business. [*Examines* MAGOON.] Nervous exhaustion; a clear case. [*Prepares some powders at a side table.*] Give him one of these powders every five minutes, in ten drops of beef tea. Nothing else; positively nothing else must go down his throat.   [*Exit.*

Irene. Here, Major, take one of the powders.

Major. You have spilled it. There's nothing in the spoon.

Irene. It is the dose the doctor ordered. You are to take one every five minutes.

Major. I am, eh! Well, now mix all at once, and I will take all in one minute, and swallow the quack if he comes back here. There, now! O, my stomach! Give me a little sup of toddy.

Mother. (*Aside.*) He's worse. His mind wanders.

First Old Lady. Ladies, I would call the colored doctor, Dr. Abram Turner. I heard of his bringing a worm forty yards long from a man who was suffering just like the Major is. He always doctors for worms.

Mother. Do you mean the colored blacksmith?

First Old Lady. Well, he was a blacksmith, and then a horse doctor, but he is now doing a regular practice. It is time we lay aside our prejudice against color. Relief is what the Major wants.

Major. O, yes, that's what I want. Send for him. He shod my horses a year ago. Toddy, toddy!

Irene. Go for Dr. Abram Turner forthwith.

Sam. Now I begins to see lite. De Majah hab a slim chance ob recobery yet. Culled pussens to de front!

Major. O Lord! give me a little more of that toddy. I am about gone; toddy! toddy! beer!

Enter DR. TURNER.

Turner. Majah, is you ill, sah! Let me 'zammin dis stomach onct. [*Examines.*] Worrum dar. Worrum hab gone insane, or he hab fits. Can feel him rippin de broad ligaments. He is coiled about de lopian tubes ob de ascendin cavy, cuttin off de blood from de front sinus ob de quadratus lumborum; and at de same time his head is stickin fast in de choly ductus docus foh shuah, closin dat 'portant tuberosity and deprivin de left ventable ob de heart ob its natral supply ob bile. Dis monster is what we doctahs calls exhurus ascaris, alludin to Judas Iscarret, de fust to hab him; and dat's why Judas betrayed he massa. He be known to hab hydrofoby and fits. You hab only one ob him at a time. I will pass him or pacify him. Make dese roots into a quart ob tea and gib it to de Majah berry hot and fast. [*Exit.*]

Major. (*Picking at the air.*) I see gnats — brush them away; a little more toddy; toddy; toddy!

Mother. (*Fanning him.*) He is failing, poor man.

Major. Where is my Irene? Where is my bride?

Irene. Here I am, my dear Major. What can I do for you?

Major. Nothing, nothing; give me some toddy; the doctors don't understand my case. They have murdered me.

Enter TUBBS.

Tubbs. What! may the devil take me, is the Major sick? Why, Major, how do you do?

Major. O, Tubbs, is it you?

Tubbs. May the devil boil me for an owl if it ain't.

Major. Yes, Tubbs, I'm sick, sick, sick! Let me have some toddy.

Tubbs. Have you been a takin' o' this doctor stuff? If you have, don't you take another bit; may I be damned, but it'll kill you.

Irene. We have tried all the doctors, and he is getting weaker. Poor, poor man.

Tubbs. Calomy doctors?

Irene. Yes, he has had calomel and jalap, and croton oil, and a bushel of other stuff.

Tubbs. May I be damned, but the calomy'll kill him. As for me and mine, we never take doctor stuff; but if I must have a doctor give me a steam doctor or give me no doctor at all. Now, do you send and get the old man Slabbs; he's an old steam doctor and a man that knows a heap. He'll gather a yarb that grows fernenst his barn; he'll bile it down and make it into a tea, and give it to you; and if the pain's not in the bones, but under and fernenst the ribs, it'll cure you in an hour; but if the pain's in the bones, it's the calomy, and may I be damned, but it'll kill you.

Major. Well, send for old man Slabbs; I know him well; he is mainly in the hoop-pole business. Give me some toddy. [*Irene gives it to him.*]

Tubbs. So he is, Major, but he's a mighty knowin' man. These calomy doctors! I hate to swear afore ladies, but may I be damned, if they oughtn't to be in the penitentiary. I'll fetch Slabbs myself, but it's no use. Calomy once in the bones is thar. [*Exit.*]

SCENE III.—*A street. Enter* SAM.

Sam. De berry debble is to pay. Heah is a chance foh doctah Abram Turner to 'stinguish hisself, and dey keeps heavin in de medicines dat works agin de doctah's tea, and makes de worrum madder and madder widout killin' ob him. De fool Tubbs hab gone foh de erb doctah, and

I is commanded to watch de street foh doctah Slash, whom it is de inwarible rule to call when it is dun shuah dat de patient will die anyhow.

Enter DR. SLASH.

Sam. Ah, doctah! you is wanted at de bedside ob Major Magoon. He married last night and he will die to-day; darfoh dey wants you.

Slash. What ails your master?

Sam. Massa! I has no massa, sah! I is a gemman, sah, if I is culled. I mobes in good 'sciety.

Slash. You do, eh? Well, now let me see you move.

[*Exit, kicking him out.*

SCENE IV.—*The bedroom.* Enter TUBBS *and* SLABBS.

Tubbs. Here's a man, Mr. Slabbs, that's been a takin' o' calomy and other doctor stuff, and may I be damned, but it's a killin' of him. Blow me, but I'd give him lobely and get it all outen him as quick as the devil 'ud let me.

Slabbs. That's the first thing to be done. Here, Major, down with this, or you are a dead man. [*Major swallows it and immediately begins straining to vomit.*]

Tubbs. Gentlemen, he's bad. Lobely's not a goin' to cure that man. I'd recommend you to send for Dr. Slash. He's an old calomy doctor that makes a sure shot—invariably kills, because he's never sent for till the patient has the death rattle. If he could get a sight at a man only half dead he'd save him. Why, here he comes.

Enter DR. SLASH.

Slash. Why, what is the matter? Major, rouse up here. What's the matter? How do you do? How do you feel?

Tubbs. May I be damned, but he feels like a man that's been a takin' o' calomy till he's about dead. [SLASH *gives him a look and gets one with interest back.*]

Slash. Have you had the doctors here?

Irene. O, yes, doctor, all of them, and he seems to get no ease.

Slash. There is need of promptness. [*Mixes and gives him a dose.*] Now give him plenty of hot whisky.

Tubbs. May I be damned, but it's more calomy. [*Aside to* SLABBS.] That man is dead. Salt won't save him.

Major. (*Faintly.*) Yes, give me the whisky. That's my medicine. Toddy, toddy, hot toddy! I'm freezing.

Tubbs. You're right, Major. Whisky is a good medicine. If it won't save you, nothing will. [MAGOON *gasps;* IRENE *takes his hand.*] May I be damned, but the Major's dead. The calomy's killed him.

SCENE V.—*A country place.* ARGO, *walking moodily, meets a laboring farmer.*

Farmer. Good morning, sir. Taking your usual ramble over the fields, I see, sir.

Argo. Yes, my good friend. I hope I do not intrude or trespass to the detriment of the owners.

Farmer. O Lord, no, sir. Our people are much interested in you. You are the subject of much wonder and gossip, sir. The country girls are agog to learn your history; they have observed you, and think some great sorrow must weigh upon you.

Argo. Poor girls! true to their nature, whether in halls
Of polished marble, or in cottage lowly;
Curiosity and love for the mysterious
Are still their ruling traits: and little foibles

Do prettily become the pretty creatures,
As butterflies the smiling face of nature,
When clad in vernal bloom.
Live you here, hard by, my good man?

Farmer. Yes, sir, this is my farm ; yonder is my house. I have worked hard here for twenty-five years, sir.

Argo. Then you are pretty well-to-do, and don't have to work now.

Farmer. Well, not so very well-to-do, either, stranger. My family has been to raise, and now that the boys are pretty well grown, they give me trouble ; and the girls must be dressed in the fashion ; and the old woman is in poor health, doing for so large a family ; and the fact is, sir, I had to mortgage my farm to keep up with the demands of the times, and for some time I've had to work harder than ever to save it from forfeit ; and I shall have to keep it up for a few years yet. But I am beginning to find that work goes harder with me than it used to, and sometimes I am almost discouraged. Still I keep plodding on, in hopes of better times for me in the future.

Argo. What age are you, my friend?

Farmer. I am just turned of fifty ; but I think, sir, that I am good for several years yet. My father lived to eighty.

Argo. And you want to live on, sir.

Farmer. Well, yes ; old folks want to live as well as young people, I suppose, sir.

Argo. But why, my friend, would the old man live on?
What is there in existence in this sphere
That man should struggle to prolong his stay?
His early years, when he looks back on them,
Seem as a war in which he took a part,
Being on the weaker side ; and fighting bravely,
Was subject to defeat and disappointment.
And save the few bright hours of infancy,
When life was opening like a new blown rose,
He scarce can name a year he would recall,
And for the few poor comforts it afforded,
Fight its rough battles over. His prime and strength
Are spent in fighting for a little footing,
Amongst his fellows ; but accumulation
Of years and troubles compass him about,
And come upon him ere his work is finished :
He falls and is forgotten ; like the horse
That tugs in heavy harness many seasons,
Till worn and weak, the winter of his life
Finds him upon the common naked, where
He lays his weary bones. O heavy life !
Where fifty years bring nothing but regrets,
And find you even too naked to eke out
Life's little remnant, but with daily effort :
Your offspring round you, each a separate care ;
Perhaps a separate sorrow. O poor man !
What fascinates you at this stage of life
To grovel for extension of your lease ?
Your past is strown with broken loves and hopes,
And wrecks of castles builded in the air ;
With memories of mistakes and many errors,
Now past correction ; and your present ! —
What is in it but a fresh troop of wants,
That cry from every faculty and organ
For remedy or rest, and gather strength

5

As you grow feebler with increase of years?
Cut off from pleasures that diverted youth,
Yet racked with pangs that youth was stranger to:
Made petulant with petty plagues and piques,
As stiffened joints, loose teeth and failing sight,
With nameless other small annoyances:
Aged and infirm, unhoused and unprovided;
Or have you goods, perhaps inheritors
Become impatient for a distribution,
That waits on your departure.   Thus at fifty:
And what is there in the few years remaining,
But aggravation of developed evils,
Which still develop others?   Then, poor man,
Here lay your armor off: your life has failed:
You weary others by a longer stay,
And you have nothing worth the staying for.
Seek you some sweet brain-soothing anodyne,
Which taken in excess promotes that sleep
From which you wake into eternal life,
Or sink into oblivious rayless night,
And find surcease of pain.

Farmer. O, I see now.   You are one of them theater fellows; you're
a player.

Argo. I am, my friend, a player like yourself;
I play a heavy part that wearies me,
And profits not the stage.

Farmer. Well, sir, you spoke a great deal of truth in that little piece.
I've often had just such thoughts as you express in your stage style,
which I love, but haven't the learning to appreciate fully, I fear.   I hope you
will call at my house when you have leisure.   My folks would be glad
to make your acquaintance, sir.

Argo. Thank you, my honest friend ; I will make it convenient to
call upon you.   Farewell.   [*Exit* ARGO.

Farmer. He's a right-down smart young fellow.   Crazy, I do believe;
but he has a power of hard horse sense about him.   Well, I shall not
seek his brain-soother yet awhile ; but the truth is, I have little to live
for.   I have worked hard and lived pretty hard all my life, and I see
nothing but hard work and hardship ahead.   My old age is not provided
for, nor won't be.   There is no rest.   But I'll go and tell the old woman
and the girls what I've discovered.   I wish I could remember that fellow's blank verse — I believe that is what they call it.   [*Exit.*

ACT III.

SCENE I. — *A Gloomy Wood.   Enter* ARGO *with a revolver, a dagger and
a vial of poison.*

Argo. It sometimes happens that a man must die
To prove himself a man ; and evils come
In shapes that cannot be endured ; and death
Is sought by way of refuge, or to wring
Some heart where ours is shrined.   To yield the flesh
To putrefactive forces and to worms,
And leave the curious bones, the pretty joints
To wear and waste to native salts and earth;
Or else mayhap to be strung up on wires
In some quack's shop to frighten timid maids,

And draw from fools much idiotic question;
Or to be hid in the quack's private cell,
Where he receives his mistress on the sly,
And there stand grinning in my naked bones
In point-blank presence of illicit loves,
Dead as a post to passion; or to creep
Away on through the years into old age,
Without the charm which might have made the journey
Endurable at least; and ever conscious
Of the nine times detestable outrage
Played off upon me; and to know that he —
O hell! let me forget it! — he enjoys
My wife! for she is mine! earth's laws and heaven's
Have nothing that to love's hot oaths can add
A tithe more marrying power. — Divorced and cuckold! —
Horn'd, fork'd, spik'd, spit on! — suicide must purge ·
This foul disgrace away. And yet to die,
To die, to leave the green earth and to yield
One's whole prerogatives to other men! —
There's where the pinch comes in! — To leave one's books,
One's horses, dogs, — one's houses, lands and monies; —
All those conveniences one has contrived
And those arrangements one has just completed
To minister to ease, is hard; and harder
Is't not to know who'll be elected Tuesday;
What wars may rage in the next twenty years;
What little men loom up; what great men fall;
What women be seduced, what wives divorced;
Who'll win the horse race that comes off next week;
And there's no telegraph nor daily press
In the unknown abyss; and whether the dead
Have means whereby they can come at the news,
I fear is doubtful in the last extreme.
O, the extremity is dire indeed
That makes the young seek death; oblivious death;
Annihilation: man prefers to wear
His faculties clear out, and crawl t' his grave,
Inch at a time, snail-like, until he chokes
From failure of the emunctories to bear off
The incidental poisonous compounds
That in life's chemical workshops accrue,
In the processes and occult assays,
Whose grand achievement is the crimson tide,
Which is the food of life. We fight for breath,
Till the worn lungs no longer generate
Electric heat to vitalize the blood,
Which now, coagulate and cold, clogs up
The avenues of life; and then our elements
Seek out their kindred elements; and each
Finds its affinity, and all disperse —
But not to perish; all will re-appear
In different combinations — in the air,
The earth, the ocean, other animals,
In fruits, in flowers, in leaves, offensive gases;
Or in the damask cheek of beauty. But
Atoms to dissolution given, never
Can be combined more! But why stand here.
Philosophizing on the brink of death!

I came for slaughter and to reap revenge,
And not for argument. Am I insane?
Some people hold that only the insane
Resort to bloody violence on themselves.
Am I insane, who reason me and plead
Like an attorney, after the verdict's in!
More fool than madman, and more ass than either,
To amplify and argue at this hour:
Yet there is something in the gulph beyond,—
The uncertain sea that hath no bound nor bottom —
And from whose surge no diver yet hath risen,—
That makes us dread the plunge. The crazy man
Retains no sense of this, and makes the leap,
Not thinking of the landing; he is brave
From want of sense; while one not lacking reason,
Will pause perforce of that same reason, and
Become a coward. That is my condition:
I am afraid to die;— and yet must die:
I would not live to be laughed at to-morrow
For th' wealth of all the Indies: only death
Remains to him who hath been cut and jilted
By a false-hearted beauty — one to whom
He hath revealed the weak side of his nature,
And made his confidant! The furies burn her!
The accursed fiends could not invent a trick
One half so sure to cut a proud man off!
Hack-drivers, loafers, waiters, chambermaids,—
The very bootblacks knew Irene was mine:
The peanut venders, apple-women — all
Knew us affianced up to the very hour
When she skipped nimbly to the old banker's bed!
I'm laughed at by the raggedest boy 'n the street!
I'd die for this if hell had nothing hotter!
Now come grim murder with your goriest hand!—
One sweep of this keen dagger cuts my throat,
And ends the matter quickly; still I am
Opposed to all barbarity in killing.
I never stoned a bird nor drown'd a kitten,
I who want my own blood have shed no blood!
But I am shaken with my bloody purpose,
And with my trembling hand may botch the job,
And being discovered wallowing in my gore,
Be set upon by surgeons and be saved
To my intense disgust. I cannot stab;
Fire-arms are best — a bullet through the brain
Doth pass like lightning and is scarcely felt;
And there's small chance of failure — 'tis less brutal
To spring a trigger than to cut a gash;
Still it may snap or my unsteady aim
Cause worser havoc than a half cut throat.
Perhaps 'twere better to engulph this poison —
'Twill kill without a pang; you sleep to death,
And never know the moment you depart.
Yet I'm no judge of drugs and may have looked
So like a kill-sheep dog when ordering this,
That the pert pill-box nosing out my purpose,
Being wise as new-fledged quacks perforce must be,
Brewed me an anodyne or vile emetic,

Instead of the life-suffocating chloral
To give me riddance; and even now perhaps,
He dogs me here to witness the result;
Thinking to laugh while I do heave and vomit,
Or else to lull my wronged, indignant spirit
In a composing sleep — thus cheating me
Into some hours of life, and thwarting me
In my most fixed and settled purpose — thus
By a foul swindle, making me appear
Thrice more ridiculous than I am already!
I will not touch it. But what shall I do?
I will not live, yet scarcely dare to die;
I'll plunge this dagger to the spinal marrow
And end the parley straight! But not too fast;
I may not make a decent looking corpse,
And when the coroner's rag'muffin jury
Come to inspect me, they may scoff or jeer,
Or pass some jest that should not go unpunished,
And show the body of a bashful man
Stark naked to a mob of gaping fools,
Of after incidents the most abhorrent
To all the senses. Is there no escape?
But for the coroner's jury I could do it.
Let me consider coolly — must I die?
Die for a woman? Are there not concealed,
In earth or hell some direr helps to vengeance?
By living grimly on through all my years,
And hating all the women all the time —
Doing to them every unkind, ugly thing —
Writing against them — preaching against them —
Backbiting them — making faces at them —
Pinching their babies — making their husbands jealous —
Slandering them, (if it were possible) —
Seducing them, (if it would plague them any) —
By these means might I not spite them a little,
And feed my vengeance some?
I'll try it for a time, though I may reap
Less vengeance than vexation.
I trust no eye hath seen me: I'm ashamed
Of my irresolution — it is fear,
Or I would else be fly-blown and the buzzards
Be here at conference. O Irene, Irene!
To what extremity I've come for thee!
Where is the precious estimate of woman
I had but yestermorn! At dead of night
While my muse ranged the universe for flowers,
And rainbow tints and rubies to adorn
The coronet 'twas weaving for thy brow:
Even then thou wert locked in conjugal clutch
With a worn lecher! and myself, greenhorn —
I, duped idiot, was contorting rhymes
To sound thy virtues! Fie! But I am cured
To the thoracic duct.
A careful estimate of woman's faults,
Would shock the devil; we see not her faults,
We're blind to everything except the toy
She keeps to tantalize us; but for that
She'd get her dues from bards and other writers

Whose flattery is measured by their lusts.
I see her as she is, and, being impartial,
Say she is treacherous, vain, deceitful, giv'n to lying;
To eating clay and gum; slate pencils, chalk;
She has hysteria by the year — the yellow jaundice,
Dyspepsia and chlorosis; polypus;
With lead marks under the eyes — these half the time;
False teeth, a tapeworm, corns — infallibly these.
She most delights in dress, balls, fooling men,
And being fooled; for there is bawdry in
Her bones, her blood, in each particular drop.
These are a few of her most marked defects,
But there is not a trouble known to mortals
But she's at bottom of it. I do hate her,
And am well rid of her.

SCENE II. — *A room.* IRENE *in mourning.*

Irene. Occasions make the actors they require,
And great emergencies sometimes bring forth
Immense resource, and develop strength
In individuals or in nations whence
We looked for weakness only: will is power:
My purposes are great and I am strong.
They take me for a vain and idle woman,
A slave to fashion and to avarice;
And think that as I have come into fortune,
I will come out a flaunting butterfly;
But I will fill their ears with other stories;
I'll show them that a woman's head is full
Of plots and strategies, and that her heart when swoll'n
With love or hate can dare death, hell, the furies!
I'll have him back — I will lose all or have him.
I did obey my mother as in duty,
For who can tell what mothers bear for children!
What pains, what cares, what sleepless nights and days,
Must the poor mother bear to rear her baby!
Which, when grown up, too often makes return
In disobedience and ingratitude.
I sold myself and broke my vows to buy
Some little comforts for my failing mother;
As she when I was little would have sold
Her dearest treasures to procure me food.
And now as heaven hath taken away my husband,
And left me that which he could not take with him;
And as my mother is provided for,
And I have leisure for some further business,
I will put on the stage another play,
And win fresh laurels or throw all away.

Enter Lawyer, with legal papers.

Lawyer. Good morning, good lady. You are looking well. Weeds
become you mightily.

Irene. Have you drawn the papers as I directed?

Lawyer. They are ready for your signature. [IRENE *reads and signs the papers.*] I hope the young man will prove worthy of your confidence.

Irene. Please, sir, keep the matter strictly private until I remove the confidence. There is some money in bank to your credit. By examining enclosed papers you will see what disposition to make of a part of it. Please carry out the written instructions, and keep all quiet.

Lawyer. I will take pleasure in executing your commands, Madam. Farewell. [*Exit Lawyer.*

Irene. Farewell, sir.

How many sickly doubts and fears assail us,
If we make pause to listen to their tongues,
While we are lugging lame irresolution
To the front door of action; after all
How easy is performance when the mind
Is well resolved and settled in its purpose!
Now for another chapter.

SCENE III. — *A studio. Enter Publisher and Critic.*

Publisher. We have lost on that volume of the crazy fellow Argo, have we not?

Critic. It may turn out so. The fellow has genius, but he is imprudent. He makes reckless assaults upon the vices, beliefs and prejudices of men and women; and people won't pay money to be told of their follies and absurdities.

Publisher. Have you examined his last production?

Critic. I have looked it through. It has merit. If the fellow had a name to give it a start it might have a good run.

Publisher. Perhaps; but we can't afford to lift unknown authors into prominence at our cost. We must deal with those who are already famous. I have written declining his book.

Enter Lawyer.

Ay, sir; glad to see you. Pray be seated.

Lawyer. I called on a little business. Have you in press a volume by the young fellow Argo?

Publisher. The work was offered, but we were compelled to decline it. The author is laboring in a field where few succeed and many fail.

Lawyer. Is there any merit in his work?

Publisher. That is not so much the question, sir. We think there is more risk than money in it. If the author had an established reputation the work might be received with favor.

Lawyer. Then it would seem that it is the name of the author rather than the character of the work that takes with the public.

Critic. Exactly so. The world is full of literary trash that would fall, but for the popular names that sustain it.

Lawyer. May an author possessing no solid worth be lifted into public favor by money and puffery?

Critic. Undoubtedly he may, and without them he has a poor show, unless his abilities are very rare indeed.

Lawyer. A party that must be unknown in the affair desires you to advance, as if from your firm, ten thousand dollars to the young author Argo, on the work you have declined. The order for the publication will be given hereafter. Here, sir, is a check for that sum.

Publisher. That is liberal, sir. Some enthusiast, with more money than discretion, I presume. But we will attend to the matter.

Lawyer. That is not for me to judge, sir. Farewell. [*Exit.*

Publisher. We must seek out the crack-brain. This money will bring him to the surface.

Critic. His work is worthy, and we will undertake him now that he has backing.

SCENE IV. — *A studio.* ARGO *reading a letter; tears it and rises.*

Argo. Declines the work, but thanks me; a cold lie!
No matter, though; I will not struggle more;
A further effort in an honest way,
In view of these rebuffs, would be unmanly;
Occasions rise when villainy is virtue,
And when you may employ the devil's weapons
To fight his armies off. When one is in
A war with villains he must be a villain.
Man is the villain waging war on me;
He will not give me foothold in the world,
And I must fight for it. The wolf and lion
Are kindlier to their kind than man to his.
The sturdier swine that, gobbling up the slop,
Crowd off and crush the weaker, are less brutal
Than men who crush their struggling fellow-men,
Nor help the weak to rise. Inborn is villainy;
Your average man is every inch a villain;
Nine-tenths of every ounce of him are villain,
And the other tenth is tyrant. So I find him.
Cheated by men, I never trusted woman
Who did not put herself to extra trouble
To craze my soul with love but to betray it.
Are all like these? or does some crooked chance
Present me ever the worst specimens
Of women and of men? It must be fate,
Fixed by the adverse stars when I was born.
There was a time when I did seek for fame,
For honor and distinction in the world,
Long did I struggle in the mad pursuit,
But fate did thwart me so I caught them not,
And now the chase is ended. All my arrows
Are shot awry; and my most cherished hopes
Lay limp and withered like to early corn
Nipped by untimely frost. That man's a slave
Who hath a cherished hope or aspiration,
And who hath none is free; now having none
I'm free, and will give nature rein; and like
A baulky racer able to win the race,
I'll only rear and plunge. I will become
A misanthrope with hate so hot that it
Shall make my eyeballs vomit fire and fix
Upon my brow a scowl to shed the plague;
Set my firm jaws and make my aspect such
That men who see me bolt as from the devil,
And grazing herds stampede, though I approach
No nearer than a mile. I'll be men's ague,
And shake them like an earthquake; and their fever,
And burn them like the sands on torrid plains.
I'll work upon their passions with my pen,
I'll make wild havoc in the social circles,
By hell invented stories that shall point
To infidelities crossed forty ways;
Backed up by circumstance so probable
That wives shall lose all faith in husbands; husbands
In wives; mothers in daughters, and daughters
Believe their mothers bawds; when all may be

As innocent as babes.
My chiefest study shall be men's designs,
And when I fathom their complots and plans,
And find from whence each draws his chiefest bliss,
Then, with red vengeance reveling in my brain,
I'll lay my little plans and counterplots
And subtle schemes to trip them. This I'll do —
Ay, fifty other fell, malicious things,
A million other foul malpractices;
(Which, like a merchant counting up his means,
I will enumerate and classify,)
Will I employ to vex and worry men.
　　So much for them, — and now for women — O!
Bring me a chisel and a mallet quick!
That I may pummel off these amorous bumps,
The bane of all my life! O woman, woman!
Thy loadstone doth attract me and repel! —
Now I adore thee, now I loathe thy name;
To-day I worship, but to-morrow weep!
Thou shouldst be faithful, but I find thee false;
Sweet source of all my hopes, haps and mishaps,
I cannot live with thee, I die without thee;
Like a wrecked seaman, famishing from thirst,
Which he attempts to swage with briny drops,
And thirstier grows with drinking! — O, thou art
The wide Atlantic which my thirsty soul
Is cast away upon — it needs must drink;
For drinking not it famishes to death,
And drinking, dies for drink. Thou lov'st me not,
Tho' with a Pagan's mad idolatry,
Have I pursued thee — O, thou art my sun,
My moon, my star, my stumbling block, my steam
That doth propel me. O excelling creature!
I had resolved to be a thorough villain,
But thoughts of thee will shame me from my purpose.
How can a man be other than a man
When woman's observation is upon him?
O heart of man! a riddle art thou still;
Here have I softened to a very lamb
From the most roaring lion, at the thought
Of woman, woman, woman! Why, I should —
No doubt I should — if the particular woman,
Even she herself, the falsest and the fairest,
Who has deceived me most — I should be slow
To do a scaly trick if only she
Were witness to it, and if I were sure
She would be struck with death the very instant
She read me out a villain.

　　　　　　[*Knocking at a door.*]
　　　　　　　　Come in!
　　　　　　　Enter IRENE.

Irene. You are alone. Now for the very worst;
　　Though you may stab my heart with cruel speech,
　　The music of your tongue will heal the stabs
　　As fast as words can make them. Noble youth,
　　Turn not away, but hear my piteous prayer.
　　If thou canst not forgive the grievous wrong

Inflicted on thee by a thoughtless girl,
Yet do not move till thine unwilling ears
Have drunk the mournful tale of my remorse,
And floods of pity rising in thy soul,
Supply thine eyes with sweet forgiving rains
To wash away my sins.

Argo.   . Is this reality?
Or faulty action of the o'erwrought brain,
Lending this vision life?' Am I awake?
Art thou not Irene, relict of Magoon?
And reck'st thou of remorse!

Irene.   O, say not relict!
A wife, a widow, but a maiden still.
The old man died of surfeit in his cups;
From drink and gourmandizing at the feast
That followed the unholy nuptial tie,
He fell in cramps, on rising from his chair,
And made his exit, after much ado.

Argo. I heard of it, and from his age and habits,
I wondered less that he had died in drink,
Than that he had seduced my wife's affections,
And lured her from my side. Two claps of thunder,
Your marriage and his death, crashed on my ears
At the same instant, and their mingled roar
Did raise me from the earth.

Irene.   I am a victim,
A thousand times more wretched than yourself,
If there be such degree in wretchedness;
But my affections were not stol'n away.
Alas, alas! I came to make my peace,
To offer explanations — and alas!
I find I have no words — O, pity me!

Argo. Weep'st for the old millionaire?

Irene.   O, kill me, Argo!
Kill me where I stand, for that were kindness;
But till you place yourself in my position,
And argue from my heart, O, do not kill me
With too severe a censure.

Argo.   O poor girl!
And art thou wretched with so fatal powers
To make thy votaries so?

Irene.   You know me not:
I am a martyr, yet I may have erred:
But every error was a special virtue,
Working specific good.

Argo. Didst thou not love deceased?

Irene.   I! — I loathed him!

Argo. Then he too was deceived.

Irene. He knew I loved him not — I told him so —
But knew not I loved you.

Argo.   And I knew not
My girl was pledged to him; both were deceived;
Thus hath it been since Eve wore fig leaves; but ——

Irene. But 'twas your fault, you crack-brain; you resolved
To win a name and fortune ere you married:
Our broken fortunes, my poor mother's needs,
Called desperately for desperate remedies,
And I was sacrificed. But I am here,

In helpless innocence and scalding tears,
To plead for pity! Argo, on my knees   [*Kneels*]
I ask forgiveness! Mercy, mercy, mercy!

Argo. (*Taking her up.*) Kneel not to me and earth, rush to the sun
In twenty seconds if I show not mercy,
(If any gracious act of mine be mercy,)
And if I do not pour forgiveness out
As lavish as Niagara's rushing flood
Pours o'er its craggy brow, to wash away,
(If that will wash away,) the heavy grief
That weighs upon the sweetest woman's heart,
That ever yet did plead to swinish man
When he should plead to her:—then fly with me—
Fly off with me, ye just, avenging gods,
To some bleak rock, and turn me there to stone—
Fixed in my tracks, a statue that may mock
The touch and tooth of time;—that through the ages
Sick lovers may troop thither, and may read:
"This stone was once a man, whose flinty heart
Refused forgiveness to a piteous maid,
Who, in an evil hour, in tender years,
And through advice of an ambitious mother,
Forgot the pledges she had made to him;
And but for fate, which ordered otherwise,
Would have become another's—then repenting,
She came with tears to melt his frozen heart,
To own her error and sue for pity;
But this denying, the malignant powers
Changed him to stone as here you see him stand,
With visage grim and a forbidding frown
On his unyielding brow!" I am in fault:
My peevishness and pinched-face poverty
Have wrought this ruin. Pardon me, Irene!
I should have bent me to thy girlish ways:
I should have had more gold and less ambition—
For love itself must compromise with gold,
And aspirations, noble in their nature,
And fraught with blessings to ourselves and others,
Decay before their bloom beneath the frosts
And chilling blasts of poverty. And wants,
The grinning troop of wants that harass life,
Led by the skinny hag, the want of gold,
Embitter all the hours that else were sweet,
Seal up promotion, and, like hungry wolves,
With hydrophobic teeth and gummy eyes,
Pursue and bay the impecunious wretch,
And hound him to his hovel or to hell;
For any place on earth is hell to him
Who hath no bank account.

Irene.   And any place
Where love is absent is a barren spot,
And where he is, a heaven. Do you believe
That love's infatuation may possess us,
And make our lives as sweet as zephyrs playing
Amid magnolia groves in southern climes,
And we not know it? Is there an infection
So subtle that it steals into our tissues,
Till it is, as it were, our very essence,

And we not know its source, nor feel its presence,
Till some familiar voice, scarce prized before,
Is lost in death or distance? I was happy
Till wealth and station came within my reach,
To gild the hours and make that happiness
Perennial as the pines, as some would think : —
Not so for me; because, alas! when lost,
I found my Argo's voice had made the music
To which the gold-fringed moments danced away
So lightly that the hours appeared as minutes
Then had I owned a ton of golden coin,
I would have bartered half of it away,
If that the shining treasure would have bought me,
With its delicious sweetness, back again
One hour of Argo's love.

Argo.   But all that gold,
With all the other treasures superadded,
Would fail to buy a husband worthy
A woman such as this. But still the rich
Speak slightingly of riches. Thou art rich,
And I congratulate thee. But to me
No more may come the rainbow-tinted moments;
The rosebuds and the singing birds of summer,
The aspirations and the hopes of youth,
The consciousness and pride of manhood's power,
The thirst for fame and the applause of men;
And the heart-hopes more precious than all these,
The yearnings of the soul to win at last,
The approbation and the eye of woman,
O, all farewell! Life's craggy coast affords
No shelter, and no gap to let me forth
To the green fields beyond.

Irene. Why, Argo, are you mad? Must I not fear
That you have given color to the rumor
That somewhere in your brain there is a crack
Across the healthful structure? Like the winds
You list and roar by turns. You cannot take
The evil with the good, the bitter with the sweet,
As here in life they are inseparable,
And thus presented to us. There are those
Who will not take the world in which they move,
A little period in their rounds through space,
As they do find it: but are ever seeking
To make it as they fancy it should be,
And to reverse the fixed laws of nature.
They would conform all appetites and tastes
To their own standard. But the level mind
Takes circumstances in and makes the best
Of the combined surroundings; patiently
It bears with evils unavoidable;
And to the fullest it enjoys the pleasures,
And sweets within its reach.

Argo.   A woman still!
O, that philosophy is worth to me
More than was ever preached. Dissatisfaction,
Impatience, petulance, ye saffron devils!
Depart ye hence, and leave me! O Irene!
I will reform me! Make me what you will;
Like the glass blower, you can blow me into

What shape you please; or the confectioner
Who moulds his batch in shapes to suit the tastes
Of customers who buy; so you can make me
That shape which sells the best.

Irene.   Then you shall be
Made into sugar kisses, and I'll keep them,
And only I shall taste them.   [*Kisses him.*]

Argo.   O infection!

Irene. O confection sweet!   [*Kisses him again.*]

Argo.   You joke when I would weep.

Irene. You've wept too much already.   So have I,
I came to break your heart and break my own,
Or heal them both at once; although unwomanly
The action may appear.

Argo.   Are you my girl?

Irene. Heart, lungs, and liver, every atom yours.

Argo. Shall we renew our vows?

Irene.   It is superfluous:
And yet perhaps 'tis best, for those I made
Were doll babes of a child; now I am grown
And know the force of words; and so I pledge
Undying love and duty.

Argo.   So I pledge
Undying love to thee; and furthermore
I pledge myself to kick the seedy spook,
Which men call genius, till he shabs away;
I'll starve with him no farther: I will work;
At daily labor; I will get a berth
As brakeman on a hog train: I'll achieve
A little money; then a house and lot;
A cow, a pig, a horse; what else?

Irene.   A wife?

Argo. Why, yes, a wife, when I have got a home
To shelter and protect her; not till then.
I have mistook my calling and have tried
To earn distinction by the force of mind,
While it has brought me supperless to bed,
And I have borrowed money from a drayman,
To buy my breakfast.   Freight me not with talent
Poor truck is genius in the open market;
I'll put my bones and muscles to the proof.

Irene. O noble Argo! wise is your resolve;
For labor brings sweet sleep and peace of mind;
And it is right and honorable to labor;
And pleasant is a cottage with content;
And genius may put forth the passion-flower,
Even in the poor man's hut.

Argo.   But hut of mine
Will never know content nor have a sleeper,
Though wooed by weary limbs to soft repose,
Whose slumbers will bring healing on their wings,
To cure the heart-ache; for upon my pillow
My Irene cannot rest; she now is rich;
She cannot take my poverty, nor I
Assume her riches with dependent role —
O misery, I'll embrace thee!

Irene.   Still the yellow fiend,
The epileptic spook that waits on thee,
Doth trip thee up!   Be still and hear the truth.

Argo. The truth? the naked truth? Why I will hear it,
And bray it to the moon with throat of brass.
It is that we did love, do love to-day;
That thou art rich, and I am poor and proud!
I'll make a song of it; set it to music;
And have the nimble elbows in the orchestra,
The groaning viol and the brazen horns,
(Cheek splitters to Mienheer with the mustache;)
And crashing plates give it uproarious discord!
The truth! By all means give us truth! Here's more:
The lack of money kept me from your arms,
Excess of it will keep me from your arms;
As I had none I could not wed with you;
As you have much I cannot wed with you;
So money still must keep true love at bay;
Whether we have it or we have it not:
Possession is as bad as want of it;
For either brings the other's evils with it,
And works our bane.

Irene.   I have no money, Argo,
You see me as I was before the marriage,
That brought me wretchedness as well as riches;
So I have not a dollar to my name,
And am dependent on my mother now
For sustenance of life. Oppressed with gloom,
And in despondent and dyspeptic mood,
And charging riches with my wretchedness,
I did determine to adjust the score,
And be avenged on that which wrought my ruin;
And so I called a lawyer armed with quibbles,
And stock of heretofores and stale preambles;
Well-timed whereases, the saids and aforesaids;
And did bequeath, devise, give and convey,
Conformably to law's extremest letter,
My whole possessions, moneys and effects,
Unto a friend held dear; and this the rather
As it did place me on a footing level
With my erratic poet.

Argo.   All but poet!
Talk not of poetry, for we are poor;
But the wise law permits the poor to marry;
If like cures like, one's lack shall cure the other's;
And lest some other fat man comes 'n the way,
I will espouse thee straight; let's to a justice.
                    [*Knocking without.*]
Sit down, my darling, in this easy-chair.
                    [*More knocking.*]
Come in! Come in! — a pest upon intruders! — (*sotto voce.*)

                Enter Publisher and Critic.

How now, gentlemen? Take chairs; take chairs.
Do you desire to see me on any special business?
Publisher. Excuse us, sir; we have not time to sit. But did you receive a note from me?
Argo. Yes, sir; I did.
Publisher. Well, sir, on a more careful examination by our literary critic, to whose decision we refer such matters, he has decided that your work has high claims to public favor.

Critic. It is a fine production, sir. It will take well. My first examination was rather hasty. We have heaps of rubbish to wade through,
and a gem may sometimes escape notice.

Argo. Do not popular names give currency to much rubbish?

Critic. True. The public ear will tolerate much discordance from
voices that have casually charmed it.

Argo. Then there is more in the man than the matter.

Critic. That is very true. Popular names gloss over much that is
stupid.

Publisher. Here, sir, is our check for ten thousand dollars as an
advance on that work.

Argo. Ten thousand? That is a large sum, sir, for such a trifle?

Publisher. O, well, sir, we are content. We will confer at another
time in regard to the style of the book. A good day to you, sir.

Argo. Farewell, gentlemen.   [*Exit Publisher and Critic.*
  A freak of fortune; she may frown to-morrow;
  Come hither, pet; now happiness I have thee.

Irene. But may I not your arguments employ,   [*Embraces* IRENE.
  And plead your money and my lack of it,
  In bar of marriage?

Argo.   No, no; not to-day.
  I'll no more pleading; bring me to the 'squire!

Irene. But how about that hog-train and that hut?—
  That lowing kine, whose lacteal supply,
  Was to afford your babies nutriment?
  And that sleek swine—must he untwist his tail,
  And squeal perpetually for buttermilk?
  Your genius, also, that starv'd spook which you
  Did banish and abjure—will you recall him?

Argo. I will until he make me voluble,
  And rich with proofs and pleadings to refute
  The slanders I have said against thy sex;
  And till he bring and burn me up the arrows
  Which I have impotently fired at Fate;
  Because I could not pry out the decrees
  He ever writes in cradle of the baby,
  To fashion its career—and fought against them
  While inexorably each written role
  Was acting to the letter. I'll invoke
  The discontented ghost of poesy,
  Until he help me to undo much folly,
  In one grand flight; and till the work be done,
  Give me fish diet only.

SCENE V.—*A cemetery. One gravestone inscribed Major Magoon.* Enter
  SAM *and* DR. ABRAM TURNER.

Sam. Poah Majah; dar you is, while de crazy man hab youh wife
and money.

Dr. Turner. Is dey married?

Sam. Dey is and dey ought to be. Dey is boff alike. Dey raves at
nuffin, boff uv 'em. Dey is allers in lub; allers in trubbel, and dey biles
ober like a pot o' soapsuds wheneber dey meets or parts. Ize heard 'em
ravin, den kissin and makin frens. Tell you, doctah, dey lubbed like
hosses. Well nuff de ole Majah died. Ef he hadn't dat gal wud a loped
wid de crazy fellah in 'bout nine days.

Dr. Turner. 'Tween us two, Sam, warn't dat marriage a sot-up job
on de ole Majah?

Sam. Lor' bress you, no. De Majah done it all hisself. Course she married foh money, spectin' to come out a surwivin' widah, as she did.

Dr. Turner. Tell you what, Sam, ef I warn't done shuah dat de crotum oil struck a function and killed de ole Majah, I wud swar dat he war pisened.

Sam. Course he war pisened. Didn't dem doctahs pour dar pisen and whisky down his froat?

Dr. Turner. Dat's truf, and dey nebber paid de slightest 'tention to dat tape worrum.

Sam. Doctah, you ought to seed de larst ravin' fit dat crazy fellah took. Arter dey war married he foun' out dat she had made ovah to him all de Majah's property soon as de bref war out ob de Majah. Den you bet he raved.

Dr. Turner. What 'bout? War he mad?

Sam. 'spect not. He 'spaciated on de lubliness ob de female sec, an' de power and beauty ob true lub. An' I tell you, doctah, lub is powerful, as I knows myself, ef I is culled. I lubbed dat gal, an' ef I hadn't a been culled I'd a got her. But some folks has a prejudice 'ginst cullah; an' she called me a niggah, too! But, howsevah, Ize boun' to hab a white gal. Ize nebber gwine to marry a niggah, ef I is culled.

        [*Exit* Sam *and* Turner.

Enter Argo *and* Irene, *strewing flowers on the Major's grave.*

Irene. Peace to the dead; from thine eternal sleep,
  Love nor ambition, lust nor avarice,
  Can ever rouse thee. Rest thee in thy shroud,
  Whilst we who come to heaven by thy death,
  Will keep thy memory green.

Argo. Rest thee, poor man; thou hadst thy little day,
  Thy little pleasures and thy schemes for more.
  It little recks him who doth sleep below,
  That I enjoy his revenues, his wife.
  The happiness of those who live and move
  Works no disquiet to the eternal sleeper,
  Nor does their wretchedness. We travelers
  Upon time's whirling train have each our station,
  And are pitched off, while the swift train moves on —
  Here is thy stopping place.

MALACHI AND MIRANDA.

PERSONS REPRESENTED.

BRYAN DUKE, *alias* ANSON GLUGE.
EDNA, *his Mistress.*
SADDIE, *his Wife.*
MACKAPEE McCOY, *a Spiritualist,*   } *Confederates of* BRYAN.
BENDER, *a Drunkard and Ruffian,*
TEDDY O'RAFHERTY,   }
BRIDGET, *his Wife,*   } *Servants at* BRYAN'S *House.*
DIXIE, *an old Negro,*   }
BASIL DUKE, *brother to* BRYAN.
ANNABEL, *his Wife.*
MALACHI,   } *Son and Daughter of* BASIL *and Wife.*
MIRANDA,
MICHAEL DALE,   } *Sailors, afterwards* JUDGE DALE *and* SHERIFF MAGUIRE.
BARNEY MAGUIRE,
BLANTON DALE, *son of* MICHAEL DALE.
BELL MAGUIRE, *daughter of* BARNEY MAGUIRE.
A Detective, a Pastor, a Doctor, Superintendent of Insane Asylum, Clerk of Court,
  Bailiffs, Spectators, Guards and Masked Lynchers.

ACT I.

SCENE I.—*The coast of California. Enter* MICHAEL *and* BARNEY *bearing*
  children.

Barney. Was ever escape so miraculous? We alone are saved.

Michael. The ship seemed to disappear as if by magic. You had barely received the children in the boat, and I turned to help the mother down, when the vessel made a lurch. I knew all was over then, and I instantly loosened the cable, threw a noose of it around my body and sprang into the sea.

Barney. The lights went out like the flame of a candle in a midnight dungeon. If the poor gentleman and lady had taken to the boat at first, and not attempted to save their effects, they might have been saved.

Michael. I suppose all the passengers were asleep in their berths, poor souls.

Barney. I saw none stirring but the pair with these babes.

Michael. I never heard of a ship going down so suddenly and so unexpectedly.

Barney. Well, it is light now. Let's bring up the plunder that cost two lives. It ought to be valuable.

Michael. Right, comrade. I think we can't be far from San Francisco. We had better make our way in that direction. There must be inhabitants hereabouts. [*They lay children down, retire and return with a basket and some traveling sacks.*]

Barney. Let's break open; perhaps we'll make discovery. [*They produce two lockets and a lady's watch, together with large packages of bank notes.*]

Michael. We are made forever, Barney. This is more money than I ever saw before. Whoop, hurra!

Barney. By old Boreas, enough to make us rich as Jew David. Now, it is impossible that anybody else escaped, so we had better keep this

6

thing to ourselves; divide the money; put the children in asylums; leave part of the money to raise and school 'em, and do the best we can on the remainder. What d'ye say, Mike?

Michael. The money is ours by luck, but these poor babes have a better title to it.

Barney. True for you, Mike; but it isn't often that a poor sailor gets a fortune in his hands all in good money.

Michael. By advertising we may find relatives for these children.

Barney. Yes, and claimants for the money!

Michael. We needn't confess the money.

Barney. True. But still I think we had better say nothing about it. Do the square thing for the orphans, and wait for what will turn up. This sweet babe can't be a year old.

Michael. And this chubby little boy — isn't he pretty? His age may be some two years. My boy, Blanton, is a little bigger, bless him. I will now be able to educate him. I will make a lawyer of him and this one, too; and blow me, Barney, if I don't quit the sea and study law myself. Money will put me through. Poor little boy; what is your name, sonny? Don't be afraid.

Boy. Where Ma? My mamma.

Michael. Is this Pa? [*Opens a locket and shows child a picture.*]

Boy. (*Reaching for the locket.*) Pa — pa — pap.

Michael. (*Opening the other locket.*) Is this your ma?

Boy. (*Seizing it.*) Mamma!

Michael. Poor little creature! (*hugging the child.*) Barney, the curse will light upon us if we wrong these babes.

Barney. Never a wrong will we do 'em, Mike. Did you ever see anything so greedy as this little innocent? The poor mother — how thoughtful in that terrible moment to put the child's bottle in the basket with it. We must skurry the coast for cottages and fresh milk. I will name this sweet babe, Mike. I will name it after my poor wife, rest her soul. It shall be called Miranda. Poor Miranda! she is in heaven if there be a heaven. My little babe, Bell, now with its grandmother, is just about such a cherub as this.

Michael. Well, Barney, you be a father to the girl babe and I will to the boy. He shall be called Malachi, after my little son that was drowned in East river. Now let's divide this money into four equal parts. I will take my part and the boy's and return to my family in New York. I will adopt, rear and educate the boy, and will invest his money so that he will have something when he reaches manhood.

Barney. Agreed, comrade. I will do the same for the babe; but I'll leave it in San Francisco, if we have luck to reach that place. There I will deposit its money and my own safely, and try my fortune in the mines.

SCENE II.— *Windsor, Canada. A family-room. Enter* BRYAN DUKE (*as* ANSON GLUGE) *and* EDNA.

Edna. What have you now in hand? May I not know?
When will you stop and be a quiet man?
We have enough, and if you risk no more
Old Pinkerton will fail to fix on you
The heavy robberies that have of late
So stirred communities and so enriched
You and your fellows; for your stealthy tracks
Are so well covered that, without betrayal,
All the sleuth hounds in old Pink's kennel house
Will never smell them out. O, then be wise;
Fulfill the promises you made to me

When I fled home and friends for love of you,
And threw in scales against your solemn vows
My honor and my all. How long, how long
Must I live mistress where I should be wife?
Remember, love, the tender vows you made;
Remember my devotion to yourself;
Remember how my parents cut me off
Without a farthing for my love of you;
Keep me no more a scorned, a scarlet one;
Make me your lawful wedded wife, and then
If you desire it, I will go away
And never see you more; or drown myself!
O, any fate, or any death is preferable
To such a life as this.

Bryan.   Peace, wrangler! hush!
Let me not hear another word from you.
Are you not clothed and fed? are you not housed?
Have you not servants to attend on you!
Have you not money to your heart's content?
You are a quarrelsome, discontented shrew,
And but for your unrivaled penmanship,
That counterfeits so cunningly and apt
That bank officials know not their own hands
From those you write for them, whereby false checks,
And other forgeries do open vaults,
I would a beggar set you down again,
Beneath the window whence I stole you forth
A dozen years ago. You will betray me?
You shall be watched; I'll have your liver out
Before your rebel lips can fairly lisp
Ten syllables of treason.

Edna. (*Weeping.*)   Do not fear;
She who hath risked her life and falsely sworn
So many times to save you, won't betray you,
Though beaten every day.

Bryan.   Then cease to whine.
Your tongue is on the wag from morn till night,
Whenever I'm at home;—the same old theme;
I'll not endure it; ere I'll be so badgered
I'll rake ten miles of hell for remedies.
There are more women; you are not the purest;
The unlawful tricks you do with me, no doubt
You do with others. She who yields to one,
Outside of wedlock, will so yield to any.
So mistress, mind your cues; I don't suppose
You fast when I'm from home; I've still in mind
The sharp detective you were flirting with
While I was late in jail.

Edna.   O viewless sprites,
If you protect the innocent, stand forth
All palpable to naked mortal, sight,
To vindicate me here! Let him behold you,
That he may know he has the truest woman,
That ever sinned for love.

Bryan.   No sprites appear;
But you may yet be true; their non-appearance
Makes you no less so; I must take your word,
Though a lame witness, bringing feeble force

Against the circumstantial evidence
That points to guilty joy; yet I will take it,
(As you have no other,) making due allowance.

Edna. The man you speak of sought me as you know,
In sleek disguise, in hopes to get some clew,
Or some confused or contradictory statement
As to your whereabouts one certain night.
He measured arts with mine and he was baffled;
And thereupon was hanging your own life;
Had I been fool or false you would have swung.

Bryan. Is that all, darling? Why, upon my soul,
I did suspect a measurement of noses;
But starving love still feeds upon suspicion.
Well, well, let's say no more; you know, my love,
When I am angry I am sometimes rash;
I love you, and will make my pledges good,
When we can get our hidden wealth together,
And the lynx eyes of Pinkerton shall sleep,
Till we can slip off to some foreign clime,
Where his detectives do not lie concealed
In every bush and closet and pervade
The daily walks of men. Go, gentle Ed,
Prepare us supper; I am off to night;
If I do prosper I will soon be back;
If not — you'll hear from me.

Edna.   Now you do speak,
Like that brave, gallant youth, called Anson Gluge,
Who won my girlish heart. I will not question,
But wait your safe return. I hope
You are not bent on perilous enterprise,
And will not further stain with gore the hands
Too thick with blood already. You shall have
My blessing when you leave.   [*Exit* EDNA.

Bryan. She is becoming dangerous; I must watch her;
I must revive her hope to keep her quiet;
I must re-light her love or she'll do mischief;
She's yet amenable to blarney as
A miss of fifteen summers; but of late
I have been troubled and have used the jade
Rougher than is my wont;— these women need
A dreadful sight of blarney and small talk
To keep them half in sorts. I'll flatter her,
And ply her with the old worn arts of love
That did achieve her; I cannot succeed
Without the jade, or I would fat the fishes
Upon her delicate flesh! But breaks the day
When every tongue that could plague me in court,
Must cease to wag, and her's among the first.

Enter MACKAPEE *and* BENDER.

Ha, boys, how do you both? Are you quite sure
You are not shadowed? Wherefore come you here?

Mack. Less for our liking than to save our lives;
Here's reason why. (*Showing money.*)

Ben.   We cracked a safe and skull.

Bryan. Why did you crack the skull?

Mack.   'Twas Bender's whim;
He had a drop too much; the appalled cashier,
Blindfolded, gagged and tied, might have been spared.

Ben. As I was passing out, my sledge in hand,
He strained his head far back upon the floor,
And strove to peep along beside his nose;
And I did see, between his cheek and bandage,
His eye wide open; then I swung my sledge
And smashed his skull for luck.

Bryan. Bender was right;
But Ben, old fellow, look you, curb your thirst,
That flask will bring you to the gallows, boy;
Your tongue is limber when you are in drink;
Your hand too swift, and your hot head too bold;
In the performance of a dangerous act,
Be it as fair as truth or foul as sin,
The actor should be sober: mark you this,
And curb your appetite.

Ben. I think quite different.
There's nothing like good drink to nerve a man;
It whets his wits and makes him strong and bold;
Gives him assurance and contempt of danger;
It drives weak pity and wry-faced remorse
From lodgment in the brain; and makes you lap
Hot blood as cats lap milk; and these, I take it,
Be graces that become a man o' the world,
As wags the world to-day. I've had more luck
When half-seas over than the ablest man,
Like circumstanced, could hope to win when sober,
And with his mind befogged with doubts and fears,
That cloud the sober brain; and drunk, I've gone
Through perils that no sober man could pass;
I've suffered falls that would kill any man
Who had no liquor in him. On my word,
I tell you, Anson, that in love or war,
At rape, at robbery, or at murder, or
At any fracture of the law whatever,
A man must have assurance — impudence,
And go about it drinking.

Mack. You're a fool!
No man has yet done that when he was drunk,
Which he had tried and failed to do when sober.
Drink, in its first wild thrill, may make you strong,
But that false strength entails a fatal weakness.
Drink hath degrees: if you could take the first,
And not the second, third, the fourth and fifth,
It would not be so bad; but you cannot,
The First, (Exhilaration), is a fire
That heats you for the second, (Recklessness;)
This leads you to the fighting stage, the Third;
From which you settle to the Fourth, (Dead Drunk,)
A hoggish, helpless, sleep; thence to the Fifth,
With tremors, trembling tongue and eye askance;
With snakes in boots, and grinning fiends in bed;
Thence to more liquor and to repetition,
Whereby you graduate into the gutter;
A sot confirmed, a loathing to yourself;
Or reach a prison, or the gallows; for
In all of these degrees, except the first,
Your reason's gone; you are a roaring fiend,
Or trembling idiot; and in either case,

You'll break the law, and break it clumsily,
So that observing eyes will take your measure.
Alike to honest men and knaves does drink
Bring more disaster than all other causes:
All history teaches this.

Bryan.   But wherefore, Ben,
When at love-making, would you be in liquor?

Ben.   Because that women, timid in themselves,
Are ever pleased with boldness in a lover;
They most admire that quality in us
Which they themselves do lack. Your sober man
Is nervous and has doubts, and fears to speak,
Where one bold word would win her. Drunkenness
Breaks up the ice at once, dives to the bottom,
And comes off with the prize. Once in my youth
I hung up to a girl a half a year,
And all that time I could not nerve myself
To ask her for a kiss, much less to take it
Without the asking for; made bold with drink,
I seized her in my arms one Sunday night,
And without hesitation she returned
My kisses two for one. Here I had starved
Six sober months for that which drunkenness
Did win me in a minute.

Bryan. Most cogent reasoning; but adventurous deeds
Require great caution and strict reticence
For their success; and both of these are out
When too much drink is in. Be wary then.
How long are you in Windsor?

Mack.   Scarce an hour.

Bryan. That job in Iowa? was't that, my lads?

Mack. It was, my boy; here are the bonds and cash.

Bryan. I read the account, and did suspect as much.
These we will bury here; and now, my lads,
You come in nick of time; just now we have
Some heavy work in hand. Are you quite sure
The hounds have snuffed no scent? How came you off?

Mack. I held my seances and my lectures there,
After the deed was done, more than a week.
Bender did warble off with tools and swag,
As viewless as the spirits.

Ben.   Yet you say:
Ben drinks too much; it takes a sober man
To act a difficult and dangerous part.
I did not sneak away. I hid the tools,
And with the swag in this old carpet sack,
Tied with a string, foot-sore and woe-begone,
In tattered soldier clothes, I made my way
Out of the country, selling recipes
For making patent soap.

Bryan.   Had you your flask?

Ben.   You bet I had. Your sober-minded thief,
Lacking the daring which good whisky gives,
Would have gone skulking off at dead of night,
When every line of exit swarmed with spies,
And would have stretched a rope. I came by day;
John Barleycorn did pass me through the guards;
So here's good luck to him. [*They drink from the flask.*]

Bryan.   I merely touch my lips.
Now boys, prepare for work. We'll have some supper,
And then we must go separately away,
By different routes, but meet and join our friends
In Seymour, Indiana; where the boys
Have plans to crack the trains on both the roads.
Through trains from California, at some point
Between Vincennes and Seymour, will be sacked;
For late those trains bear heavy sums in gold.
But first a night train north upon the Jeff,
Is to be seized at Marshfield, a morass
Remote from telegraph, or station, so
That with the engine and the baggage car,
We can make off, with time to rob the safes
Ere we reach Seymour; and in thirty minutes
I'll be upon the O. & M., going east,
With all the bonds and bills that can be carried;
And be in Canada before the news   •
Is fairly on the wires. The messenger,
The engineer and fireman will be killed
Or tumbled from their posts. With lights put out,
The engine may be run close to the town
Where we will scatter; you two go on foot,
One east one west upon the O. & M.,
As laborers seeking work; and make your way
As best you can back here, with naught about you
To indicate your craft. If there be gold,
Or other heavy plunder it will be
Secreted safely by the Seymour boys,
Who each will have an alibi in soak,
As I, as usual, shall; for no good general
Provokes engagement with his rear exposed,
Or his retreat cut off. He steals not well,
Who has not all the conduits of detection
Estoppled ere he steal.
Mack.   And swift on this
You'll strike the other road?
Bryan.   Exactly so;
For when a general ventures from his works,
He should strike heavy blows at different points,
Thus to appall and paralyze the foe,
That through distraction and confused assays,
He fights at random, while his rear is gained,
And his supplies and treasures carried off;
We'll stir them when we start.
Ben.   Here's luck to you;
We'll take a drink on that; and all I ask
Is that the deaths required to hide the deeds,
Be left to my discretion.
Bryan.   Be it so,
Provided you are sober. Now to supper.   [*Exit.*

SCENE III.—*A room in same house.* EDNA *rising.*

Ed.   O, what a thorny path that woman treads
Whose early error blights her future hope;
Whose gentle nature, tenderness and truth
Revolt at crime and immorality,
While she must seem pleased with their fellowship.

She, like a rosebud cankered at the core,
May bloom, but gives a sickly odor off,
And withers early. O poor fallen woman!
False to thyself and sex, yet true to man,
Thy tempter and destroyer! — Wretched girls,
Who put their confidence in lovers' vows;
All valueless when vantages are gained.
Your lover is your slave; his goddess you;
But yielding virtue, you become the slave,
And he your tyrant master. Trusting still
For the redemption of his broken vows,
And hugging love's delusion, you go on
Sinning to retain your slender hold on him,
Until he tires of what he fancies cheap,
And rudely casts you off. Is there no power
To visit retribution on the wretch
Who plays with nature's costly jewels thus?
And blurs her daintiest tints? O victim! slave!
O fallen woman! heavy is her load
Who lives the life she loathes. How like the thrush,
Charmed and enfeebled with the serpent's eye,
From whose magnetic and malignant spell
She cannot break away! — I'm in too far;
I must go onward; there is no retreat;
While he is robbing, murdering far away,
I must appear in his apparel here,
A counterfeit so perfect of himself
That Pinkerton cannot detect the cheat:
Thus am I an accessory to murder,
How much against my will! and this the fruit
Of the old-time early fall!

ACT II.

Scene I.— *Cincinnati. A room in* Bryan's *mansion.*

Teddy. I'll be afther putting out the lights and closing the house. A bad business, be me sowl. The masther'll be ruined and Bridget and I'll be thrown adthrift widout a ha'penny. Murther and confusion! I was shure it was the masther himself whin he put his pug in at the duar the other marning. [*Sudden knocking heard.*]

Come in if ye be not the divil, and don't be bating down the duar.

Enter Bryan.

Bryan. How now, Teddy? Why, up so late? and alone? Where is Mrs. Duke?

Teddy. Howly Moses! Is it yerself, or the other feller?

Bryan. Why, Teddy, where are your wits? Don't you know me? Has a year so changed me?

Teddy. Know ye, is it? I know ye will enough, and yer brother, too, but for the life av me I can't detarmine in me mind which ye most resimble.

Bryan. I am myself, Teddy; I had only one brother and he was drowned twenty years ago.

Teddy. Dthrowned or not dthrowned, he was here, and we thought it was yerself, and the misthress rushed into his arrums, and Bridget jumped up and down for joy. But he said he was not yerself, and that ye are not yerself, but mistaken or an imposther.

Bryan. Is this possible, Ted? Where is he?

Teddy. He is in the city, shure, waiting to see ye. They say the properthy was all his and ye'll have to give it up.

Bryan. Where is my wife, Ted?

Teddy. Retired to her vartuous chamber, sir, long ago. I'll be afther waking her, for its the proud woman she'll be. [*Exit.*

[*Detective emerges from a side door and steals (unobserved by* BRYAN) *across the stage and out at another door. He has his coat, vest, and boots in his arms.*]

Bryan. In the name of all the fiends, what now is up!
Can this be Basil, or his ghost come back,
Haunting the loved scenes of his life-time walks,
With power to rehabilitate himself
In form, contour, and fashion as of old,
With voice and motion manifest to sense,
With pertinent remark and circumstance,
That leave no room to doubt identity?
They do assert that spirits have this power;
That the dark void betwixt the dead and living
Is now and then pierced by a gleam of light,
By which the restless spirit sees its way
Back to its earthly idols. Mackapee
Is a believer in this spirit power,
But he has got the glassiness of eye
That goes with latent madness. But this brother —
Soaked in salt water twenty years or more,
Ate up by fishes, these by other fish,
And yet come back to claim possession, and
Unsettle titles! Was the ocean's maw
Too delicate to hold this lively fish
That it hath cast him up? But if't be he
Alive and in the flesh and water-proof,
I'll try if lead hath power to lay him out,
And if he will come back to claim his lands,
After his throat is carefully cut across
Down to the very bone.

Enter SADDIE, *hastily dressed,* (TEDDY *peeping out at a side door.*)

Saddie. (*Rushing into* BRYAN's *arms.*) O darling, darling husband! have you at last come home to your faithful, faithful, lonesome, lonesome wife? O my head! [*Faints.*]

Bryan. (*Hugging her furiously.*) O my precious jewel! My spotless wife! What! has she fainted! [*Lets her fall to the floor.*] Help here! help here! Water! water!

Teddy. (*Rushing in.*) Wather! wather! Bridget! Dick! ye spalpeens! hurry!—the misthress has swoonded!

Enter BRIDGET *at one door with a pitcher and* DIXIE *at another with a bucket.*

Bridget. Is it fire there is, that ye rear for wather? [BRYAN *snatches the water and sprinkles* SADDIE's *face.*] Is this the man that said he was not the masther nor his brother nather? and has he kilt her for the properthy?

Dick. (*To* TEDDY.) It's de massa hisself; but if it is de udder fellah, I'll dun him foh my wages anyway.

Teddy. (*Aside.*) Be the powers, that's put on: I could spake six words that 'ud make her jump to the sailing.

Saddie. (*Reviving.*) Where am I? O my husband! is it you?
Bryan. 'Tis I, sweet wife; I'll help you to your room,
    And there give you a history of my travels,
    In foreign countries in pursuit of health,
    And knowledge that will fit me in the future
    To serve my country at some foreign court,
    Where, if I be appointed, you shall go
    And mate with titled dames. [*They retire, and exit servants.*

Enter Detective.

Detect. I have him now; I overheard all this.
    He is the man we want, and I will pull him
    When all the wires are laid. But by my soul,
    Had it not been for honest Ted to-night,
    The scoundrel would have had a pull at me.
    I have an itching that no salve can cure
    Except that villain's blood. I want his wife,
    And I want him for various other reasons,
    But none so pressing and so hot as this.
    Must I stand, with revolver loaded, here
    While she is in this villain's arms up-stairs,
    And I a warrant here to take or kill him,
    And not approach and burst his head with balls?
    But patience; I must yield her; she knows not
    The man she married, and she knows not me.
    I'll kill him, but she must not know 'twas I;
    Nor must old Allan know I have the bonds
    She gave to me, not dreaming they were stolen,
    But only hidden by her husband's whim
    Secure from thieves and casualties of banks —
    Gave them to me, as she believed, upon
    The eve of our elopement. If she knew
    That she has in her arms great Anson Gluge,
    The noted thief and forger, and I her lover,
    Am a detective warm upon his scent,
    Would horror not consume her? Or if he
    Should miss his bonds, or learn by any chance,
    Of her seduction and intended flight,
    Shrewd and malignant as the villain is,
    Would he not swiftly track the author out,
    And make this little world too hot for me?
    On second thought I'll start him; 'tis unsafe
    To leave her with him; he is well aware
    That he is wanted and will not show fight
    If he has room to run; but hand to hand
    I do not care to meet him. I'll retire,
    And suddenly assault the outer door
    With clamor for the forger, Anson Gluge,
    Ere they be yet in bed.   [*Exit.*

Enter TEDDY, BRIDGET AND DICK.

Bridget. Shure an' there's thrubble brewing. I've had bad drames for a fortnight. I doubt that being Misther Duke at all at all, and he's gone to bed wid her. I'll warran him to be the same chap that was here the other day calling himself Misther Duke, and poking about the place like a ghost.

Dick. I tell you, folks, Ize gwine to dun him in de mornin' foh my wages, and if he knows de sum 'greed upon, it is Massa Duke, udderwise he may be a duke or de debble.

Teddy. Be jabers, I shall not slape to night! Me nurruves are shattered entirely. [*Sudden and loud knocking.*] O mother of Moses!

Dick. O lor-a-massa, lor-a-massa!

Bridget. Perleeee! perleeee! the whistle! Fan me, O'Rapherty, darlint! [*Voice without.*]

Unbolt the door; we want one Anson Gluge,
Who has sought shelter in this lady's house.
Let him come forth and yield.

Bridget. We're ruined sowl and body: here'll be adulthrey committed and murther discovered.

Teddy. Howly angels, fan us with the wings av ye! It's meself that knew the imposther.

Dick. If none ub you is gwine to open de doah, Ize gwine to show de fojah de back-way out ob de house. Mabe he'll gib ole Dixie a fibe dollah bill. [*Exit.*

[BRYAN *passes from a hall stairway across the stage, carrying his boots and a revolver. Shakes his head and throws a roll of bills to* TEDDY *and* BRIDGET, *and disappears at a back door. Knocking ceases.*]

Bridget. (*Seizing the money.*) A noble thafe; the heavens protict him.

Teddy. Give me the money, Bridget. We'll kape it sacret.

Bridget. Ye'll be afther spinding it for whasky, Ted.

Teddy. Divil a cint. I'll buy a race-horse or a farrum.

Bridget. (*Giving him the money.*) See that ye do; here comes the misthress.

Enter SADDIE *weeping and wringing her hands.*

Saddie. Is he well gone?

Teddy. He is. Did he know if it war himself?

Saddie. It was himself. They seek the other man,
Yet he had reasons not to be seen here
Till he is more prepared. Open the door
And let the police in; I wonder much
Why he should fear to meet them.
[TEDDY *goes out and presently returns.*]

Teddy. They are not at the duar, mom; the spalpeens have left.

Saddie. They do pursue him. O, what shall I think?
My head is in a whirl; I will retire,
And sob myself to sleep. [*Exit.*

Teddy. An' Bridget, we'll retire and count this money. Come on, ould gal.

SCENE II.—*Mouth of a cave.* BENDER *and* MACK *emerging.* BRYAN *approaching.*

Bryan. Ha! comrades! here you are, as I supposed;
How fare you both? [*They shake hands.*]

Mack. Jolly, Great Duke, and you, I see,
Look every inch yourself. Did all go well?

Bryan. Not quite so well as Marshfield; there is left
A clue to my detection; but meantime
The other boys are safe with lots of gold.
I shall be crippled and must hide me here;
But for Ben's rashness they could not have traced
Those robberies home to me. He needs must kill
And so took time to kill a trembling fool,
Already paralyzed with mortal fear.
I did not want to hurt the passengers;
It is bad policy to murder; for

Of all the crimes in the black catalogue
It is the hardest to conceal, and surest
To work exposure; and aside from this,
That soul that has upon it murdered blood
Though to a ruffian linked, will never rest —
Will never know repose and tranquil sleep;
And rove in slumbers midst th' elysian fields —
The dream-lands of the innocent. As you saw,
In warding blows aimed at a helpless man,
By crazy Bender, there, my mask fell off,
And ere I could adjust it, prying eyes
Did photograph my physiognomy.

Ben. I told the fellow to hold up his hands,
But still he fumbled as if for a pistol;
His eye showed mischief, so I shut it up:
If all the rest had been shut up like his
You need not fear identity till doom.

Bryan. Well, say no more; 'tis fixed that some should die,
That others may have happiness and wealth.
How oft a single life is all that stands
Betwixt us and the goal of our desires.
A case in point;—my sister whom we killed,
By going hence gave me my brother's lands,
And I felt safe as sole inheritor,
But now that brother, drowned a score of years,
Has been cast up by the uncertain sea,
And claims his late estates; and it would seem
That he so strikingly resembles me
As to mislead my servants and my wife,
And the detectives, for they have him now
Arrested for the robbery of that train,
And other feats set down to my account.

Mack. Then let them hang him if you want your lands.

Ben. And if they clear him give him o'er to me;
I'll give the coroner a job next week:
Your brother would have lands? — I'll give him lands —
A hole in Potter's field.

Bryan.   Bravo, my lads;
Here's money; help yourselves; this is your own.
Now this man must not live, whoe'er he is;
On Wednesday next his case comes up in court,
On his petition for release on bail.
Dress you like gentlemen of ample means;
(For rich attire gives testimony weight;)
Report as victims and as witnesses,
But not together — strangers to each other —
Identify him — fix on him the murder
That Bender did commit: if let to bail,
Dog and despatch him; if remanded back
Inflame the mob and have him lynched at night.
Away! despatch! you have no time to lose;
I will await you and the issue here.

Ben. And we will bring you back a good report;
Perhaps your brother's scalp.

Mack. (*Aside.*)   Ay, or your sister's ghost.
                [*Exit* MACKAPEE *and* BENDER.

Bryan. Go, murderers, tools, fools! soon your time will come,
Kill you my enemies and then will I

Kill you, not that I hate you, but because
I'm bound to kill the secrets you possess.
But when I have killed all and covered up
All traces of my past career — what then?
Will I be happy? will I have no dreams?
Will spectres not appear? my sister's face —
Wet, pale and pleading for her gentle life,
As last I saw it, when her pure young heart
Received its death stab from this bloody hand,
Which now is raised against a brother's life?
O bloody work! that calls for fresher blood!
To wash out older stains! — as falsehood forged,
Requires the forging of more falsehoods still
To fortify the first! Am I a fool?
I'll be a man. This brother, killed for me,
Gives me advantages — takes off pursuit,
Brings present safety and secure retreat.
A useful brother — view him as you may:
A treasure drowned — a very fortune hanged.
I will be cheerful; there is light ahead.
I'll in and hide me 'til they do report. [*Enters the cave.*]

SCENE III.—*A court-room in Cincinnati.* MICHAEL DALE *as Judge;*
BARNEY MAGUIRE *as Sheriff;* BLANTON DALE, *Attorney for accused;*
MALACHI *as Prosecutor; Officers and Spectators.*

Judge. Bring in the accused; we'll try this case at once
But let the witnesses remain outside;
When they are called, admit one at a time,
And do not let those going out confer
With others yet to come, lest some collusion
May jeopardize the prisoner's rights at law.
When prejudice sets hard against a man,
The office of the law is to protect him
Till he is fairly tried, and then, if guilty,
Its office is to fix the penalty,
And see to its enforcement. Bring him in.

BASIL DUKE *is brought in.*

Judge. Are you prepared for trial, gentlemen?
Malachi and Blanton. We are, your Honor.
Judge. (*To prisoner.*) You are cited here
By writ of *habeas corpus* to show cause
Why your detention is unjust, and why
You should be let to bail. What say you, sir?
Blan. Your Honor, we appear with odds against us.
My client is mistaken for a man
Who is much dreaded by community;
He is not guilty, but we cannot show it
Unless he is enlarged and given time
To make up his defense. He is a stranger
But can pledge money for sufficient bail.
Judge. Are you not Anson Gluge, as here set forth
In these indictments, sir?
Basil. I am not he; my name is Basil Duke;
I suffered shipwreck many years ago,
And found my way to India, thence to London,
Where I did prosper much and tarry long.
But love of country brought me home at last,

Where here hard by I once had some possessions,
Which I had hoped my sister did enjoy —
She being my only heir; but I have learned
That she was murdered, and I find my house
Possessed by people who affect to see
In me resemblance to one of my name,
Traveling in Europe for his health and pleasure,
And who it seems has titles to my lands,
Which he usurps.

Judge.   Had you a brother, sir?
Basil. I had a brother, Bryan was his name,
But he was crushed by cars when but a boy;
Myself did see him buried.

Mal.   Please the court,
This story is too thin, and yet ingenious;
But we have here the cunningest rogue extant,
Who knows his life is forfeited to the law;
There is no hand he cannot counterfeit;
His soul is blackened with too many crimes;
He is a murderer whose red hand is damp
With human blood, shed in pursuit of gain;
He knows no mercy, and should meet with none;
No jail will hold him, and no safe defy;
Locks offer no impediment, and law no point
That he cannot evade; tame though he seem,
With air of truth and candor well put on,
So like a broken-hearted victim; but
As there you see him, there your eyes behold
The bloodiest criminal, the guiltiest man
That ever went unhung.

Judge.   Bring in the witnesses.

Detective, MIRANDA, BELL MAGUIRE, *and* BENDER *and* MACKAPEE (*as
        gentlemen*), *are brought in.*

Now, Mister Clerk, swear me these witnesses.
Clerk. Hold up your hands; be sworn. You each declare
Your testimony in the case now pending,
Wherein the Commonwealth is plaintiff, and
One Anson Gluge, defendant, shall be truth,
Without evasion, prejudice or favor,
As you do hope for mercy. [*All retire but Detective.*]
Mal. What is your business, sir, and where your home?
Detect. I am on Pinkerton's detective force;
I have no special home.
Mal.   Know you this man?
Detect. We know him as a noted robber, sir,
And have had him in custody ere now;
I have his photograph, you will observe,
The likeness is correct. Three nights ago
I tracked him to a house here in this city,
And aimed to take him, but he did escape;
I followed, and he's here. I know him well
From the description and his photograph,
But personally I never met the man,
Prior to the events I here am speaking of;
He has disguises and some *aliases;*
We know him best as Anson Gluge, the forger.
Blan. You say you know him by description only?

Detect. True, sir; but still I know him.
Blan. That is all. [*Retires, and* MACKAPEE *takes the stand.*]
Mal. Your name and occupation,—residence?
Mack. Mark Robbins, gentlemen; San Francisco.
Mal. What know you of the prisoner at the bar?
Mack. In transit to the East, the 20th ult.,
At night, in Illinois, the train was stopped,
Masked men possessed the cars, with guards at doors;
We all were robbed; the express safes carried off;
A passenger plucked off this fellow's mask;
This fellow killed him; ay, sir, you are he.
Mal. A narrative succinct. Take you the witness.
Blan. I have no questions; Robbins, you can go.   [*Exit.*

Enter BENDER.

Mal. What is your name, my friend? Where do you live?
What is your occupation?
Ben.   Rearing stock;
Near Austin, Texas; Smith, sir, is my name;
John Smith; I am one of them.
Mal.   A singular name;
Well, tell us, Mr. Smith, about the train,
Robbed near Vincennes, the 20th of last month —
If you were there, go on and tell the court
What there occurred.
Ben.   Your Honor, I was thar.
The whistle blowed down brakes, and bang we stopped;
Masked men rushed in crying, ' Hands above your heads."
When traveling, please the court, I pack a flask,
And always drink on entering on a muss;
I took a drink, then gave the thieves a pull,
For which they passed me by. Just then this man
Stabbed one poor man who had not raised his hands.
He cut him several times, and then the man
Tore off the fellow's mask while falling dead.
This is the murderer; own up, fellow!— see!
Here is the flask you took that liquor from.
Blan. If the court please, I enter my protest
Against this rudeness to my client here.
Court. The witness will address the court, and not
The prisoner at the bar. Go on.
Ben. I have no more to say.
Blan.   You are excused.
Bring on your witnesses; we'll see you out.
Mal. And we shall see you in — in jail, you know.
Court. Keep order, gentlemen, and hurry up your work.

BENDER *retires and* MIRANDA *enters.*

Mal. Look at this man; have you seen him ere now?
If so, say when and where.
Mir.   A month ago,
The date I do forget, this man and others
Waylaid and robbed a train near to Vincennes.
I saw this man pass through the sleeping car,
Demanding money with revolver drawn;
There was a scuffle and his mask fell off,
And then we saw him plainly. This is he.
He took my watch and locket with a picture —
Will you return them, sir?

Bas.   I wish I could;
          I was not there; you are in error, dear;
          And yet so honest in your error that
          I half way doubt if I be not the man
          I must so much resemble.
Mal.   Wait awhile,
          And we will show you that you are himself;
          You are improving. Take the witness, Dale.
Blan. Is this the man that killed the passenger?
Mir. Not he; he struggled to prevent the killing.
          'Twas one of them who seemed to be half drunk,
          And wild for blood. While pushing this man back
          His mask fell off.
Blan. You're sure of this, Miss Vail?
Mir. I am; my recollection is distinct,
          Though I was badly frightened.
Blan. That is all.

          Exit MIRANDA *and enter* BELL MAGUIRE.

Mal. This is the sheriff's daughter, please the court,
          Miss Bell Maguire. The twentieth of last month
          An east bound train was plundered near Vincennes.
          Were you upon that train? If so, be pleased
          To tell the court, fair lady, what transpired
          In your immediate view.
Bell.   I crossed the plains
          To meet Miss Vail, whose friendship I had won
          While in attendance on the Golden coast,
          Upon a school kept for young ladies, by
          The Sisterhood of Mercy. She, a nun,
          Was very dear to me. Five years ago
          My father brought me here against my will,
          For all I knew of him was that he claimed
          To be my father, and came once a year
          To pay the Sisters for their care of me.
Blan. Your Honor, this is all irrelevant;
          I hope the lady will restrict herself
          To what she witnessed in that sleeping car.
Bell. I begged to be excused from testifying,
          But Mr. Dale would have me on the stand
          In hope to save his client. Now I must,
          To vindicate myself, tell why I was
          Upon that luckless train, when father, here,
          Supposed me in New York amongst our friends.
Blan. I beg the court to stop this story, and
          Restrict the lady to the simple facts
          That bear upon the case.
Mal.   Let her go on;
          You are uneasy, Dale. It may come out
          That you yourself were in that car, if not
          A masked robber, still a runaway.
Blan. Please the court, I must inform the gentleman
          That I do very much despise his jeers
          And weak attempts at wit.
Judge. Well, let the case proceed. It seems to me
          The witness may have latitude to state
          The circumstances bearing on the point
          How she became a witness; if not regular,
          It is perhaps the quickest way to come

At the main facts. Go on, and tell your story.

Blan. I take exception to the ruling, Judge.

Judge. They shall be noted.

Mal.   Now proceed, Miss Bell.

Bell. The glowing letters did persuade my friend
To leave the Sisters and take shelter here,
If I could come or send her an escort,
She being unused to travel and the world.

Blan. Your Honor, I must once again protest——

Judge. Be patient, sir. The witness will proceed.

Bell. I being affianced to your son, your Honor——

Blan. I ask the mercy of the court, and beg
That this fair witness may be now excused.

Judge. Go on, fair lady, I will hear it all;
The advocate will please to keep his seat;
His interruptions do impede the court.

Bell. I being affianced to your Honor's son—
Himself most honorable and chivalrous—
I did enjoin him to go for my friend,
To be my bridesmaid; telling him
I would not wed him till my charming friend
Did stand a pleasing witness by my side.
I, and your son, together with his aunt,
Went out to California, got my friend,
And took immediate leave for home again.
She is the lady that preceded me
As witness on this stand. At East Saint Louis,
Somehow, your son and his good aunt were left,
And came upon a train a few hours later.

Mal. I see my friend is fortune's favorite,
Else he would have been robbed by his own client.

Sheriff Maguire. All this is news to me; but I declare (*Aside*)
It is most entertaining testimony.

Judge. Saw you this man the night the train was robbed?

Bell. I did; he and two others searched the passengers.

Mal. How do you recognize him, Miss Maguire?

Bell. One of his comrades stabbed a poor old man,
Which he endeavored to prevent; and in
The scuffle that ensued his mask fell off.
And there he stood revealed.

Mal. Is this the man?

Bell.   That is the face I saw.

Mal. We rest our cause.
Take your fair witness, Dale; in future learn
Just what a witness will avouch before
You put him on the stand; this fair one brought
To clear your client has convicted you;
Ask mercy of the court.

Blan.   Miss Bell, you say
The prisoner struggled to prevent the murder?

Bell. He did, and in that act was he exposed.

Blan. You can retire, my dear.

[*Sheriff goes out with her;* BLANTON *follows and presently returns.*]
If the court please,
I cannot urge my client's innocence
Against this proof; still he is innocent
Beyond a doubt or question, and can show it,
If given time and the fair course of law.

7

My client is an honest man, your Honor;
He has great wealth in England, and can pledge
Undoubted vouchers for a half a million,
If he may be enlarged. He seems to bear
A fatal likeness to a noted rogue,
But he is not that rogue.

Judge.   The evidence
Is clear as to identity; and so
The prisoner is remanded without bail.
Two witnesses declare he did the killing;
His case will come up at the regular term,
Now close at hand. The court will stand adjourned.

SCENE IV.—*Interior of a prison. Enter* BASIL, *Sheriff and* BLANTON.

Blan. This prisoner is innocent, Maguire,
And we fear nothing but a frenzied mob
Of half drunk men. So double you the guards;
The signs are ominous.

Sher.   I do believe
This is not Anson Gluge, the robber chief;
And I will fortify for his defense;
No mob shall have him while I am alive.
          [*Locks* BASIL *up in a cell.*]

SCENE V.—*A street at night.* BLANTON *walking; enter meeting him* BASIL
          DUKE, *in female attire.*

Bas. O lucky circumstance — is that you, Dale?
Blan. The gods protect us! Mr. Duke, you here!
How came you out? where got you this attire?
Bas. It is a dream, my friend — I scarcely know.
A woman came — the sheriff said: Your sister;
The bolts turned on us, then she put her hand
Upon my mouth, and straightway she disrobed
Herself and me — mechanically I helped her,
And in five minutes more she looked like me,
And I like her, perhaps. Then kissing me,
And bidding me draw close my veil and sob,
She motioned to the sheriff as he passed,
And asking him to let me in next day,
She gently shoved me out. Bewildered quite
I was repairing to your office, sir,
To seek advice and get some fitter garments.
Blan. This is another blunder, sir; no doubt
That woman is a pal of Anson Gluge;
She's read of his reported troubles here,
And played this desperate game to let him forth.
The looks that got you into trouble, sir,
Have got you out again — so far so good.
Errors are oft impartial, and sometimes
Mistakes do speed us when true efforts fail;
As now this blunder gives you that relief
Which neither gold nor well-directed effort
Could have effected. But let us go in;
You must be off and sail for calmer seas
Till we have fairer weather.

ACT III.

SCENE I.—*Interior of a prison. Sheriff and guards. Shouts and pounding without.*

Sheriff. Gird up your arms; the mob will break the doors.
 Stand firm, and shoot the first that dares approach —
 Hold! do not fire; there are too many men;
 We cannot fight them off.

[*Mob rush in masked and armed*— BENDER *and* MACKAPEE *leading Guards knocked down and guarded.*]

Ben. (*Knocking the Sheriff down.*) Yield up the keys!
 You monkey-visaged scoundrel, yield the keys!
Sheriff. I have not got them; get them how you can.
Mack. Who cares for keys! come, break the door, my lads!
Ben. Come out, you safe-blower! out, you thieving wretch!
Mack. Here! here! that rope! string up the villain, here!

[*Rope put round* EDNA'S *neck.*]

Edna. (*Throwing down her hair.*)
 But, gentlemen, you will not hang a woman
 Who hazards thus her life to save a brother!
 The man you want is many miles away —
 Safe from your fury. I am but a woman;
 A poor weak woman — see my naked arms.
 My only error is to shield my brother
 From such rash men as you.
Ben. (*To* MACKAPEE, *aside.*) It is poor Edna! gallant, gallant girl!
 She thinks 'tis Anson she has sent away;
 She must be saved; be quick.
Mack.   Well, gentlemen,
 I have a weak side for a woman's love,
 And admiration for a daring act;
 I move that this girl be allowed to go.
 The man we want cannot be far away,
 And we can find him if we stir ourselves.
All. Let her go.
Mack. Then, sheriff, bring her garments.
Edna. I have a trunk just at the depot here,
 If some kind gentleman will go for it.
 I will arrange my toilet in the cell,
 And then go hence, if you permit me to,
 Leaving my blessings here with you, good men;
 And hoping you will not pursue my brother,
 But leave him with his life and to repentance.

[BENDER *and* MACKAPEE *go for the trunk and return.*]

 Please set it in the cell, good gentlemen,
 And presently I'll go with some of you,
 And crave protection till I find a lodging,
 For I am poor, and am a stranger here.
 O, gallant men, so cruel to each other,
 And yet so kind and tender to our sex.

[*She enters the cell and presently emerges a fine lady.*]

Mack. O beauteous woman! lady, in the world
 There is no fairer creature than yourself,
 And were your brother good as you are brave,

Lovely and sweet and gentle in your looks,
He then were worthy such a charming sister.
Come, lead the way, we'll see you safely housed.
                    [EDNA *takes his arm and all retire.*

SCENE II. — *The cave.* BRYAN *sitting near.* *Enter* MACKAPEE *and*
                              BENDER.

Bryan. A thousand welcomes to you, noble lads!
        How seems the world to stand?
Mack.   As if about to fall,
        And we must stand from under, gentle boy.
Ben. Things do not look so bright, but I will drink;
        I have not felt my liquor for a week.
                    [*Drinks and hands the bottle round.*]
Bryan. Can you report his death?
Mack.   No; he's at large.
Bryan. Then Satan burn you in his hottest pit!
Ben. Go slow, old fellow; we have done our best,
        And would have had him but for Edna's zeal:
        She read of your arrest, and as a sister,
        Sought you in jail, changed habits with your brother,
        And sent him weeping out.   .
Bryan.   So big a fool?
Mack. Not much fool either — he's as like yourself
        As one black ram is like another. Why,
        His gait, his voice, his gestures are your own,
        His hat sets on him as does yours on you,
        From front, or rear, or viewed from either flank,
        He is your counterfeit. 'Twas hard, indeed,
        To make poor Edna understand the facts,
        For she knew nothing of this brother business
        Until we told her.
Ben.   Well, we should have hanged him;
        We swore him out of bail, and raised the mob,
        We quelled the guards and sheriff, broke the door,—
        Was in the very act of hanging him,
        When he pulled off his hat, and there was Edna,—
        A stranger to the mob but known to us,
        Who, unrevealed to her, in our disguise,
        Became her instant champions, taking in
        The situation at a glance — at once
        We set the mob upon your brother's track,
        For he was scarce a half an hour away,
        And spirited brave Edna to a house
        Where we had rooms; and there disclosed ourselves.
Mack. And come for counsel and to make report.
Bryan. A pretty mess you've made! — all the black furies
        Vent here their plagues upon you! eat you up
        With foul corroding ulcers! starve, burn, freeze,—
        Rack you with toothaches, nightmares,— blow you both
        With nitro-glycerine to nothingness!
        You fools! you dolts, you asses, idiots, infants!
Ben. What in the devil ails you, Bryan Duke!
        I'll whip this dagger in your carcass, sir!
        Damn me and you! I will not take it, sir! —
        McCoy may take it, if he, coward, please!

Mack. (*Standing between them.*)
    Put up your weapons, Ben; and Bryan, you!
    Put down that pistol! Peace, I say!—be still!
    What! are you drunk entirely!
Bryan. (*Throws away his revolver.*) Pardon, boys—
    I am too fast, too fast—give me your hands—
    Give me your hand, brave Ben; and yours, good Mack;
    You are my friends; I love you as my sons,
    And should not anger you; but O, good lads,
    You know not how you have destroyed my hopes
    By letting Edna know I have a wife,
    By which that wife will know I have a mistress;
    For that mad girl will work the matter up,
    And all my schemes will fail!
Ben. (*Throwing down his weapons.*)
              Here's pardon, Bryan;
    Give me your hand, and kick me for a fool;
    I am ashamed—here, let us take a drink,
    And play the fool no more. [*They drink.*]
Mack. Here let it drop—all men at times are rash,
    And friends should bear with friends, because we oft
    Heap most abuse on those we love the most,
    In freaks of passion, trusting in their love
    To make allowance and take no account
    Of what is said in anger.
Bryan.   True, good Mack,
    And so we'll say no more. I do suppose
    As circumstanced, you could do nothing better,
    And well I know you acted for the best.
Mack. We did, and as the case had got mixed up,
    We came here for advice.
Bryan.   Well, we must act.
    That brother must be stopped. Our hidden wealth
    I yield to you when you can say he's dead.
    And Edna,—boys, that woman is insane;
    I love her as my life—she's saved us oft;
    But I have noticed for a year or more
    A wandering of her mind; sometimes she stands
    And looks upon the wall, her lips in motion
    As if in whispers to a spirit there;
    Then will she pause; then suddenly turn away,
    And with a sigh walk straightway from the room;
    And then, as if remembering, she returns
    With cautious tread, like some one in the dark,
    Seeks her piano and begins to thrum
    Some old-time strains familiar to my ear,
    As was her wont in her proud father's home,
    In girlhood's halcyon hours. This is a sample,
    Of the disturbed relation of her senses
    That terrifies me so.
Mack. Is't possible! then this explains her manner;
    For when she asked us why we'd kill your brother,
    Supposing he was such, and we explained
    That he was rightful owner to your lands,
    And home in Cincinnati—that your sister
    Had been dispatched to clear the way for you—
    So much vexation, yet to lose your home—
    She made no demonstration—merely shuddered:

Like a proud horse long whipped, at last despairing,
Receives the lashes without sign of feeling,
Save a faint tremor in his bleeding flanks,
And fixedness of frowns.

Ben.   In some mad freak she may betray us all.

Bryan.   That's what I fear; and precious as she is,
I could almost rejoice were she in heaven;
We are not safe while that poor girl retains
Her speech and motion, with a mind removed
So far from healthful action.

Ben.   The way is clear — knives, powder, poison cheap;
She may find heaven with a little help.

Bryan.   Who gives her that small help, helps me to peace,
For I do fear her very much of late.
Go, boys, and watch her movements, and my brother's
That brother must be killed as Anson Gluge;
And if so killed it must be quickly done
By you or by the mob; if given time
He will establish an identity
Distinct from mine, and there will be no place
Upon the earth where I can rest in peace.

Ben.   Tut, man! cheer up! — we'll have your brother's hide,
And you shall live to rob a continent;
Let's go about it, Mackapee, at once;
We will return when we have welcome news.
Another drink, and part. [*They drink.*]

Mack.   It did transpire
In his examination that this man
Bears on his person papers that do call
For large deposits in a foreign bank.
You, Bryan, if we get him, can go on,
(And it is best you were abroad awhile,)
Looking as like him as two eels are like,
And lift deposits on the vouchers' face;
I spy a speculation in this death,
As well as salt to save our tainted meat.

Bryan.   Joint actors in the enterprise, you shall
Be sharers in the profits. Fare you well.
[*Exit* BENDER *and* MACKAPEE.
I do distrust them, and I will pursue;
There is too much at stake; who wants good work,
Himself must do the work; blows must be struck;
Four deaths — my brother's, Edna's, Mack's and Ben's, —
Must be scored up; I am no free man else;
I am a slave while move upon the earth
Four persons, — ay, one person — who can swear
My neck into a halter; bloody deeds
Must seal up deeds of blood. Edna, I come,
And you must walk the plank! — you first, because
You are least wanted and most dangerous.
I will assume disguise and after them,
And if they fail to cut each other off,
I'll be on hand to help.

SCENE III.—*Bed-room in a hotel.* EDNA *making her toilet.*

Edna.   By which am I deceived? — by these false men,
Or the sure evidence of my true eyes?
The light was dim; I would not let him speak;

In fact I did not scan him, knowing him
At the first glance, and never dreaming that
There might be such another man as he.
They speak of him as being Bryan Duke,
Who by the murder of a sister got
Possession of his drowned brother's lands,
And mansion in this city. Here's a thread;
I will unravel. Be he Bryan Duke,
And not the Anson Gluge I have so loved,
And if he have a home and family here —
Then O poor me! but I will know the worst.
These men have known his secret and have kept it;
I true to all, and only I betrayed.
O, how unselfish is that woman's love
Who hugs the phantom when the form has flown;
Who bears neglect — abuse, but struggles still
To gild with gold the idol turned to brass!
Poor woman's love clings to its early dream,
And to the dear one mirrored in that dream,
All down the rugged path the vicious tread:
The sot, the thief, the felon in his cell,
May yet be shrined in some poor broken heart,
May have the halo of some woman's love,
Softened with rose-bud tints of life's sweet morn,
Shedding its saddening radiance o'er his wreck,
And wreathing a garland fringed with golden light
About his aching brow.

SCENE IV.—*A room in* BRYAN'S *house.* BRIDGET *fussily arranging the furniture.*

Bridget. Shure an its meself that has all the wurruk to do. Ted dthrunk and the nagur not wurth his salt.
[*Door-bell rings. She opens the door.*]

Enter EDNA.

Good morning, mom. Is it the misthress you'd be seeing?
Ed. Well, yes, my good woman; but I am in no hurry. I will take a chair. Does Mr. Duke live here?
Brid. Shure an' he does, barrin' the fact that he's niver here. More'n a year we hadn't seen the face av him, bad luck to him. Well, the tother day he put in an appearance, he did. But it wasn't himself even thin, but another like him as two geese; an' he wint away. Thin they said the propperthy was his and not Bryan's at all. Thin Bryan did come himself; but the perleece come pounding around and wanting to find Gluge, the express thafe; an' Bryan didn't know what the villains meant, an' he wint aff. Since that we've heard from nather av them.

Enter SADDIE.

Here is misthress Duke herself.
Edna. (*Rising.*) Good morning, Madam. I am a traveling correspondent of an Eastern magazine, and wishing a quiet home in your city a short time, I was recommended to see you.
Saddie. My husband is so much from home that I entertain a few ladies for their company, and not for gain. I think you may join us awhile. Pray walk into the parlor. [*Exit.*
Brid. Another one to pound the pianer an' to do for; an' the nagur and Ted not wurth their salt widout a masther. Dthrunk ivery day; I wish I had a divorcement or the divil had Ted.

SCENE V.—*A room. Enter* MACKAPEE.

Mack. At first it was deception played for gain,
But that deception is deceiving me,
Or it is no deception, but the dead,
That manifest themselves. I am the medium,
Through which some dreadful power, either good or evil,
Is struggling for expression. I am shaken
As if by agues; voices from the dead
Do chatter in my ears at night, and shadows dim,
As if of spirits, flit before my eyes;
Raps made by me at first, repeat themselves —

[*Sharp rapping — he starts.*]

There! there they are! — the instant I'm alone.
My eyes being shut, still have the power to see;
And faces of the murdered come near mine;
(With stony eyes,) so close I feel their breath;
My ears being stopped, yet hear; and voices stilled,
In whispers plead for lives. I have no rest;
And by continued wakefulness and torture,
I have grown timid and am not myself;
Is there not some relief?

Enter BENDER.

Ben. Still gloomy, Mack?
Try some of this : Your liver is too cold;
I think our prey is lurking in the city;
We must keep stirring till we come upon him.
Mack. I have lost appetite for this employ,
Since Edna must be slain at Bryan's whim.
I tell you, Ben, I will not harm that girl,
Come what may come of it.
Ben. Nor I; I did assent to Bryan's views
To sound him merely; he is tired of her,
And wants a newer mistress — nothing more.
But in the taking off of Basil Duke
There's money and promotion.
Mack. What promotion?
This man who kills his sister, brother, mistress —
Who rails at murder in a general way,
Yet does it in detail — where will he stop?
He has no friend so dear but he will kill him;
His earliest theft was covered by a murder:
Has he ne'er told you this?
Ben. Not he; how was't?
Mack. At sixteen years he robbed his father's safe,
And then he coaxed a comrade of his age
To change apparel with him, which he did
Down to the smallest garment. It was night,
And the two lads went forth to steal a ride
Upon a passing train; when on a sudden,
The unsuspecting lad was shoved headlong,
And crushed beneath the wheels; the murderer, Bryan,
Sprang on the train and entered thence upon
His life of crime, far from his native haunts,
While the crushed body of his little friend
Went to the grave as his.

Ben. A murderer born;
And yet he chides me for excess of murder!

Mack. He kills his friends in preference to his foes;
That you do not. May we not be the next?
What say you, Ben?

Ben. No fear of that;
Gluge is a careful man, and only strikes
Where blows are needed; he is true to us,
And will keep faith to the last dollar, Mack.

Mack. Thus far he has. Well, I am out of sorts,
And see with jaundiced eyes. Give me your flask;
The drunkard's sleep is dreamless — make me drunk,
So every sense may sleep; drink, drink to-night;
To-morrow night we'll work. [*They drink.*]

SCENE VI.—*A parlor in* MAGUIRE'S *house.* MIRANDA *and* BELL.

Mir. Well, why does Mr. Dale desire to postpone the wedding?

Bell. O, his law business is pressing him so. We had arranged a wedding tour, and it will be two months before he can spare the time.

Mir. If you had married before you set out for California, that would have been a splendid wedding trip.

Bell. That is just what Blanton said. But I wouldn't think of marriage until we returned. I don't know what made me so foolish, as everything was ready, and it would have saved time and money and trouble, and have been more pleasant too. What do you think of Malachi, Miranda? I believe he is dead in love with you.

Mir. I think him a very proper young man, and very romantic and ardent.

Bell. Do you know he was once a suitor of mine?

Mir. Gracious, no! Was he?

Bell. He was; but we had a misunderstanding and were both too proud to make any concession. It almost broke my heart. But during our estrangement, Blanton, who was also my suitor, received my plighted faith.

Mir. Do you love Malachi still?

Bell. You oughtn't to ask me, my dear; but if I do, a woman's heart can entertain love for two men at the same time; which they say is impossible.

Mir. I am sure both of them are lovable young gents; but I have no experience in love matters. Malachi is the first man that ever said love to me.

Bell. So you have been courting!

Mir. O, no, but both the young gentlemen have paid me pleasant compliments.

Bell. Both? Why, dear Miranda, I shall become as jealous as a gander if Blanton falls in love with you too.

Mir. O, I will be very circumspect. You shall have no cause for jealousy.

Bell. Suppose you and Malachi make up a match, and we have a double wedding. It would be so nice.

Mir. O, gracious, Bell! Malachi wouldn't think of marrying a girl with no fortune, and of uncertain parentage.

Bell. Wouldn't he! Well, if I mistake not you will find out differently. And besides, the watch and locket may be found and lead to your parentage. You may come out an heiress. [*Bell rings.*] Our tea is ready.

SCENE VII.—*A lawyer's office.*   *Enter* BLANTON.

Blan. If I had never seen her all were well;
I thought I had the fairest lady living;
I had no idea there had ever breathed
A sweeter girl than my angelic Bell.
And I did love her with consuming passion —
With that ecstatic agony of love
That aches the heart and kills all appetite
Except the thirst for love; and now I loathe her —
Not that, but I don't want her; she is sour;
She's bitter, ugly, old, malicious; O!
That tempting apple from the golden slope
Hath stol'n the apple of mine eye; until
Mine eyes beheld that rare exotic flower
I thought I had the sweetest rose of summer:
Now mine is withered — withered on my hands!
Miranda! O Miranda!— how — O, how
Will I achieve thee! O, it cannot be;
My honor is at stake; come, faded Bell;
Here is my hand — here is my naked hand;
My heart I have not; it is with your friend,
The graceful goddess of the Golden State,
The queen of California. So it is;
Comparison breaks up our dearest charms;
Corrects the erring eye and shows defects
In pictures where perfection seemed to rest,
Till ranged with others of diviner finish;
Miranda! O Miranda!

Enter BELL, *hastily.*

Bell.   O Miranda!
She is out walking with dear Malachi!
I called for you so we could join them; but,
Miranda, O Miranda, is the song
I find you singing, sir!
Blan.   Well — and — indeed ——
Bell. Well and indeed!— the truth is, Blanton Dale,
You are in love with my bewitching friend;
And would break off with me.
Blan.   Well — and — indeed ——
Bell. Love has tied up your tongue!— well and indeed,
You iterate as idly as a parrot:
You stand dumbfounded, a convicted lover,
And false to iron-clad oaths.
Blan.   Well — and — indeed ——
Bell. Has she took all your wit! have you no speech!
Was it for this I broke with Malachi,
And took you in his stead!
Blan.   Indeed, indeed ——
Bell. Indeed me no indeeds; I want to know
If you do love Miranda?
Blan.   In very deed ——
Bell. Tut! tut!— You are a fool! if you have speech,
Pray tell me why you called upon Miranda
In plight so lackadaisical and woe-begone;
With arms outstretched as if to pluck her form
From the invisible air?

Blan. Indeed, my dear, let me have time for speech.
Bell. Speak, speak; I'm dead to hear.
Blan.   Well,— well,— in fact
I was composing some tremendous verse,
For Malachi to fire at your fair friend,
For he has fallen so in love with her
That he raves furiously by day and night,
Crying Miranda, O Miranda dear!
Even in the public streets; and so I wove
Her name quite frequently in the blank verse
Which I was conning o'er.
Bell.   And is that all?
And does the poet work his visage thus,
And fling his arms about in giving vent
To passions that are strangers to himself,
But burn for utterance in his neighbor's bosom
Till he gives them expression?
Blan.   The poet's realm
Is the ideal; he lives not in facts;
His fancy is the goddess he admires,
And in whose world he moves.
Bell.   I pardon you;
But Malachi will not require your verse;
Our wedding day and theirs will be the same:
That much has been arranged.
Blan.   So hot as that?
Well then, my love, let's join them in the walk;
I must congratulate them. This is news.
Bell. Miranda would be married privately
At some good pastor's house; with your consent,
That is determined on.
Blan. That suits me to a T. ·
But better still the other girl for thee. (*Aside.*)

SCENE VII.— *Cincinnati. A room. Enter* MALACHI.

Mal. Our marriages are managed by the Fates;
And matches are made up in infancy;
And our blind efforts to pervert this law,
Are turned to naught at touch of destiny.
How madly I did worship Bell Maguire!
How resolute was I to make her mine!
But destiny designed her for another,
And put the means to bring about the ends,
In my own nature — swift to take offense,
And quite too proud to own myself mistaken.
The unobservant mind would scarcely note,
In this slight ripple in our stream of love,
The hand of destiny that made delay,
Until the far off golden gates let forth
The peerless woman pre-ordained for me,
And she was drawn by fate's resistless power,
Without an effort of her own or mine,
And placed before me on the witness stand:
But he who notes no trace of fate herein,
Is dumb as ox — blind as earth-burrowing mole:
He is too big a fool to argue with,
And is not worth converting.

ACT IV.

SCENE I.—*The street in front of* BRYAN'S *house at night. Enter* BRYAN, *partly disguised.*

Bryan. As I expected, she has sought my wife,
And Saddie knows the villain she has married.
Now vengeance whets the knife whose edge were dull,
In killing for precaution. Die in sleep!
Though I would rather kill you while awake
And begging for your life upon your knees,
So you might feel your hurts; it is a pleasure
I must forego, for there must be no noise:
I'll enter and you die.

[*Unlocks the outer door and enters.* MACKAPEE *and* BENDER *emerge from a corner and approach the door stealthily. They are drunk and partly disguised.*]

Mack. 'Tis Basil Duke; why should he enter here?
Did you not see how cautiously he moved?
As if afraid his foot-falls would be heard?
Ben. Indeed I did; he had a dagger drawn.
His business must be bloody, like our own;
Let's in and after him; 'tis fit he die
In the performance of some overt act:
Let's drink and after him.

SCENE II.—*A room in the same house. Enter* SADDIE *with* EDNA'S *shawl about her head and shoulders. She opens a rear door and lets Detective in. They embrace.* BRYAN *seen hiding.*

Saddie. Be still, my darling; now the coast is clear;
The ladies have retired, the servants sleep,
And we may feast on love.
　　　　[BRYAN *rushes behind and stabs them.*]
Bryan. 　　　　　　　Then feast in hell!
I'll ope the way for you—down! you adulteress!
　　　　[*Detective and* SADDIE *fall.*]
Detect. O fool, to risk his life to gain a woman,
When he can have so many without risk!
The fool's death do I die.
Bryan. (*Stabbing him.*) Out on you, damned villain! speak no more!
Have you nine lives?
Saddie. 　　　　　　Forgive me, O my husband!
Bryan. (*Stabbing her.*) Away to hell, and take my curse with you!
I took you for another, but 'tis well,
Since you are false as she.
　　　　MACKAPEE *and* BENDER *enter and rush upon* BRYAN.
Bender. 　　　　Hold, villain, hold! [*They fight.*]
Mack. Yield, scoundrel, yield or die! your time has come!
Bryan. Stand back, you cowards! back upon your peril!
　　[*He stabs both and they fall,* BENDER *stabbing him as he falls.*]
Ben. O Mackapee, 'tis Bryan we have slain,
And by his hand we fall!—a parting drink—
O, comrades, fare you well!
　　　　[*Fails to lift the flask to his lips—dies.*]
Bryan. 　　　　　O cursed effect
Of blundering drunkenness! Here is the end,

The terminus of strife; farewell, my lads!
You are beyond reproof. [*Falls and dies.*]

Mack.   Too many plots —
Deceit and scheme engrafted upon scheme;
Deceivers while deceiving, more deceived;
Your mines for others sprung by other mines,
And these by others — life is a web of schemes,
Which death can but unravel! Let me hence! [*Dies.*]

Enter EDNA.

Edna. What dreadful work is this! O horrid sight!
What! Bender! and Mackapee! and Anson, you —
Are you all dead! Then why should I survive
Who have broken laws and hearts as well as you!
One kiss, betrayer! it was this face I loved,
And not the spark just out! One more embrace!
Now false one, loan me this!
[*Takes a pistol from his breast and shoots herself.*]

Enter DIXIE *in front, not seeing the bodies.*

Dixie. What dat shootin'? I heard a gun goin' off.
[*Discovers the bodies.*]
O lod, lod, lod, lod! Murdah! murdah! murdah! murdah!
murdah-ah-ah!

Enter TEDDY.

 Teddy. Who's kilt, that ye roar murther, ye black villain? [*Discovers the bodies.*] O murther! murther! murther! The masther kilt and the misthress! O murther and adulthrey! Ivery livin' sowl in the house dead and kilt!

Enter BRIDGET.

 Bridget. Are yez dthrunk again, ye blackguards! [*Sees the bodies.*] O howly Moses! Murther, murther! Perleece, perleece! O, fan me, darlint, fan me! [*Falls.*]

SCENE III.—*A room in Judge* DALE'S *house. Enter Sheriff* MAGUIRE, *hurriedly; the Judge seated.*

Maguire. Excuse abruptness; let me speak to you
As Michael Dale the sailor, time is precious.
Since the dread tragedy at Bryan Duke's
We know that he and Anson Gluge were one;
And that his brother who was tried for him,
Is the true man which he did claim to be.
But now prepare for wonders. He is here,
Returned to yield him to the law's demand;
And just this moment comes the coroner,
Who found upon the person of this Gluge,
The watch and locket from Miranda stolen,
As I suppose they are from her description;
Here they are, Michael, and you will perceive
They are the articles found with those babes,
Whom we, young sailors, rescued from the waves
So long ago, and which with the sweet babe
I left with pious nuns, but saw no more.

Judge. I recognize them, and I do believe
Miranda was that babe; this photograph,
The likeness of her mother; I have here,
      [*Takes it from a drawer.*
The other photograph which, Malachi,

You will remember, prattling, called his pa,
The morning after we escaped the wreck,
For reasons, Barney, you may understand,
He has not seen the picture since that day.

Maguire. (*Taking it.*) 'Tis Basil Duke, who now is at my house,
And he's the father of your Malachi
And my Miranda.

Judge.   Bring him quickly hither;
He'll recognize the picture of his wife,
If it be he.

                [*Exit* MAGUIRE *and returns with* BASIL DUKE

Judge. I'm glad to greet you as an honest man,
Free from restraint and from suspicion, sir;
We know the story of your loss at sea;
Some twenty years ago, Maguire and I
Were sailors, and escaped a sinking ship;
Saving two children, with some photographs,
Some watches, and some money; scan you this.

Basil. (*Kissing the picture.*)
This is the picture of my wife! O men,
Where are the children now?

Maguire.   Gone to their wedding.
The youth that prosecuted you in court,
Reared by the Judge, who named him Malachi,
Is your own son; the witness called Miranda,
Is, we believe, your daughter and his sister,
Who, ignorant of their dear relationship,
As all of us have been until this hour,
Are at the pastor's house this very moment
To solemnize their marriage.

Basil.   Haste we thither —
O, lead me to the house, good gentlemen!
We yet may reach it to arrest the marriage.

Maguire. We have no time to loose; this is the hour;
All further explanations can be made
When we are more at leisure.   [*Exit hurriedly.*

SCENE IV.—*A room in pastor's house.* MALACHI *and* MIRANDA *and*
BLANTON *and* BELL *standing before the pastor to be married. Company
in attendance.*

Pastor. Join you your hands. [*Loud knocking.*]
Voice without. Open the door; we do forbid the marriage.
Pastor. What may this mean?
Malachi.   Some merry friends, perhaps,
Who have divined our purpose, and have come
To give us a surprise.

        BASIL, *Judge and* MAGUIRE *rush in.*

Basil. Hold! hold! I do forbid! — you are my children;
You, fair young lady, are the very image
Of your dead mother; and this fine young man
Has got his mother's eyes. O you, my daughter,
Did make me think of her when in the court
So that my heart was broken. [*Attempts to embrace* MIR.

Mal.   Hold, good sir:
Has this man gone insane?

Judge.   He is your father;
And that fair girl beside you is your sister;
Embrace him, Malachi.

Mal.   Are you all mad?
Maguire. We are not mad; the stolen goods are found;
            Here, sweet Miranda, is your mother's picture,
            And this was once her watch. This will explain
            Why we are here to interrupt the marriage;
            Your bridegroom is your brother — ample proof
            Have we at hand to verify the fact.
            But explanations fuller in detail,
            You shall have shortly — now salute your father,
            Whose heart is gushing for his long lost babes.
Mir.   He looks so like the man that took my watch,
            That I do shudder; should he be my father,
            I fear I cannot love him; but I know
            That robber is no more.
Judge.   He was your uncle;
            His ways were bad, but he has paid the debt;
            Your watch and photograph were found upon him;
            Which Barney and myself do recognize;
            For we were sailors in our youthful days,
            And from a shipwreck saved two little babes,
            The parents being lost, as we supposed;
            But here the father is — the children you,
            Whom he has mourned as lost for twenty years;
            Remembering them as prattlers on his knee,
            Whom the devouring waves had swallowed up,
            With their young mother, whom he mourns to-day,
            Though his lost babes who know and own him not,
            He has recovered unexpectedly.
Mal.   Dear father, welcome, I will doubt no more,
            But wait the history at greater length
            With very great impatience.
Mir.   Father, I
            Do here salute you with a daughter's kiss:
            And I look like my mother?
Basil.   O, so much,
            That my soul wanders back to sunny hours
            Of courtship, love and marriage.
Mal.   O Miranda,
            Haply not my wife; now I may love thee,
            But with a brother's love; — the husband's hopes
            Die here like early flowers: I have a pearl
            Where late I had a diamond — precious still,
            Though in a different sense; I gain a sister,
            A father too, but lose so dear a treasure!
            There's no expression nor analysis
            For this conflicting war of the emotions!
            Perplexity of passion! — pain with pleasure!
            Torture with ecstasy, and glowing heat with ice! —
            One gentle kiss at parting, O my bride!
            And sister, one at meeting!
Mir.   Farewell, husband,
            O, farewell, farewell! — and brother, brother, hail!
Blan.   That marriage, then, is off.
Pastor.   Shall we proceed with yours?
            [JUDGE, BASIL and MAGUIRE *confer aside.*]
Blan.   These ladies, sir, have made a girlish vow
            To live in maidenhood till the same hour
            Sees both made happy brides.

Judge.   Miss Bell, and you, Miranda — you, my son;
And you, good Malachi, almost my son:
Give me attention. It is known to us,
That both young men love both of you young girls,
With almost equal ardor. You, my son,
Do love Miranda.

Blan.   (*Aside.*) Nine billions more than Bell!

Judge.   You, Malachi, do love fair Bell Maguire;
Go, take her for your bride, and give your sister
To Blanton for a wife; then you will have
A wife and sister, too, and sweet Miranda
Will have a brother's and a husband's love,
And all paternal blessing.

Mal.   Gentle Bell,
Will you exchange your husband there for me?
And take the place of my transformed wife?

Bell.   With his consent I will; it was yourself
That first taught me to love.

Blan.   Well, darling Bell,
With all my heart I yield you to my friend,
If I may have his charming sister there,
To fill the void made in this faithful heart,
By your unlooked-for loss. My dear Miranda,
Will you stand here my bride?

Mir   What says my father?

Basil.   He wishes you to wed the worthy son
Of this good man, who with his comrade here,
Snatched his poor children from the hungry sea,
And here restores them.

Mir.   Father, I obey.

Blan.   Then once more take our places on the floor;
Come, rose of Yosemite.

Mal.   And you, my flower-de-luce;
The old flame shall be fed upon your lips,
Till it consume all other.

Past   Once more join hands. You here take, each of you,
The person whom you now hold by the hand,
For your companion, confidant and friend,
Above all other friends; and promise never
To do an act which you would wish concealed
From your companion? this day's covenant
To end but with your life? You give assent;
Then you are married.

Basil.   And each couple here,
I do endow with fifty thousand dollars,
A father's wedding gift — much more will follow:
Go with my blessing, while I do retire
To my old home, and there in solitude
Bewail the loss of your dear mother during
The remnant of my life.

Enter Doctor, Superintendent of Insane Asylum.

Dr.   Excuse intrusion:
By much inquiry I have found at last
The person whom I seek. You, sir, I think,
Are Basil Duke, who suffered shipwreck once,
And who here late was tried as Anson Gluge,
The famous robber: — are you, sir, the man?

Basil.   I am, my friend.

Dr.   Your recent trial, sir, ·
Was published in the papers, with your portrait,
As you appeared in court. One of these papers,
Came by the merest chance, here recently,
Into the hands of a poor crazy woman,
Whom we have had in charge in the asylum
For more than twenty years. I should have said,
I am from San Francisco, in which place
I superintend an asylum for the insane;
How this poor woman came there is unknown;
She was most lady-like, with dreamy eyes,
Expressionless, but steady in their gaze.
She never smiled, nor wept, nor did her tongue
Give any token of intelligence.
Though she was oft conversing with herself,
No question put to her received reply;
Yet when addressed she gave you rapt attention,
As if in hunger to devour your words,
But without power to comprehend or speak;
Nor would she speak when any one was near;
But when alone her voice was often heard
In low, sweet accents, talking to her dolls;
For her sole occupation was the nursing
Of two doll babies like a little child.
At first she made them from her dress or shawl,
But, seeing her bent, two dolls were bought for her,
A little boy and girl; these she embraced
And straightway ran and hid; and from that hour
She hid them from the intruder; but alone
She nursed them constantly, and could be heard
Telling them that their pa would soon return;
And singing snatches of old nursery songs,
And lullabys to them. Well, as I said,
One of these papers came into her hands;
I happened to be present when her eyes
Fell on the portrait; instantly her hands
Were clinched, as from an overcharged battery,
Then she seemed reading calmly several minutes,
When with a strangled, gurgling shriek she fell
Prostrate upon the floor. She then was bled,
And slept composedly some twenty hours,
When she awoke and asked us where she was.
The eye had lost its stony, vacant stare,
And through the pupil came the spirit light
That spoke the language of the healthful brain.
In short, the lady was restored to reason,
Though twenty years of life were blank to her:
She thought it was but yesterday she stood
With her loved husband and her Ralph and Rose,
Upon a vessel's deck. [BASIL *falls.*]

Paston Haste to the gentleman, good people, all;
See! the poor man has fallen!

Basil.   Gently, friends:
Let me lie down; 'tis but a dizziness:
Thank you, my daughter, for a sup of drink:
Go on, good doctor; where was't you left off?
I will stand up and hear you to the end.

8

Dr. I said the lady was restored to reason:
She gave her history and was so assured
That you, sir, are her husband, that she begged
To be brought hither.

Basil.   Am I still in the earth?
Or in deep slumber have I stol'n away
Amidst the spheres, and found some whirling planet,
Peopled with spectres, riding on the winds,
And phantoms taking shapes of dear ones dead,
Flitting in mockery, half obscured the while,
Athwart my troubled vision? Do I sleep?
Did you not say the lady was brought hither?
Where is she? May I see her?

Dr.   Here she is:

Enter ANNABEL.

Let me remove your veil. Is this your wife?
[*Rush into each other's arms.*]

Basil. Have you come from the dead, my Annabel,
To join me once again?

Annabel.   O my dear husband!
I've dreamed of you throughout a troubled sleep,
That seems to me an age!

Basil.   And I of you.
Now let us think of nothing more at present,
Save that we are alive.

Annabel.   But Basil, dear,
Where are the children?

Miranda and Malachi. (*Both embracing her.*)
Here, mother, see your children!

MISCELLANEOUS POEMS.

The miscellaneous pieces which follow here, with a few exceptions, have appeared in various publications, running back to 1849; and several of them possessed local or general significance at the time of publication, which, perhaps, gave them their only value.

CARRIER'S GREETING.

WRITTEN FOR THE MADISON, IND., DAILY BANNER, JANUARY 1, 1852.

FAREWELL, farewell, old year! thou hast departed
   Upon Time's turbid and tempestuous sea,
While chastened, and subdued, and heavy-hearted,
   We turn to take one lingering look at thee;
While memory worketh — worketh as the bee
   Works in her hive — it worketh in the brain;
It reveleth in the past incessantly —
   It pointeth to past peril, pride and pain,
And vanished vagaries, all valueless and vain.

It holdeth up a mirror to the mind
   Where it hath painted pictures of the past —
The fairest faintly, while alas, we find
   The foulest figures most securely cast!
Shades of shortcomings! rush ye thick and fast
   In memory's mirror, ye tormenting troop!
Away with you! since loved ones ye outlast!
   O, could we sweep ye with a sudden swoop
Into forgetfulness! — ye grim ungainly group!

Sad things, indeed, are by-gones. to review —
   Hopes wrecked — foes made where friends did once abound —
Hearts that beat for us when the year was new,
   Now putrifying pulseless in the ground,
And loves that warmed us once, but lived to wound,
   And lights that lured us late have lingering died:—
What change one year hath wrought on all around;
   What millions it hath stricken in its stride!—
Mind ye the beau, the belle, the bridegroom, and the bride;

The aged, the infant — rich, poor, great and small
   All round ye in the past year stricken low? —
As they have fallen, shall ye surely fall;
   As they have gone, as surely shall ye go! —
Then be ye ready — sudden is the blow —
   The aim unerring — short the warning given:
Uncompromising is man's common foe —
   He's conquered all with whom he yet hath striven.
Alas! what noble hearts his thunderbolts have riven.

And *thou*, my generous and warm-hearted friend,
    In the full vigor of thy bright career,
All sudden — prematurely death did end
    Thy march of manliness and glory here.
O death! remorseless ever and severe,
    This blow of thine was all too sternly dealt;
Too painfully it stunned the public ear:
    By many a friend its freezing force was felt;
And many a manly heart to mourning did it melt.

Thou gifted one! — a stranger to thy face,
    Still thy bright genius did I long admire;
Nor days can dim, nor distance e'er erase
    Its impress from my spirit, set in fire!
Alas, alas! that I should tune my lyre
    To chaunt the dirge of the best friend I had!—
Even while aspiring as he did aspire,
    I come in ashes and in sackcloth clad,
And set about my task, all sorrowful and sad.

How recently the BANNER at its head,
    Bore forth thy name, and in its strength and pride,
The fire and fervor that thy spirit shed,
    It scattered in its columns far and wide:
We have the paper here, but thou hast hied
    To distant climes — hast vanished like a dream
Upon oblivion's ne'er returning tide: —
    Didst give the world an intellectual gleam;
Then sink to rise no more, in death's mysterious stream,

O, could we read the writing on the wall —
    Blind to our own, each see his fellow's fate —
How gently we would deal with one and all!
    How we would prize the gifted and the great! —
To thee I offer tribute, although late
    And all too homely may the homage be:
Love, virtue, honor, genius, consecrate
    The spot where resteth thy mortality.
And so, dear JONES, adieu! a last adieu to thee!

Now let us pause a moment to reflect
    On things about us, serious or absurd;
The march of science and of intellect
    Is onward still; — strange tales are daily heard
Of odd discoveries — wonders just occurred; —
    Inventions made — to be perfected soon —
If one were told, he'd scarce dispute the word,
    That some adventurer had, in a balloon,
Went stumbling o'er the stars, and stove against the moon!

Time still turns up things that confound the brain;
    Sage, songster, fiddler, fool, philosopher —
Fire made from water by Professor Paine,
    While spirit-rappers with the dead confer! —
In fact a fellow is afraid to stir,
    Lest he be "done for," "taken in," and "sold,"
By some vile humbug, that might just occur
    To Barnum, Beelzebub, or bores as bold! —
Who give us, with new tricks, revampings of the old.

To get a rage up, and to "raise the wind,"
  No scheme was happier, recent or remote,
Than the late tour of tuneful Jenny Lind,
  With Barnum buttoned to her petticoat:
Gulled crowds sat gaping till fair Jenny's throat
  Was properly ahem'd, and fairly cleared;
But when she wheezed the first unnatural note,
  The initiated like mad furies cheered;
  The balance bellowed too,—all fooled, and many scared!

How we Americans delight to be
  "Sucked in," "cajoled," "bamboozled," and "humbugged!"
We fuss and foam about our liberty,
  While to our hearts vile slavery is hugged;
Then how we welcome outlaws who have tugged,
  To free their countries?—here they're safe enough!
For since Old Albion's lop-ears last we lugged,
  And Europe's starving stomach still we stuff,
  All nations really hate to see us in a "huff."

Unlucky Lopez! thou who didst concert
  Plans to set mongrels and mulattoes free:—
Adventurer, patriot, or whate'er thou wert;
  A passing notice seemeth due to thee:
Dark was thy doom, and stern thy destiny;
  And they who slew thee were but slaves of slaves;
And servile slaves they should forever be—
  Should toil in chains, and rot in menial graves!—
  Vile, worthless braggarts, beggars, cowards, negroes, knaves!

"Adieu, dear Cuba!" was the latest sign
  Poor Lopez breathed with the last breath he drew!
And like a hero he did calmly die—
  All nobly—proudly—scarce regretted, too!
But for his comrades whom those cut-throats slew,
  Or chained in bondage, tears were shed, tho' vain:
How galling to endure (if even their due)
  That free Americans should wear the chain
  Of cowardly and corrupt, priest-ridden, rotten Spain!

LINES TO INZA.

ON RECEIPT OF A BOUQUET.

EVEN while my spirit strives with gloom,
    Like a maim'd eagle with the storm,
Like incense comes a sweet perfume,
    Even from my fair one's angel form:
None but the spirit spurned too oft,
    Knows how a gentle look may thrill;
It comes upon one like the soft,
    Sweet murmuring of a mountain rill:
Even as the honey to the bee,
    Rare tribute, art thou unto me.

This free-will offering to my muse,
　　Comes welcome as a shower of rain
To the parched earth — as pearly dews
　　Unto Arabia's thirsty plain!
Fair flowers! ye breathe of the sweet girl
　　Who culled ye from your parent stem;
The ocean caves have not a pearl,
　　The East hath not a diadem

That were as rich a gift to me,
　　If given by other hands than thine,
As one sweet pink, when culled by thee,
　　And offered from thy heart to mine!
Sweet pleaders for your mistress dear!
　　What would ye say to me of her?
Did she suppose your presence here
　　Would bless her lonely worshiper?

And did she say your sweet perfume
　　Must represent her languid sighs?
And that her love should re-illume
　　The plain o'er which my pathway lies?
O, what a glorious night is this!
　　The moonbeams fall as softly now
Upon the wave as dreams of bliss
　　Upon a slumbering virgin's brow!

On such a night as this how sweet
　　To wander forth alone with thee,
With this bright river at our feet,
　　Reflecting back thy form to me!
To shield thy slight and tiny frame,
　　From every chilling breath of air —
To read in thy sweet eyes the flame
　　That love for me hath lighted there!

O, fair one, couldst thou feel the fire
　　That glows in this deserted heart —
The longing, languishing desire
　　For such a being as thou art —
A being that in boyhood's hour,
　　Was imaged in my dreamy mind —
That Fancy decked in every flower
　　That could embellish woman kind.

Ideal idol of my heart,
　　Through all my life I've worshiped thee;
But now thy glorious counterpart
　　Appears in mortal guise to me:
Appears in thy sweet form, dear love,
　　Fair as my fancy could portray,
Pure as a spirit from above
　　Art thou, O lovely Queen of May!

Bright as midsummer's brightest beam,
　　Chaste as the full, soft, silvery moon,
Dear as a lover's earliest dream
　　Art thou, O sweetest rose of June!

Rich as the robes of Eastern queens,
  Soft as the down that doves bedeck,
Is thy dark hair, which half way screens
  Thy swan-like, alabaster neck.

O, thou art altogether bright —
  Thy sweet eyes, like the evening star,
Diffuse their love-inspiring light,
  And shed their glory from afar!
But death will dim those love-lit eyes,
  Still thy dear name shall live as long
As hearts are thrilled by maiden's sighs,
  And there are light and love and song:

For it shall linger on my lyre
  Through every clime — in every age,
Nor love, nor hate, nor flood, nor fire,
  Shall blot thine image from my page!
And while I hew my way to fame,
  With this elastic pen of steel,
Still linked with mine shall be thy name,
  In peace, in war, in woe, in weal!

Thy God my God, thy home my home —
  Weep thou, or laugh — even so will I:
Where'er thou roamest I will roam,
  And where thou diest I will die!

THE CHOLERA.

WRITTEN DURING AN EPIDEMIC.

THOU scourger of the world,
  Whose presence doth appal;
Whose viewless banner is unfurled
  O'er many a city's wall!
When will thy reign be o'er,
  Destroyer of our race?
Alas, alas, how many more
  Must feel thy cold embrace!

In thy black charnel-house
  Thy greedy whelps are fed;
And there thy furies hold carouse
  About thy victims, dead!
While thou dost sweep the earth
  Alike by night and day,
Turning the world from joy and mirth
  To terror and dismay.

Thy fearful presence known
  But by its dire effect,
For all the arts that chemists own
  Thy form cannot detect.

And yet, without disguise,
  At noon-day, and at night
Thou walkest forth before our eyes
  In all thy dreadful might.

Thy fatal essence still
  Eluding every test —
Mocking at all the drugs and skill
  Physicians e'er possess'd.
Death rides behind thy car
  Upon his whited steed,
Hurling his poisoned darts afar,
  Wherever thou dost lead.

Where'er thou dost appear
  Thy pestilential breath
Contaminates the atmosphere,
  And poisons man to death.
'Tis plain thou carest not
  On whom thy work is done —
Now smiting the degraded sot
  Now the abstemious "Son."

The vigorous and the faint,
  The wise, the foolish, too,
Alike the sinner and the saint,
  The Gentile and the Jew;
The master and the slave,
  The wealthy and the poor.
The honest man, the scheming knave,
  The famed and the obscure:

The maiden in her charms,
  The matron in her pride,
The infant in its mother's arms,
  The husband at her side;
The convict in his cell,
  The school-boy in his glee,
The dashing beau and haughty belle,
  Alike are food for thee!

What is thy fearful aim?
  What is thy frightful form?
Dost thou inhabit flood, or flame,
  Or revel in the storm?
Or doth thy venom pass
  In the electric fire?
Or is it in some subtle gas
  That animals respire?

Or com'st thou on the winds,
  From an offended God,
To scourge us for our many sins
  With thy avenging rod?
And was thy dreadful path
  Mark'd out by God on high?
And did he tell thee in his wrath,
  How many had to die?

Alas! thou may'st be sent
 To fill a fearful trust!—
Wilt thou depart if we repent
 In ashes and in dust?

- - --   - -

TO MISS ADALINE S——.

SWEET maiden with the silvery voice,
 And with the bright and lustrous eye,
And smiles that make all hearts rejoice,
 Save those which thou wouldst doom to die;
While at thy shrine doth daily fall
 The brave, the gifted, and the gay,
Let one, more luckless than them all,
 The homage of a pure heart pay.

Let them in poetry and prose,
 Each daily urge his amorous suit,—
They cannot prize such orbs as those,
 Like him whose warm soul must be mute—
Like him who sees thee as thou art,
 Pure as the snowy, feathery flake—
Would give his life to bless the heart
 That dooms his own to break.

Thy sylph-like form, thy slender waist,
 Thy jetty curls, thy polished brow—
Thy sense so charming, wit so chaste,
 Enchant me, and I meekly bow;
Nor can I break the charmed spell
 Thy beauty hath thrown over me—
Therefore, my blushing, blooming belle,
 In silence let me worship thee.

—   --   ——

EDEN AND ITS FLOWERS.

THE veil of darkness long had hung
 O'er nature's face ere Adam's time,
Nor tree nor flower had ever sprung
 In all the void and barren clime;

Nor had the loneliness profound
 Been broken by a warbling bird,
And never had the cheerful sound
 Of any human tongue been heard.

Thus stillness long her vigils kept,
 And all was dark and doubt and gloom,
While Nature 'midst the darkness slept
 Like one who sleepeth in the tomb:

Sleepeth until redeemed — recalled —
The day that endeth not in night
Shall dawn and he be disenthralled —
Robed in habiliments of light.

Thus Nature slept for many an age,
How long — how languidly although
We cannot glean from history's page —
Ne'er knew — alas, can never know!

At length the Almighty disapproved
The lethargy of Nature's sleep,
And his mysterious spirit moved
Upon the surface of the deep:

It moved in its mysterious might,
And Nature from her slumbers woke,
And vivid gleams of living light
Throughout the climes of chaos broke.

And now the God of boundless powers
In love and mercy did create
Trees, vines and fields, and fruits and flowers
The new-born day to decorate.

On every flower, on every tree —
In every grove, in every glade
The glory of the Deity
Was stamped and imaged and displayed.

And many a blooming forest wild
Bespangled Nature's radiant face;
And many a roseate valley smiled
In beauty's most bewitching grace.

And glowing with a golden hue
Were all the young and verdant trees,
While countless beds of violets threw
Their fragrance on the balmy breeze.

While every zephyr was perfumed
With spices, frankincense and myrrh,
The lilies of the valley bloomed
In groves of cedar, pine and fir.

The vine, in clustering fruit arrayed,
Formed many a wild and shady bower,
While daisies bloomed in every glade
Along with the magnolia flower.

The playful roe, from hill to hill,
Went feeding on the lilies then,
And there ran many a murmuring rill,
Through many a glade and forest glen.

And the glad birds among the flowers
Sang many a wild and warbling note,
Which, ringing through the forest bowers,
Went sinking on the winds remote.

In the wild bowers a charm was wove
  So bright and so serenely gay,
One would have thought the God of love
  Had robed them for a bridal day.

O, yes, a charm, a soothing power,
  So formed to ravish — to entice —
That angels might have thought each bower
  The prelude to a paradise.

Yes, to each bower a heavenly store
  Of such enchanting charm was given,
That they were bowers in bloom no more
  Than they were blooming bowers in heaven.

But one was still more brightly clad,
  And did so far outshine the rest,
It seemed that beauty could not add
  Unto the witchery it possessed;

For Beauty's hand had sweetly wreathed
  Her fairest garlands brightly through it,
And the Almighty had bequeathed
  A spell of dear enchantment to it.

Throughout this blessed bower there were
  Such varied charms so sweetly blended,
One would have thought a bower so fair
  Was for the immortal gods intended.

It owned such heavenly witchery,
  The Almighty must have been enchanted
When walking in the garden He
  With His own blessed hands had planted.

All kinds of fruit and every flower,
  And every herb and every tree
That could be formed by love and power
  Were growing here luxuriantly.

And summer reigned forever here,
  No cloud was ever seen above,
While birds filled all the atmosphere
  With songs of everlasting love.

The Lord God, seeing all was fair
  That He had formed to deck and bless it,
Then placed his creature, Adam, there
  To keep the garden and to dress it.

And Adam gazed with joy intense
  On everything that met his eye,
Yet looked for something more, from whence
  He felt he could not tell, nor why:

Even while it made his pulses thrill
  To gaze on Eden's loveliness,
He felt a charm was wanting still
  To fill the measure of his bliss.

The Lord, who saw this shade of gloom,
   And knew the source from whence it sprung,
Caused yet another flower to bloom,
   To which a charm so potent clung,

That, filled with wonder, love, and awe,
   And reverence, Adam viewed the flower,
For without blemish, fault, or flaw
   Was this, the queen of Eden's bower.

This capped the climax — Power, and Art,
   And Beauty could devise no more;
And rapture glowed in Adam's heart,
   Where there was aching void before.

And this last fairest flower that he
   Did from the Almighty's hand receive —
Was that sweet queen of witchery,
   Bright woman — 'twas the enchantress Eve!

WINTER.

FULL many a year hath fled since last I roved
   In this lone wood, where now unseen I stand,
Like a sad ghost that haunts some spot it loved
   Ere it was summoned to the spirit land.
I cling to this lone wood, where summer flings
   Her fairest flowers to beautify the grove,
As the subdued and sorrowing spirit clings
   Unto the memory of a mother's love.

For I have wandered in this wood alone,
   When May-day flowers were blooming fresh and fair;
Here I have bowed to the Eternal Throne,
   As all should bow, who know how frail they are.
Yon withered rose-bush, for which few would care,
   Wakes in my bosom memory's vivid rays;
As oft a chance note from an old-time air
   Wakes in the soul sweet scenes of happier days.

'Twas Spring, and many a lovely little bird
   Was singing sweetly from the blooming boughs,
When here we parted, here the angels heard,
   And Heaven recorded our undying vows:
But, like a flower, borne from its fragile stem
   By ruthless winds, my love was borne away;
And I, like one who drops a precious gem
   In the green billows, mutely stand to-day.

As one awakened from a summer dream,
   Whose magic scenes still in the fancy flit,
Just so, ye birds, that sung by yonder stream,
   Your songs of love live in my memory yet.
Drear Winter reigns supreme, his icy breath
   Hath frozen up our once loved trysting spring,
The fishes in the brook are chilled to death;
   The murmuring brook hath ceased its murmuring.

O'er all the earth a dreary shade is cast,
  And o'er the hills the howling north wind blows,
And o'er the valleys, where all summer last
  Bloomed the meek lily and the blushing rose,
The sun, while sinking in the far-off west,
  But faintly sheds his feeble, cheerless ray;
Like rays of hope in the poor exile's breast,
  Still doomed to wander from his home away.

O, this cold night, though friendless and alone,
  I feel for those who are poorer still than I;
I almost hear the widowed mother's moan,
  And the poor shivering little orphan's cry.
Black clouds are gathering in the northern skies,
  Like clouds of horror in a murderer's soul;
The sun's last glimmer meekly, dimly dies,
  While wailing winds assume their wild control.
On come the black clouds in their fearful flight,
  Flinging their flaky fleeces, white and pure:
Ah me! 'twill be a cold, inclement night—
  God shield the poor!

CALIFORNIA.

FIRST PUBLISHED IN FEBRUARY, 1849.

'TIS said that California's plains
    Are glittering now with gold;
And sure 'tis turning people's brains
    The stories that are told;
For there is not an earthly doubt
That thousands would at once set out,
    If it were not so cold;
It is too bad to wait till Spring,
One cannot think of such a thing.
        How will the virtuous people go
            Who languish for the mines?
        A stupid ox-team is too slow
            When tempting gold so shines;
        And he who doth attempt to cross
        Upon a jack, or mule, or "hoss,"
            Quick to his sorrow finds
        That he can make but sorry speed,
        While Lo makes off with scalp and steed.

I s'pose one might get on a ship,
    If he had cash to pay;
Yet that would be a tedious trip,
    For many a weary day;
And then it cannot be disguised
That vessels are sometimes capsized,
    And crews are cast away;
And little do gold-seekers wish
To give their bodies to the fish.
        Besides, while on your tedious route,

Around by Panama,
O'er there they're clawing gold dust out
  With desperation's claw!
This thought doth rankle in the brain,
And fire the blood in every vein,
  And on the vitals gnaw!
Ah me! is there a miner born
Could wait to go around Cape Horn?

O Genius, canst thou not invent
  Some strange and startling way,
By which the public can be sent
  To San Francisco Bay?
O, do provide us all with wings,
Or air-balloons or some such things,
  And that without delay!
O, how 'twould make the people laugh
If they could go by telegraph!
  The cobbler flings away his awl,
    The carpenter his tools,
  The loafer leaves the public hall,
    Professors leave their schools;
  The lawyer leaves his trade of tricks,
  And preachers, doctors, "cut their sticks;"
    Great men and greater fools,
  Together in confusion scud,
  To dig their fortunes in the mud!

Poor California! thou wilt hold
  A desperate set of men;
Full many a rogue in search of gold,
  Will leave his hiding den;
Thou wilt be lucky if there be
Amongst the hordes that swarm to thee,
  One righteous man in ten!
How many a dark and bloody crime,
Must soon pollute thy sunny clime!
  All lands and nations far and near,
    Will vomit forth their gall,
  And flood thy shores the coming year,
    With villains great and small.
  New York is fixing to unpack
  The rogues she hopes will not get back;
    A mongrel crew, withal:
  The murderer, swindler, gambler, thief—
    The pirate and the bandit chief.

Yet, California, don't suppose
  That all are rogues who come
To steal thy gold; tho' no man goes
  Unless, indeed, he's "some."
No man would venture over there,
Who could not whip a grizzly bear,
  Or knock a bison dumb!
And live upon wild oaten cakes,
And sleep with wolves and rattle-snakes!

'Tis said that famine threatens thee,
  Yet that cannot be so;
For o'er thy plains are wandering free
  The bear and buffalo;
And all historians boast about
Thy monstrous salmon and thy trout,
  And surely one might go
And hook a fish or shoot a bear,
That is, if he had time to spare.

No doubt the prices of produce
  Are most exorbitant;
Gold is so plenty, 'twere no use
  For husbandmen to plant;
In fact no man can sow his grain
While gold is glittering on the plain,
  That every one will grant;
Yet he must barter gold for bread,
And at an awful loss, 'tis said.
    The recent war removed the cause
      That curbed thy spirit so,
    It freed thee from the unstable laws
      Of fickle Mexico;
    No emigrant would settle down
    Where Mexico's accursed frown
      And jurisdiction go;
    But now the flag of freedom waves
    O'er thy emancipated slaves!

And thy bright valleys will attract
  The virtuous to thy shores,
Thy sunny vales are worth, in fact,
  More than thy precious ores;
For thy serene and heavenly clime
Is but an endless summer time,
  Where wintry wind ne'er roars,
But ever comes the healthful breeze
From snow-clad mounts or briny seas.
    The invalid with hectic cheek
      Will seek thy sunny vales;
    The poet there, subdued and meek,
      Will weave his fairy tales:
    For lovely flowers forever bloom,
    And with their dulcet breath perfume
      The life-reviving gales!
    Upon my soul I think that I
      Will seek thy valleys by and by.

Perhaps this everlasting cough,
  Would give my diaphragm
A long respite if I were off
  Where all is mild and calm;
Besides, upon thy golden coast,
What pleasure it would be to roast
  The oyster and the clam!
I am about resolved to go,—
Yoke up the steers, my boys!—haw, whoa!

I doubt if I can urge an ox
From now till judgment day,
Three thousand miles across the rocks,
With Indians all the way!
And bears and wolves upon the route!
Ge! Brandy! ge!—(your tongue is out!)
Ge, Buck!—G'lang! I say!
Ge up! ge up!—confound the luck!
Ge, Brandy!—damn you, haw!—You Buck!

TO HAYNAU.

THE INFAMOUS AUSTRIAN GENERAL.

FIRST PUBLISHED IN 1849 OR 1850.

INCARNATE fiend of countless crimes
    Beyond the briny seas!
Thou bloodiest monster of all times!
    Is thy black heart at ease?
Canst thou, with conscience calm and clear,
Look back upon thy past career
    And barbarous butcheries?
Nor feel a shudder at thy heart,
All black and bloody as thou art?
        Thy victims' blood is on the ground,
            Its incense fills the air;
        And Christian nations stood around
            While thou didst spill it there;
        Nor voice nor arm was raised to save
        The young, the gifted, and the brave,
            Old men, and maidens fair:
        Nor rank, nor age, nor sex was free
        From thy inhuman butchery!

Thou mighty man! thou valiant chief!
    Thou warrior of renown!
All thy commands were blunt and brief,
    And at thy slightest frown,
Some victim (whom it mattered not)
Was stripped and tied, and flogged, or shot!
    And who e'er sacked a town
Or burnt a church with more delight
Than thou! most brave and gallant knight!
        And she* who periled her pure life
            To set her lover free,
        The fair, the fond affianced wife
            Who rashly trusted thee,
        In hopes her bravery and her youth,
        Her sex, her sorrow, and her truth,
            Love, faith, fidelity,
        Would soften and subdue thy heart,
        And she be suffered to depart.

---

* Referring to the betrothed bride of a Hungarian prisoner of Haynau's, who took his
place in the cell while he escaped in her attire. In the morning she was deliberately shot
in his stead.

How was her deep devotion prized?
  Were grace and favor found?
Were her fond wishes realized
  When morning rolled around?
No! thou accursed bloodhound, no!
Her noble blood was made to flow
  From many a bullet-wound! —
Accursed forever be thy name!
Thy breast a hell of torturing flame!
    Thou libel on the human race!
    Thou fiend of deepest dye!
    Away! and hide thy hideous face
    From every mortal eye.
    Go claim companionship with owls!
    Go where the wolf forever howls,
      And fierce hyenas hie!
    And mate with beasts and birds of prey,
    For thou art savage more than they.

Lean, lank, and luckless, lone and lorn
  Mayest thou hereafter be;
And may thy hours, from night till morn,
  Be hours of agony;
May devils howl about thy door,
And demons haunt thee evermore,
  And nightmares harass thee;
And mayest thou still, with sleepless eyes,
In tears retire, in torture rise!

WOMAN.

O IN that name there dwells
    A music void of art,
Whose harmony expels
  All sorrow from the heart.

The youthful and the old,
  The fettered and the free,
The warm heart and the cold,
  All love and worship thee.

Through fortune good and ill,
  Even from our earliest breath
We're blest by thee, and till
  We fall asleep in death.

Thou art an angel bright,
  Who scatters care and gloom,
And cheers with heavenly light,
  Our pathway to the tomb.

The lightning of thine eyes
  Dissolves our cares away,
As gloomy darkness flies
  Before the opening day.

Thou art the living spring
  Of all our earthly bliss,
The dawn and opening
  Of endless happiness.

Without thee there would be
  No loveliness in flowers,
No charm in poetry,
  Nor joy in idle hours.

O, let her have the reign,
  And wear the royal crown,
And we will kiss the chain
  By which we're fettered down.

The youthful and the old,
  The fettered and the free,
The warm heart and the cold,
  All serve and worship thee.

LETTER TO LIZZIE H****S, OF NEW JERSEY.

O FLY from the land of the cedar and pine,
    The magnolia blossom, the cranberry vine;
The barrens where ripen the bilberry blue,
The hills where we hunted the whippowil-shoe,
The bay on whose bosom our bark used to ride,
The beach where we rambled, down by the seaside;
The sedgy salt marsh where in springtime we strayed
For the eggs that the wild goose and sea gull had laid:
The groves (where the grapes cluster high over head)
That border the fens where the panther hath tread,
Where the mocking bird daily his wild harp attunes,
And the purple swamp-huckleberries hang in festoons:
The apple so rich, and the melon so rare—
The cherry, the plum, and the peach and the pear—
The orchard, the arbor, the ocean, the bay—
O, leave them, Liz—leave them, and hie thee away!
I offer no apple, no cherry, no plum—
I ask thee to leave them, love—leave them and come;
Desert thy sweet cottage, down by the blue sea,
And haste to the Hoosier State—hasten to me!
For I'll give thee my love for the land thou wilt lose,
I will hunt thee pawpaws for the whippowil-shoes;
For the cedars I'll give thee the sweet sugar tree;
Great rivers and lakes for the bay and the sea:
I will give thee, for orchards long nurtured by rule,
Wild forests, romantic, green, shady and cool;
For the beach, and the barrens, and sedges, and fens,
I will give thee green prairies, and mountains and glens.
O, list to my lay!—'tis an old lover calls;
I will wait for thee here, at the Ohio falls;
I will show thee Kentucky—the Hoosier State, too,
And thou shalt have both for our lost Jersey blue.
O, since I have left thee I am stricken and sad;
They have died, all the loved ones but thee, that I had.

There are none here that love me — 'neath sorrow I bow;
Then hasten, dear Liz, to thy lone lover now!
Come away! come away! come away to the West!
My angel, my goddess, my guardian, my guest!
I have bought thee an arbor — I have built thee a house —
Come be my companion, my sister, my spouse:
Come, leave thy lone cottage, love, by the blue sea,
And reign in the halls I've erected for thee;
But first send a line on the lightning to cheer
My heart till thou comest. Good night to thee, dear!

THOUGHTS OF THE DYING.

THE fearful hour has come at last,
  And Heaven has signed the stern decree;
One moment and I shall have passed
  The threshold of eternity.
Such is, O God, our darksome fate,
  That we who live and move to-day,
To-morrow lie inanimate,
  And ghastly forms of putrid clay!
And yet we should not fear to die;
  For O, the weary heart and head
Find no repose until they lie
  Among the calm and peaceful dead.
But when we feel the icy sting,
  And know we must so soon depart,
There doth a dread unbidden spring,
  From the deep fountains of the heart.
And yet, indeed, it is not strange
That mortals dread the awful change,
For O, how bright a world is this!
How decked in fairy loveliness!
The flow'ry earth, the azure sky,
The stars that twinkle from on high,
The moon that sheds her silvery light
Upon the waters calm and bright,
The birds that carol wild and free, .
  From every bower and breezy grove,
And fill the air with harmony,
  And teach the human heart to love!
And dearer still those cherished ones,
  That move around us daily here,
Shedding their light, like vernal suns,
  Throughout our wearisome career!
O, think of these, and who will say
  That this is but a dreary. earth,
Where beauty, love and joy decay,
  As swiftly as they spring to birth?
'Tis true that sorrows oft destroy
The bloom of love, and hope and joy;
And some have chattered in our ears,
That life is but a vale of tears;
Yet still the sober truth is this:
Our life is one of woe and bliss;

A scene of trials, joys and woes:
Each in its turn successive flows,
And still doth the immortal mind
Regret to leave these scenes behind.
Not many hours have passed away
  Since I, not dreaming once of death,
Went forth to hail the coming day,
  And drink the morning's dulcet breath.
And as the morning zephyr stole
  Among my locks in wanton glee,
It seemed to tranquillize my soul,
  And give new vigor unto me.
But never more, alas! shall I
  Be by the morning breeze caressed;
The morning breeze will shortly sigh
  Above my lowly bed of rest!
And tho' perchance the lonely spot
  Be bathed anon in memory's tear,
Still I shall shortly be forgot
  By all who saw me daily here.

And now before another hour
  That mystery will be known to me
Which baffles all the boasted power
  Of learning and philosophy!
But, O, I never can disclose
  What I shall learn to mortal ears;
Within the grave it must repose,
  Or live with me in other spheres!

LIFE.

LIFE is an ocean
    Of ceaseless motion:
With strange devotion
  We mortals cling
'To hopes that treat us,
To smiles that meet us,
    Like rosy spring;
    And fondly bring
    Sweet ravishing
Alas! to cheat us
    With sorrow's sting.

Fond hopes deceive us,
And falsely leave us,
And new hopes weave us
    Their garlands fair,
Which scarce are braided
Ere they be faded:
    As lightning's glare
    Lights the night air
    With fitful flare,
Then earth lies shaded
    In dark despair!

And joys are fleeting
And still repeating
Their swift retreating
  As we draw nigh,
And still pursue them
And vainly woo them,
  Still, still they fly;—
  Or tasted lie
  Where Reason's eye
Can calmly view them
  With sorrowing sigh!

God's blasting power
Blights friendship's flower;
Misfortunes lower
  O'er life's short day,
And woe incloses
Love's dulcet roses:
  Loved ones decay —
  They come — and stay —
  And pass away;—
Death interposes,
  And where are they?

O, death is reaping,
Devouring, sweeping;
The laughing, weeping
  Alike are slain!
And mirth, and gladness,
And gloom, and sadness,
  Each in its train
  Brings woe and pain,
  Fatigues the brain;
All, all is madness!
  All, all is vain?

TO AN ALBUM.

BRIGHT book, why cam'st thou unto me?
  One might suppose thou wouldst be moved
Amongst the gay, the fair, the free,
  The wooing, loving, and beloved.
How durst thou wander round so much?
  How durst thou unprotected go
For every pen's unhallowed touch
  To soil thy virgin leaves of snow!

Fair emblem of dear woman's heart!
  The letters, once inscribed in thee,
Become of thy own self a part,
  If not a part of purity.
Thy leaves will keep polluting stains,
  Or song that purest love awakes,
As woman's heart till death retains
  The love-tints that it earliest takes.

Yes, when that cherished urchin, Love,
  In woman's heart has left his trace,
No charm below, no power above,
  Can e'er that darling line erase!
How sacred will sweet woman's breast
  Still bear the love which first it bore;
And how much more would man be blest
  If woman's love were valued more!

Bright woman! if thou wert not here
  How dark this sunny world would be!
For all that's perfect, pure and dear
  Belongs to thee, and only thee!
Sweet being! how I long to paint
  The wild idolatry I feel
For thee!—thou bright, thou blessed saint!
  And sketch it with poetic zeal!

Tho' many a bard has sung thy worth
  Long ere I felt thy gentle sigh,
Yet, O! that mortal ne'er had birth
  Who loved, adored thee more than I.
I would not cause thee aught of pain
  Nor wring from thee one tear of grief—
Nor would I write a thought profane
  Upon this white and glossy leaf.

Go, lovely book, and do not dare
  From thy sweet owner to depart;
Go—go, and tell her to beware
  Who writes upon her virgin heart!

I'M WEARY OF THIS LIFE.

TO EMMA.

LOVED one, I'm weary of this life,
  And pining to be free;
This sunny world with joy so rife,
  Hath not a joy for me!
And saving thee I have no friend
  For whom I'd longer live;
Life hath not now a charm to lend,
  The grave no hope to give.

Tho' once bright hopes lived in my soul,
  Like birds in summer bowers,
And sweet dreams o'er my slumbers stole,
  Like soft winds o'er the flowers;
And still, like the green vine that clings
  Unto a blasted tree,
Sweet visions come on memory's wings,
  And softly cling to me:

Fond memories of vain hopes and schemes
  That lured life's early day
Melt in my soul like soft moonbeams
  In ocean's foaming spray.
But the sweet charm that latest clung
  To my deserted heart
Was rudely from its chambers wrung
  When we were torn apart.

For never till I met with thee
  Did spirit speak to mine;
And like ripe apples on the tree,
  Or grapes upon the vine,
Thy smiles did lure my longing soul,
  Which lost their light too soon,
And which attends thy soft control
  As tides attend the moon.

'Tis not thy face, so strangely fair —
  'Tis not thy faultless form —
'Tis not thy dark and wavy hair,
  And lips so soft and warm —
Nor yet the witchcraft of the eye —
  The tongue's enchanting tone —
The magic glance — the melting sigh —
  That make me all thine own.

No, no! — not all of these combined,
  Unrivaled tho' they be,
Could madden thus my brain, and bind
  My spirit thus to thee.
Then what — what is this potent spell!
  What mortal can define
This power that madly doth impel
  My own to seek for thine! —

This wish to have dissolved and lost
  Loves, hates, hopes, thoughts in thee,
Like snowflakes by the tempest toss'd,
  Dissolving in the sea!
But like a summer bird, that hies
  To sunnier climates hence;
Or like to dreamed bliss that flies
  Before the waking sense; —

So thou hast fled, my gentle dove,
  And robbed the world of light!
Our planet lacking thy sweet love,
  Seems always in the night.
O, no! — no light to him is borne,
  Who must not see again
The form that in the heart is worn,
  And woven in the brain!

TO MARY.

WRITTEN ON THE FLY LEAF OF A BOOK.

DEAR Mary, shouldst thou turn these leaves
 When I am far away,
Think of the stricken heart that grieves
 For thee by night and day —
Of him who like some mateless dove
 Bemoans his lonely fate,
And sighs and sickens for the love
 Of his dear absent mate.

Yes, Mary, dear, remember him,
 Whose heart doth pine and break —
Whose eye with weeping still is dim —
 And sleepless for thy sake.
I know thou wilt remember me,
 My own beloved dear,
And pine as I will pine for thee
 When I am far from here!

THERE IS NO MATE FOR ME.

TO MAGGIE.

THERE is no mate for me — O, none!
 I sail o'er life's dark sea —
I tread life's path alone — alone;
 There is no mate for me!

I grope my way without the light
 That woman's warm love lends;
O, sadly passes the dull night,
 In gloom the long day ends!

Bound fast by Fate's unhallowed tie —
 Unlov'd, and yet not free!
Alas, alas! how lone am I —
 There is no mate for me!

And yet the hours with bliss are freighted,
 The world is full of love ;
Birds, insects, animals are mated,
 Around, about, above.

It seems that only I am sad;
 Yet she — O, where is she —
The maid who pines — in mourning clad —
 My loving mate to be!

O gulf — impassable redoubt!
 Why hide me from her charms?
O frowning heights, why hedge me out
 Forever from her arms?

Her pale, wan face, her tearful eyes,
  Her aching, breaking heart;
Her silent tongue, her constant sighs,
  Proclaim that we're apart.

But, maiden, by the stars above thee,
  I swear, tho' fate may sever,
To think of thee, and love thee — love thee
  Forever — ever — ever!

THE HAUNTED RING.

TO MARY ———.

FAIR girl, I bring thee here
    A ring of rarest gold,
'Twas forged for thee, my dear,
    And ne'er was bought nor sold.
There's a secret goes with it! —
    'Tis haunted with a spell! —
But still, love, it will fit
    Thy taper finger well.

I found a wizard skilled
    In black and devilish arts!
I paid him, and he filled
    This ring with magic parts!
So while thou'rt true thou'lt see
    The ring still pure and bright;
But once prove false to me,
    'Twill turn as black as night!

'Tis frightful, but 'tis so,
    Nor all heav'n's floods of rain,
Nor all thy tears of woe
    Can wash it bright again!
There is an artery lies
    In thy finger near the bone,
And this the heart supplies
    With blood, and it is shown

That while the heart is mine
    Thy blood will keep this ring
Bright as the stars that shine,
    Or a gay bird's gaudy wing;
But shouldst thou prove untrue,
    And love and fervor lack,
The blood thy lungs will brew
    Will turn this bright ring black!

The wizard quizzed me sore —
    Said woman was not true —
He said the girl that wore
    This ring would live to rue
The hour she saw it first,
    For it might tell the tale
(She would not have rehearsed)
    That love like hers can fail.

So, loved one, search thy heart ;
    If it can my faith betray,
Tempt not the wizard's art,
    Nor touch this ring, I pray!
But my fair one, without fear,
    Puts on the haunted gem!
And she'll wear it bright and clear
    As an angel's diadem!

LINES TO A WESTERN RIVER.

FLOW on, noble River — flow on to the sea,
    Thou flow'st through the land of the faithful and free —
Thou flow'st through the beautiful valley in which
The poor are as fearless and free as the rich.
See the emigrant vessels, how gaily they glide
Away to the West on thy glorious tide!
Where the prairie is green, and the forest is wild,
The soil is productive — the climate is mild;
Where the rattlesnakes hiss, and the prairie wolves hie,
And the grizzly bear growls in the mountains hard by,
Where the wild horses prance in the pride of their power,
And the timid doe feeds on the wild prairie flower.
Far away in the West, where the buffaloes roam,
Are the emigrant's hope and the emigrant's home;
Then flow, noble river — flow on to the sea,
Through the land of the fearless, the firm, and the free!
And O, while thy waters continue to run,
May our Empire of States be cemented in one!

MY LOVE IS NOT LIKE OTHERS.

TO MAGGIE.

MY Love is not like others —
    Who can with her compare?
I challenge you, ye mothers,
    To show a maid so fair!
Your daughters' eyes are duller —
    None can with hers compete —
Tho' I know not their color —
    I only know they're sweet.

The lilies vie with her,
    The violets in their beds,
Whenever she doth stir,
    "Hide their diminished heads."
The soft winds from the south,
    That wanton with her curls,
Steal incense from her mouth
    To give to other girls.

When her glad laugh is ringing
  The bowers and groves among,
The mocking birds quit singing
  To listen to her tongue.
But pencil cannot trace
  Her matchless charms and graces:
Hers is the fairest face
  Amongst the fairest faces.

Love lurketh in her eye,
  He lingereth on her lip,
And on her brow; for I
  Did feel the urchin skip
Thence through my heart and head
  With such a blissful thrill
That I would now be dead
  If sudden joy would kill.

And we were late alone
  While the dull world did sleep,
When the soft whispered tone
  That makes the young heart leap,
I poured into her ear,
  I poured into her heart,
Till rapture's sigh and tear
  Did both unbidden start.

But this you must not tell;
  There's not a soul must know
That she loves me so well,
  And I adore her so.
O, she is not like others —
  She is a beauty rare!
I challenge you, ye mothers,
  To show a child so fair!

LINES TO A BIRD.

O BIRD of rare beauty, come back to the breast
  Where late thou didst quiver and tremble to rest!
I found thee forsaken, thy life ebbing fast,
All alone in the cold world too cruelly cast.
In the pride of thy power thou hadst breasted a storm
Too rude and too fierce for thy frail, gentle form;
And the teardrops of heaven having wetted thy wings,
Thou couldst not soar up where thy trembling hope clings,
But timidly flitted to the bosom that sighed
So long for some loved one — so long was denied.
Had not thy fair plumage been drooping and wet
I should not have known thee nor grieved for thee yet,
And had not misfortune cast o'er thee her pall
I could not have found thee nor caught thee at all.
I caressed thee and soothed thee and gladdened thy heart,
And soon found thee again the bright bird which thou wert.

But thou couldst not be blessed in my cold atmosphere,
And hast fled from my sight while I sigh for thee here:
But, bird of rare beauty, come back to the breast
Where late thou didst trustingly tremble to rest!

THOU HAST WOUNDED ME.

TO LIZZIE.

O FAIR one, art thou not afraid —
    Dost thou not tremble, peerless maid
Lest I shall die and thou shalt be
Arraigned for wounding, killing me?
A foeman's bullet or his dirk
Does not more sure and fatal work
Than those swift arrows which do dart
From thy bright eyes to my poor heart.
O, thou hast wounded me with sighs,
With glances from those sweet, sweet eyes —
With smiles that ravished me to death —
With tones that made me hold my breath,
Lest one soft whispered word of thine
Should miss these eager ears of mine!
Dark lashes fringing lids of snow,
And wicked curls that haunt me so,
And lips where every earthly sweet
And those of heaven commingling meet!
O, with those sweets, those charms, those arts,
With these thick showers of Cupid's darts,
Has thou destroyed me, and I die
Lest thou the only balm supply!
Canst thou refuse a heart thus smote,
The only, only antidote!
O, thou who woundest me canst give
The nectar that will make me live;
Nor will it cost thee greater skill
To cure me than it did to kill.
Wert thou as kind as thou art sweet,
What heaven were ours when next we meet!

CAUGHT IN THE FACT.

ONE day not long ago there passed
    A sylph-like girl near where I stood;
One glance into my eyes she cast,
    When it occurred to me I could
Go straight to heaven, with a whirl,
If I might take this queenly girl.

In majesty she moved along
    While I stood spell-bound by her grace:
To follow her I felt was wrong,
    But yet I gave the beauty chase,

And coming up I asked her why
God gave her such a sweet blue eye.

Just then I took a closer view,
  And shrinking down with abject fear,
Said I, " My darling, is this you?
  I did not think *you* could be here!"
'Twas my own wife!—was ever quicker
An old offender caught, and slicker!

O, FOR ONE HOUR WITH THEE!

TO LIZZIE.

O FOR one short, sweet hour with thee,
    To all but us unknown, unknown!
Then I could spend eternity
    Alone, alone, alone!

My darling girl! my heart's delight!
  Thou'rt all of earth or heaven that's dear!
I want thee, want thee all the night,
  I want thee ever near!

O, could I have one hour to pour
  The story of my soul's mad fire
Into thine ears—I'd ask no more,
  Save that I might expire
Upon thy bosom, and forget
  The dreadful fact that we are parted,
Or that we ever, ever met,
  And both are broken-hearted.

ON RECEIPT OF A WITHERED ROSE.

TO MAGGIE.

WHAT wouldst thou, mystic messenger?
    What brought thee here?—how comest, and why?
What tidings bringest thou of her
  Who saw thee bloom—who saw thee die?

Comest thou with crushed and scentless leaves
  To say my history is known?
To tell my heart, although it grieves,
  Another deems that grief its own?

Remindest me of moments fled
  When life was sweet and passion young?—
Of loves that like thy leaves are dead?—
  Of blighted hopes and harps unstrung?

Sayest thou her fate is like my own?
  Her heart's young tendrils clung to naught?
Its sweet flowers blasted soon as blown?
  Its woe with its own life-blood bought?

Art thou a type of tones now hushed
  That once were sweet? — of hopes now dead?
Speak'st thou of young affections crushed?
  Of blighted loves, and blisses fled?

Back to thy dead — parched leaves, what power
  Can perfume, freshness, fragrance bring,
And make of thee the lovely flower
  Which thou wert in the early spring?

None, none! — no magic can restore
  The life and odor thou hast lost;
But can the young heart hope no more
  Whose wild, first love was crushed and crossed?

Is there no sympathetic soul —
  Is there no languid, love-lit eye,
That can assume a sweet control
  O'er the young heart half doomed to die?

Does Fate not fix its own affairs?
  Why comest thou, faded flower, to me,
Thrilling a soul oppressed with cares
  With love's quick electricity?

O, tell me, flower, with odor flown,
  Is there not some mesmeric art
The gods employ that moves my own
  To seek thy sweet young donor's heart?

Although our eyes have never met —
  Although my lips have pressed not hers —
Have not the gods some magic set
  In both our hearts that strangely stirs

Love's smouldering embers? — Speak! O, speak!
  Is there not some magnetic power
That makes some souls each other seek?
  I ask thee, flower! — I ask thee, flower!

A NEW YEAR'S GIFT.

TO MISS B. J. M'COLLUM.

A NEW-YEAR'S gift a fair one craves —
    What shall I give her? — I have nought!
O, had I corals from the caves —
  The ocean caves, with rubies wrought
Into a shining chain of beads —
  Or lilies from the valleys, where,
Unsought by man, the wild doe feeds,
  To weave a garland for her hair —
Or could I pluck a star from heaven
This would I give — those should be given!

But I have nought to give but song,
  And woman only can inspire
The impassion'd notes pent up too long,
  Like some entombed volcanic fire.

And, maiden, those sweet eyes of thine
  May well inspire the wildest strain
That ever thrilled this harp of mine —
  That ever burned in poet's brain!
Were fifty maids in some bright bower,
I'd choose thee for the fairest flower!

But why should woman still provoke
  The homage of the brain — the heart
By woman frenzied — maddened — broke!
  What solace can she *now* impart?
But I forget me; — Maiden fair,
  This New-Year's gift, what shall it be?
Wilt have the lilies for thy hair?
  Or will these verses answer thee?
Or shall I pluck from heaven's bright sphere
A star for its sweet sister here?

THE TIME FOR YOU AND ME.

TO MARY.

THE balmy day's refulgent light
    May suit, dear love, the blest and free;
But the black, dull and dismal night
  Is the time for you and me.
When darkness spreads her sable pall,
  Like funeral robes o'er land and sea,
Then what sweet light from heaven doth fall
  On you, dear love, and me!

GIVE ME THY MINIATURE.

TO MAGGIE.

DEAR Miss, give me thy miniature,
    Though in thy smiles I may not bask,
Thy sun-lit shadow, I am sure,
  My aching heart may ask.

I ne'er shall feel thy fond embrace,
  I ne'er can claim thy love nor thee,
Yet the outlines of thy sweet face
  Thou may'st vouchsafe to me.

Let me drink from those imaged eyes
  The nectar that my spirit needs,
For it may save the soul that dies,
  Or break the heart that bleeds.

Perchance the picture, by awaking
  Tumultuous passions in my breast,
May help the heart that's breaking, breaking.
  To break and be at rest.

Place in a desert parched and dry
  A miser with his wealth untold—
There rich, though thirsting, he will die
  While gazing on his gold.

And thus my soul must thirst, even though
  I have thy priceless image here;
Yet its mild light may soften woe,
  And sanctify Hope's tear.

And since thy love cannot be mine,
  Since nought but woe awaits me now,
Thy shadow shall be all the shrine
  At which my heart shall bow.

Then let me have the precious charm,
  Fresh stolen by sunbeams from thine eyes;
My throbbing heart shall keep it warm
  While life that warmth supplies.

MUSINGS OF A MANIAC.

MY Mother! is that thy angel form,
  Upon yon cloud of silvery hue,
Which, in the sunlight, soft and warm,
  Appears to my enraptured view?
It is! it is!—I know thy face,
  I know thy features mild and fair—
Through all the mist of time and space,
  My warm heart tells me what they were!

Majestic, graceful and erect,
  Thou standest on thine airy car,
Which, gorgeously and gaily decked,
  Goes floating gallantly afar!
O, comest thou from thy home above
  To gaze upon thy wretched son,
Who since he lost thy living love
  No other woman's love hath won?

And still upon thy pale, fair brow
  Sits that mysterious shade of gloom—
I see it just as plainly now
  As when they'd decked thee for the tomb!
O Mother! what doth it forebode?—
  That look of love, awe, anguish, ire?—
Seest thou marked out my future road
  O'er quicksand, mountain, marsh, and mire?

Did death, the instant that he smote
  Thy fragile frame, unmask to thee
Events to come howe'er remote,
  All hid to blind mortality?
Perchance he did—thou may'st foreknow
  The dark doom o'er thy son impending,
And hence that shade of doubt, fear, woe,
  With looks of love and pity blending

In thy sweet face. My Mother dear
  In mercy quit thy cloud of light,
And let thy spirit,—hovering near,
  Watch o'er thy firstborn all the night!
For he is ill, and there are none
  To soothe, to succor, and to save;
In all the world there is not one
  Would wrench him from a maniac's grave!

O, there is no physician here!
  For what I bear there is no balm,
And none, from what I do appear,
  Would think me wretched as I am!
O, from the body of this death
  Alas, who shall deliver me?
Its choke-damp suffocates my breath
  From nightfall till the shadows flee!

Here live five monsters in their lair,
  Upon thy son's unhappy heart,
With features grim, and eyes whose glare
  Blight all it beams on in the earth!
A she-wolf holds me while she howls,
  A wild cat clamps me with her claws,
And while I gasp a grizzly growls,
  A lioness unjoints her jaws,

In eagerness to break my bones,
  And tear my tendons with her teeth,
While screech owls, in distracted tones,
  Cry — "Haste, thou hated, to the heath!"
O God! if I could fly! for here
  There comes a ghoul in hedgehog figure:
It draweth nearer — nigher — near!
  It groweth grimmer — broader — bigger!

Help! help! O Mother! or I die —
  My life is at its lowest ebb!
Behold thy son, a feeble fly,
  Caught in a tarantula's web!
Thy boy, bewildered, bared his breast,
  And took an adder nestling in it,
And there it nightly makes its nest,
  And he that same unmindful minute,

Was palsied by a poisoned dart —
  Was by a deadly scorpion stung —
Hugged a hyena to his heart —
  Touched a torpedo with his tongue!
A monster here with many heads
  Tears and torments me all the day:
It hideth in the rooms, the beds;
  And standeth in the open way.

And she who lured my love-lorn soul
  Is off upon some shadowy shore;
She roveth where proud rivers roll,
  And music moveth evermore!

10

While dearth, and dread, and darkness, doubt,
  And death and desolation damn
All, all below, above, about,—
  And all is anguish where I am!

The tiger growleth in his lair,
  The adder hisseth in her nest,
The hydra comes with threatening air,
  The fiend with high and haughty crest —
I have not rested all the day:
  A dreadful night is drawing on!
Come, Mother, from the milky way!
  Mother! O God! the cloud is gone!

LINES TO MARY.

ONCE more, once more, my Mary dear,
  I sink in those fond arms of thine;
Once more I see thee, feel thee near;
  Once more thy pulses thrill with mine;
Once more my soul from those bright orbs
  Drinks up the light that therein lies,
Just as the thirsty earth absorbs
  The raindrops falling from the skies.

Once more I feel that balmy breath
  Upon my cheek, whose healing charm
Would rescue dying men from death,
  Or make a host of dead ones warm!
Once more I hear those whispered words,
  The low, soft voice that maddens men,
Sweet as the warbling of gay birds
  In some delightful summer glen.

Like music heard in festive halls,
  Or murmurings of some rippling stream,
Thy soft voice on my spirit falls,
  Reviving love's first maddening dream —
Love's first fond dream — that blissful trance
  In which I fell when first we met —
When love came with the earliest glance
  That on thy heavenly face I set.

And love's first thrill that cheered my soul,
  Like sunshine seen through clouds that lower,
Hath chained me in its charmed control,
  Hath held me in its heavenly power,
Till every other thought is razed
  From out my mind but thoughts of thee;
And if my seething brain is crazed,
  Why, love, 'tis blissful thus to be!

Without thee what are fame and wealth?
  Can all earth's wealth with thee compare?
Without thee what are life and health?
  Or aught in heaven, earth, sea or air?

Without thee how could there be light?
 How could the sun make glad the day?
What use were there for day or night
 Were heaven to call, thee hence away?

LINES TO MISS P.

I THOUGHT that I had loved before,
 I thought my heart had felt as much
'Neath woman's glance in days of yore,
 As heart could feel 'neath woman's touch.
But O, I see I was mistaken,
 For when I gaze on that fair brow,
I find that deeper thrills awaken
 Than ever stirred my soul till now.

I wish that we had chanced to meet
 Ere clouds had gathered o'er my way;
When suns were bright and sighs were sweet
 As early flowers in May;
And ere my trusting heart had known
 That woman's smiles to ruin lead,
And that the more of her you own,
 The more you think you need.

O, yes, I wish that we had met
 Ere I began to roam and doubt,
And tangle in some fair one's net
 Whene'er I moved about;
And ere I had conclusions tried,
 And found that choosing is a bother —
That one can be as well supplied
 By one as by another.

Then I could have been blest, I think,
 With your rare charms while they should last,
Nor, thirsting, turned aside to drink
 At every fount I passed.
But since the gulf cannot be crossed,
 That lies between myself and you,
I turn from your bright eyes, thus lost,
 To brighter ones in view.

All girls are much alike, I ween,
 If Mabel is not here, nor handy,
Or if I may not have Maureen,
 I'll make out with Amanda.
But yet I am a little sad;
 I'd rather climb where thorns defy me,
To pluck a rose I want so bad,
 Than choose from scores as sweet, near by me.

ON PARTING WITH MARY.

AND must we part to-day, my dear?
   And must I go and leave thee here?
Leave thee who art so much my own,
In tears and sorrow, and alone?
O heavy fate that still will part
My Mary from my faithful heart!
My life, my love, if thou didst know
How much, how much I grieve to go,—
How much I wish, I long to stay
Where pleasure steals the hours away;
Where every day and hour is fraught
With some new bliss that love had taught
To none till we did meet to prove
The maddening joys of mutual love;
And dearest, but for thee even now
The grass were green above my brow,
But for thy love and tender care
Where would I be? O darling, where?
Perhaps in whirlwinds blown about,—
Think'st thou in heaven?—that we must doubt,
For saving my deep love for thee,
What saving grace was there in me?
Was I not fixed in torture's rack?
Was death not baying on my track?
And who was there from death to crave
The life *thou* wouldst have died to save?
O, where was one excepting thee
Had power or wish to rescue me?
'Twas then, when less alive than dead,
That to thy loving arms I fled,
And sweetly found in those fond arms
A refuge from all pangs and harms.
No chemist ever yet hath found
Nor mixed medicinal compound
In which such healing charms lie hid
As lurketh 'neath my love's eyelid.
But time is up—I must away!
Farewell! farewell!—I will not say
How I shall think and dream of thee,
Nor ask thee to remember me,
Adieu! O God! O, break this spell!
O Mary, Mary, fare thee well!

NEW YEAR'S DAY.

LET every heart beat light to-day,
   Let hope spring forth anew—
Last night the old year passed away,
  To-day we greet the new.
    Past months and years,
    Past joys and tears,

We bid ye all adieu,
With all your blight,
With all your light,—
    Your shade and sunshine, too!

How fast the years appear to fly!
  The spring and summer hours,
And autumn's golden days go by
  Like odor from the flowers!
      Each wintry blast
      Will soon be past,
        And April's early showers
      Again will fall,
      Refreshing all
        With their reviving powers.

Peace and prosperity now bless
  The land where freemen dwell;
O, may their empire ne'er be less—
  May reason e'er repel
      The god of war,
      Rays from whose star
        Too recently have fell:
      O, never more,
      On sea nor shore
        May the harsh war-note swell!

Land of the brave! land of the free!
  Clime of our WASHINGTON!
How brilliant and how gloriously
  Shines thy meridian sun!
      Old or new year,
      We still revere
        Deeds by the valiant done:
      Whose blood did stain
      How many a plain,
        Ere Freedom was re-won!

Disunion yielded up its breath;
  Stayed was its impious hand:
And firm, till time shall end in death,
  Will our great compact stand;
      In spite of hate,
      In spite of fate,
        By freedom's breezes fann'd,
      Our flag shall wave,
      High o'er the brave,
        On ocean, lake, and land!

Arts, Science, Freedom, and the Press,
  Move onward side by side,
And naught can limit their progress,
  Nor tyrants, time, nor tide:
      Stretch forth your wire!
      God's breath of fire
        Will leap the oceans wide,
      Cementing realms
      Till light o'erwhelms
        And love and peace preside.

TO MISS ELIZA F——S.

SWEET Lize, I thank you for the comb
   You threw into my office door,
And beg that you when I'm at home,
   Will bring the pretty head that wore
This envious comb, and let me place
   It back amid your wavy hair.
May I not kiss your sweet young face
   While I adjust it?—Pshaw! how dare

I ask you such a thing as this?
   Sweet Lize, forgive me! I'm insane,
And know that just a simple kiss
   From you would make me well again!
Then come and let us talk it o'er!
   You are so gentle, I am sure,
You can't refuse a kiss or more,
   When it would work so great a cure

As bringing to your doctor friend
   His senses, which you stole away.
(I don't suppose you did intend
   To take them when you did) but say,
Will you not come when I am here,
   And let us talk this matter over?
I am your friend, my pretty dear,
   And if I could, would be your lover!

When did you rob me of my senses?
   It must have been two years ago.
Since which, without the least defenses,
   My soul has been charmed to and fro
By your bewitching, roguish eyes!
   So now I want it understood,
If you must still bewitch me, Lize,
   (And I declare I wish you would,)

You must agree, once in a while,
   To grant me something like a favor —
A pinch, a box, a glance, a smile,
   Or something that will somehow savor
Of love, or things to love allied.
   But, Lize, give us another call —
Don't fling your comb as past you glide,
   But bring your head and curls and all!

THAT PAIN.

TO MISS LEMMING.

A SWEET girl asked me yesternight
   If I by Esculapian art,
Enchantment, magic, charm or sleight,
   Could take a pain from her young heart.

And as our melting glances met
  The pain or love or something came
From her soft eyes—(I feel it yet)
  That thrilled my very soul with flame.

I know I caught the pain she had,
  For she was well one blissful hour,
And though I left her looking sad,
  Yet sweet and lovely as a flower,

Still if she suffered 'twas unknown,
  While I could scarce endure the pain —
I think she knew it was her own —
  But will she take it back again?

IF THOU WERT TRUE.

TO MISS ELIZA K.

SWEET lady, how the golden hours
  Were wafted by on angels' wings,
When first we felt the softening powers
  Of love and sweet imaginings.
Ye hours of dalliance, ye are gone,
  Yet leave behind a cherished smart;
And dear delusions have withdrawn,
  That played awhile about my heart!

Delusive hours!—they did appear
  So bright, so blissful, so divine!—
O, have they left a trace as dear
  In thy heart as they have in mine?
Sweet hours that I must not renew,
  For lady, 'twas by chance we met;
And I would never deign to woo
  To be forgotten and forget.

Yet lady, could I think that thou
  Wert true as thou would'st seem to be,
With fond submission would I bow,
  And swear eternal love to thee.
O lady, could I trust the smile
  That shed on me so bright a ray,—
Those eyes that glanced their witching guile
  Throughout my soul but yesterday!—

Yes, lady, could I think thee true,
  Thou should'st possess my heart alone,
And heaven would wear a brighter hue,
  If thy young heart were all my own.
O lady-love, had we but met
  Ere blighted hopes had chilled thy heart,
And made of thee the gay coquette,
  Which now I grieve to think thou art—

Then, then I would have dared to love —
  Then dared to trust thy plighted vow —
But even tho' constant thou may'st prove,
  I cannot, dare not trust thee now.
For now the fatal die is cast,
  And Fancy's golden bowl is broke,
And the bright visions of the past
  Were dreams from which I have awoke.

And as a summer dream will weave
  Its cherished shadows o'er the mind,
So did those visions — so they leave
  Their dear impression still behind.
But fare thee well, love, fare thee well!
  Adieu to hopes that soared above —
Adieu, sweet life! I cannot tell
  How loath I part, how well I love!

Once more adieu! But thou wilt be
  Lov'd, madly on, and ne'er forgot!
I'd give my hope of heaven for thee,
  If thou wert true — but thou art not!

O, VEIL THY FACE FROM VIEW.

TO MISS LEMMING.

FAIR girl, had every maid to cure
  The wounds her witching glances make —
The pangs that stricken hearts endure —
  The longings that like whirlwinds take
Possession of such souls as mine,
Beset with beauties like to thine —

Then thou wouldst have a patient here
  On whom thy casual glance hath dwelt,
But it would take thee long, I fear,
  To heal the wounds thine eyes have dealt;
In fact, were thy fair face not hid,
He'd be a lifetime invalid.

Because the enchantment of that brow,
  The sweets that in those soft eyes lurk,—
The smiles, the tones that ravish now —
  Would still be at their fatal work;
So that to cure wounds caused before
Thou'dst daily make a hundred more.

Then I must see thee not again,
  I must not have so sweet a nurse;
'Twere better to bear my present pain
  Than seek relief that makes me worse.
But veil thy face, I pray, from view,
Lest others see and sicken too.

I AM SAD TO-NIGHT.

TO MARY.

SWEET Mary, I am sad to-night,
Though thou art sweetly by me here,
And the dear moon's delicious light
Glads the soft atmosphere.

But still we know that lengthened miles
Must soon, too soon, between us lie —
That fate must tear me from the smiles
Which wanting, I must die!

Is this not bitter, Mary dear?
Were it not better thus to live,
In exile and in misery here,
Than, parting, gain all earth can give?

MY HEART IS IN THY HOME.

TO MAGGIE.

MY heart is in thy home, dear love —
Away, away, away,
It lingereth like some lonesome dove
Where its dear mate doth stay.

Tho' late too wretched it was free
As the wild birds to roam —
But now 'tis chained — 'tis there with thee —
My heart is in thy home.

'Tis gone just like the warbling birds
In dreary winter time;
I cannot win it back with words
To this inclement clime.

Or if I lure it here one hour,
Like a lone summer bee
That rambleth to some far-off flower,
It rambleth back to thee.

Nor earth below, nor heaven above —
No bliss, no pain hath power
To lure my lone heart from its love —
From its dear, sweet wild flower.

Ask the soft moon to-night, sweet dear —
The stars in heaven's arch'd dome —
They'll tell thee while I'm hopeless here,
My heart is in thy home.

TO LIZZIE.

I THOUGHT that passion had expired,
    And love within my heart was cold,
And blisses, hopes and fears that fired
    And crazed my maddened brain of old,
Were dead within me; but to-day
    I looked in those soft eyes once more,
And found wild passion bearing sway
    As sweetly as in days of yore.

How patiently I bore, perhaps,
    Love's first fierce fever, thou dost know;
But half cured love's acute relapse
    I cannot bear, it burns me so!
Sweet queen of witchcraft, canst not thou
    Cure heartaches by thine eyes created?
Hast cures, and wilt not use even now,
    When I so long have wooed and waited?

A DREAM.

TO INZA.

LAST night, last night, my Inza dear,
    A dream of bliss came over me,
Although 'twas marred by many a tear,
    And many a pang of agony.
I dreamed that in a gallant ship
    We sailed upon the ocean wide,
And I was pressing thy sweet lip
    As thou wert standing by my side!

While I was thus divinely blest,
    And felt thy sighs so soft and faint,
The sun was setting in the west
    In splendor which I cannot paint.
The sky was clear — no land in sight —
    No spot upon the ocean vast,
But here some clouds, as black as night,
    Went flitting fitfully apast.

A dreadful gale swept o'er our bark —
    I clasped thy form instinctively;
An instant more and all was dark,
    And we were struggling in the sea!
I kept thy head above the tide,
    Thy dark hair floating o'er my face;
"Be calm, my Inza dear," I cried,
    "Foes will not grudge us this embrace!"

All now was calm — the gale had past —
    The moon shone out as bright as day,
And I beheld a floating mast
    That the rude winds had torn away.

Just as my feeble strength was spent,
  I placed thee on the floating spar
Which heaven had thus in mercy sent
  To bear us o'er the waves afar.

I kissed thy pale brow with delight,
  As thus I held thee firmly fast,
And never spent a happier night
  Than this, upon the floating mast!
Just as from out the eastern sky,
  The sun came forth with cheering power,
We found that we were floating by
  An isle as fair as Eden's bower.

Supporting thee, I swam on shore,
  And placed thee on a mossy bank,
And then I saw and felt no more,
  But by thy side exhausted sank!
When I came to, thy angel form
  Was kneeling by me in despair,
And thy sweet tears, so pure and warm,
  Were falling on me softly there.

And then I clasped thee to my heart
  In rapture never felt before,
For now I knew foes could not part
  Whom heaven had joined on sea and shore.
As, hand in hand, we now explored
  Our bower of blessedness and bliss,
We thought that light had ne'er been poured
  Upon a fairer isle than this.

No human foot had ever pressed
  The soil on which we thus were thrown,
And we were too divinely blest
  In calling this fair isle our own.
The finest fruit, the fairest flowers,
  That ever met the eager eye,
Were growing here in wild-wood bowers,
  Beneath a bright and genial sky.

We gathered fruit from many a tree,
  And, seeking out a limpid spring,
We feasted as luxuriously
  As they who banquet with a king.
And now we sought a mossy bower,
  Where wine grapes clustered overhead,
And here, as night began to lower,
  We made our lonely nuptial bed.

We slept, and then it seemed to me
  The waves closed o'er my bride so fair —
I stretched my eager arms to thee,
  And woke — alas! thou wert not there.
And isle and ocean all had fled —
  With throbbing heart and burning brow,
I left my lone and wretched bed —
  O Inza! Inza! where wert thou?

TO INZA.

SWEET Miss, with voice so rich and rare,
  With loving look and laughing eye,
And brilliant brow, and braided hair,
  And cheeks that with the roses vie;
Permit me, maiden, to intwine
  Thy sweet name with my cheerless lay,
Because my soul has caught from thine
  A glimpse of Inspiration's ray;
And song is all I have to bring
Unto thee for an offering.

And it will be a gloomy song—
  With all thy charms to urge me on,
I cannot thrill my lyre along
  As I have done in days agone;
For all the demons of despair
  Have shed their blackness over me,
The blight of which I could not bear
  Were I debarred from seeing thee;
For there is something in thy smile
That dissipates my gloom awhile.

I knew a girl in former years,
  Who owned each charm and every grace
Which now so sweetly reappears
  In thy angelic form and face!
But Time has feasted on the fire
  That lit her eye—that lights it now,
And care in its consuming ire
  Has set its signet on her brow;
Yet it is some delight to see
Her girlish charms revived in thee.

But thou hast fled to parts unknown;
  I hear the merry voice no more
Whose many a rich and racy tone
  Rang lately near my office door!
Ever thus with every lovely thing
  That ere I set my heart upon,
Before I win it it takes wing,
  Before I grasp it it is gone!
And thou, sweet Miss across the way,
How long wilt thou protract thy stay?

For many days I have not seen
  Thy sweet form on the promenade,
And tho' the trees are robed in green,
  The fields in verdure are arrayed,
It needs thy presence to impart
  A sweetness to the flowers of May,
For all is gladness where thou art,
  And dullness where thou art away!
But whose is that sweet voice I hear?
'Tis thine—I feel that thou art near!

Thou hast returned—even while I write
  I see thee on the portico,
Thy bright eye beaming with delight,
  While health, and hope, and goodness glow

In thy sweet face. O, could I feel
  The gladness that enraptures thee,
And from my life of torture steal
  An hour of harmless revelry,
Free from the skulking fiend of care
That haunts my spirit everywhere!

Nought can I liken unto thee
  But the sweet birds of early spring,
Which, tho' they will not come to me,
  Still charm me with their chirruping;
Just so with thee, my lovely girl,
  For tho' I see thee, hear thee now,
I cannot press the wavy curl,
  I cannot kiss the snowy brow:
And there is no one save thee here
Can chain my eye, and charm my ear.

Go forth with me to yonder hill,
  Sweet maiden with the braided hair,
And let my spirit drink its fill
  Of bird-song and of balmy air;
But let me take no book with me,
  No scrap of paper in my hat,
Lest I shall lose all thoughts of thee
  In reading this, or writing that;
But let me laugh on yonder slope
To see thee jump thy skipping rope.

Let it not be the sickly smile
  Wrung from the wronged and riven heart,
Which curls the lip but to beguile
  The tears that to the eye would start;
But let it be a joyous laugh,
  Like that which springs from thy pure soul
Before which care is swept like chaff
  Before the whirlwind's wild control:
Come with me where the wild flowers smile,
And make my lone heart light awhile!

FAREWELL.

TO INZA.

FAREWELL! farewell! at last I feel
  That I can summon strength to fly;
One lingering look — love's last appeal —
  A smile, a gesture, or a sigh —
Some token that the soul may lavish
  Its lone love on through lengthened years —
Some relic the dead heart to ravish,
  While memory views the toy in tears;
A mark exchanged, however slight,
  Between the hearts that break to sever,
Then I will fly far from thy sight,
  And see thy face no more forever!

O, TAKE NOT FROM MY LUTE.

TO INZA.

O ROUND my meek-eyed, dark-haired belle
To other maidens all unknown,
There is a charm, a sacred spell,
A holy halo softly thrown!
Her minstrel, in his midnight dream,
Lives in the light her eyes diffuse,
Whose slightest, mildest, softest beam
Inspires his melancholy muse!

O, do not, do not rob my lyre
Of the sweet spell that woman gives
In glances from her eyes of fire!
O, let me live where woman lives!
O, take not, take not from my lute
The spell that woman throws around it!
Or else, unnerved, unstrung, and mute,
I'll fling it sadly where I found it!

LITTLE LUNA.

POOR little Luna's sleeping fast,
Her little sense is gone,
Her little feet have kicked their last
Until the morning's dawn.

Thy sleep is sweet, my infant dear!
While nestling by my side,
The moonbeams rest them softly here,
As through the panes they glide.

The moon? — I named thee for the moon!
And let its soft light be
Sweet as red roses blown in June,
While life shall last, — to thee!

Thy chubby little fingers lie
Beside thy little cheek,
Thy lids have closed each little eye,
And thou forget'st to speak.

Thy face and fingers do betray
The candy and the cake,
Which thou didst munch on yesterday
When thou wert wide awake.

Thy silvery hairs, my little sweet,
Steal o'er thy little brow;
Thy prattling tongue and patting feet
Repose in silence now.

I almost wish this budding rose,
In this transition state
Could stay, nor blossom for the woes
That womanhood await.

CHRISTMAS DAY.

MERRY, merry Christmas day,
   Passing cheerily away!
Little children gaily dressed,
Happy little children blest;
Tripping lightly through the street
Little, tiny, nimble feet,
Happy little voices rise;
Smiling little lips and eyes
Gladden every street and door
Till the holiday is o'er!
And the gifts of Santa Claus,
Candies, gumming little paws,
Nuts and dolls—and for the boys,
Drums and fifes, and warlike toys!
O ye little noisy crew,
We were merry once like you!
In the long remembered day
Flown away, away, away!
Romp to-day and merry make,
For too soon ye will awake;
Sorrows will come thick and fast
When the children's hour is past!
Then be merry while you can,
Little miss and little man!

TO MOLLIE.

DEAR Moll, accept from me this plain gold ring,
   'Tis like the love my poor heart bears for thee;
Unworthy thy acceptance; yet, O, yes,
Take it!—O, take it—wear it for his sake,
Whose spirit makes thine eyelid its abode
And thy sweet face its kingdom. See, 'tis plain—
O, it is simple as the words of truth
Breathed by a prattler in its mother's ear;
And chaste and humble as a piteous maid
Pleading to tyrants for a brother's life.
O, let it plead for me! Slight is its worth,
Aside from memories that cling to it,
But as a token of my deathless love,
Thy beauty is the only bribe for which
My soul would barter it. O, wear it, then!
And if thy shame or pride, or both, forbid
The wearing of so plain an ornament,
Before thy friends and in the light of day,
O, put it on when thou retir'st to rest,
And let it feel thy blood's voluptuous flow—
Glide o'er thy hidden beauties in the dark,
And revel unrestrained in each recess
Where love delights to lurk. Let it explore
Seductive clefts, smooth mounds, enchanting plains
And hillocks of delight. O, let it range

O'er all the fields of thy angelic charms,
Like a bright butterfly o'er banks of flowers
Or a bee amongst the blossoms. O, ye heavens!
Pshaw — fie — how foolish is my fervent love!
O, it doth make me like a little child,
Pleading unto its mother for a toy,
It knows it must not have. O, out upon't!
Corporeal, where is thine obesity?
Where's thy digestion and thine appetite?
Canst thou munch beans? or masticate a cabbage?
Canst eat a capon? or a codfish — hey?
Hast stomach for roast beef? for oysters? eels?
Thou'lt none of these? Then cream from love's sweet milk
Is all thou canst digest. Thy wit is gone —
So has thy flesh — thy blood — thy calf is shrunk,
And thy sharp tibia's edge hath fretted through
The pinched and purple skin; while melancholy
Hath mounted him astride thy stooped neck —
One foot in each vest pocket! Thou'rt but the ghost
Of thy late manly self — so lank, so lean —
Creeping about the earth like a sick man,
Who hath his liver full of tubercles,
Or tapeworms in his maw. O, cruel Moll!
If that thy pity with thy beauty bore
Some such relation as a circus tent
Bears to the arched and star-spangled heavens,
Thou wouldst pour on me such a shower of pity
As would at once cool down my hectic blood,
Fill up my starved veins with nutriment;
Give my abdomen its rotundity;
Cement the sinews gnawed athwart by love,
And give the shrunken and collapsed calf
The plump and graceful swell that was its pride
Before I saw thy face. Alas, within
I bear the grief that eats the entrails up;
Love's liquid lightning leaping from thine eyes
Hath such affinity for my hot blood
As quick sulphuric acid hath for water;
So when combined the heat that is evolved,
With its expansive force, explodes the vessels,
And then the starved compound pervades the tissues
Of brain, of stomach, liver, lungs and heart,
Digesting and consuming! — I am sick!
O, let me lean my face upon that cheek
In which the lily and carnation play,
And in that bosom (whiter than the snow)
That heaves with sweet emotions at my pleading,
Let my poor hand find rest! — poor shrunken hand!
Made feebly tremulous by my love for thee:
Consuming love! — how ill and weak I am!
Made so by my sweet beauty's cruelty,
Who hath the medicine to make me healthy,
Withholding which she sees me faint — I famish!
O, through those lips my course lies to the casket
Wherein my love keeps honey-coated cures;
Crazed and incautious, I will here consume them,
And I will straight be well.

JANUARY 1, 1871.

NOW like a dream that memory would retain,
The Old Year fadeth in the distant view;
'Tis gone, and yet the memory clings to it,
As clings a maiden's mind to the last words
Breathed in her ear by a departing lover:
'Tis past, and like the waves that sweep athwart
The eternal brow of great Niagara,
It can return no more. O, it brought joy,
As well as woe, and dread, and dearth and death
To many a human heart. Upon its wings
Were borne events momentous — dire mishaps,
And multiplied misfortunes — accidents,
By land and water, circumstances sad —
Strange casualties and most revolting crimes
That cut off human life.
          Let's look around:
And first this wintry day, ye who are rich
See to the poor. The poor predominate —
They're everywhere. The poor we always have.
Hunger doth gnaw and pinching is the cold!
And O, what joy would food and fuel bring
To many a widow's heart and orphan child!
Then let us search for suffering — 'twill be found —
None will have far to go, and then how sweet
Will that man sleep who makes the poor rejoice
Before he goes to rest.
          Adieu, Old Year!
We part with thee as with a dying king —
With many fond regrets and memories,
While sweet hope leads us with a smiling face,
To greet thy Young Successor.
          Hail! all hail!
Hail, glorious New Year! full of hope and promise.
We greet thee like a young bride in her bloom!
Mayst thou bring days of joy and nights of bliss,
And scenes of mirth and happiness to all.
Bright be thy suns and placid be thy moons,
Thy breezes balmy and thy skies serene.
Green be thy fields and fragrant be thy flowers,
And sweet the melody thy warblers breathe;
Bring welcome news forever on thy tongue,
And on thy wings bring honey and sweet myrrh:
Bring gentle peace to tranquillize the world;
Bring hope and comfort to the meek and poor,
And songs of gladness to the husbandman.
Bring to the maiden many dreams of love,
And hope and health and happiness to all!
Bring to each heart the joy it most desires,
And every comfort that the virtuous crave!
O, let thy hours float smilingly away,
Like a sweet bevy of young girls to church,
Or sun-lit clouds in June.

11

A MOTHER'S LAMENT.

HOW can I realize that thou,
   My darling child, art dead?
Where is thy little spirit now?
   O, whither hast thou fled?

Why didst thou leave us? — say, O say!
   Leave us who loved thee so?
Why not with thy fond mother stay?
   Thou didst not want to go!

And yet I cannot give thee up —
   My brain! — Shall I go wild!
O, take from me this bitter cup!
   O, give me back my child!

THE FATE OF FATAH.

A LEGEND OF KENTUCKY.

NEAR where the Ohio's waters calmly glide
   There stood a wigwam in the olden time,
In the dark grounds where red men fought and died,
   Ere the pale-faces trod that glorious clime;
   And in this wigwam dwelt a man of crime,
A chief who reveled in the deeds of blood,
   Then in the vigor of his savage prime, —
The giant, tyrant, monarch of the wood —
Sire of the fair Fatah, the beautiful, the good.

The rankest soil sends forth the richest fruit,
   Oft on wild shrubs the fairest flowers we find;
So, from a savage and blood-thirsty brute,
   Sprung sweet Fatah, the fairest of her kind;
   Tall, gentle, timid, stately as the hind —
In thought, in person, pure as crystal streams;
   With the wild rose in her dark hair entwined,
And flashing eye, bright as the noon-day beams,
Few forms like hers e'er lived save in the poet's dreams.

Inured to hardship — reared 'mid scenes of strife,
   And blood, and warfare, did the untutored maid
Devote each moment of her blameless life
   To deeds of mercy. Oft her tears allayed
   Her father's fury — oft her firmness stayed
The hand upraised to shed the victim's gore;
   Her father's murdering minions disobeyed
His bloody mandates when she did implore,
For tho' they loved their chief, they loved the maiden more.

But the white man o'erran her father's realms
   Ere fair Fatah attained her twentieth year;
Yet force may not subdue where it o'erwhelms,
   And the intruders found the avenger here:
   Woe to the straggler in the forest drear!

For the red warriors lurked in every brake,
  And whilst his death song grated on his ear,
Fierce hands prepared the faggot and the stake,
  And yells half drowned the shrieks that torture did awake!

One sunny morning, in the month of May,
  A hunter was ensnared by savage men,
And hurried wearily long miles away,
  Till, in the shadow of a quiet glen,
  They reached at night an Indian village, when
The furious villagers, in frantic glee,
  Rushed forth with yells to appall the captive, then
Met, to determine what his fate should be,
In dark and solemn council — death was the decree!

The captive was a youth of noble mien,
  Though slight in stature, as a lion brave;
With scornful eye he scanned each savage scene,
  Nor favor sought, nor mercy seemed to crave,
  Knowing that nought could succor — none could save
His shrinking thews from quivering in the flame —
  A milder death, perhaps, and Christian grave
He might have wished, but did not care to claim, —
A pang, a shock, a shriek, and then 'twere all the same.

At length he sank to sleep upon the ground,
  A sleep which he was told would be his last,
Nor dreamt he of the favor he had found
  With one who met him in the evening past:
  Fatah beheld him, and her heart beat fast,
As on his brow her pitying gaze did rest,
  In her dark eyes one fond look did he cast,
Which thrilled each fibre in the maiden's breast —
She did not know 'twas love — no matter — she was blest!

Her course was clear — the captive must be saved;
  Her young heart told her that he must not die:
There is no barrier that will not be braved
  When love lives in the heart and lights the eye!
  She sought her father, but 'twas vain to try
By supplication to avert the fate;
  Not only did the chief her prayer deny —
In a harangue he harrowed up the hate
He bore the captive's race — which blood could but abate!

With thongs embedded in the swollen flesh,
  Lashed to a stake, at dawn the captive stood;
The appalling yells and shouts broke forth afresh,
  While savage hands heaped round him piles of wood;
  Fatah looked on, determined that he should
Be rescued yet or that hour be her last;
  A brand was brought, but ere the savage could
Ignite the pile, high in the air 'twas cast —
The prisoner stood released — the savages aghast!

As quick as thought had Fatah cut the cords,
  And led the captive to confront his foes;
With flashing eye she scanned the hideous hordes,
  While no one moved, and not a murmur rose:
  None did applaud, and no one durst oppose,

But every eye was fixed upon the twain;
  Rash was the act—the deed was one of those
Which mocks at death, and danger doth disdain,
And one which rarely fails its object to attain.

The captive was adopted — time passed on,
  And Fatah spurned all suitors for his sake;
The days of strife and gore were past and gone —
  The battle-axe was buried in the brake:
  But Fatah's father still disdained to shake
The hand of peace — his war-cry still arose
  Upon the air, and oft at night did wake
From their deep slumbers his unwary foes —
Fixed was the fate of such — dark was the doom of those!

Among the whites at night, on noiseless feet,
  Oft did the chief steal with his stealthy crew;
Quick was the work, and rapid the retreat —
  In blood did every brave his hands imbrue!
  Then to their fastnesses the furies flew,
Bearing, perhaps, the bride, or blooming belle —
  Woe to the pale-face if he did pursue!
In the deep fen quick rifles rang his knell,
While red men sang and danced his death-song in the dell!

And the strange love had strengthened night and day
  Which for the youth the faithful Fatah bore;
Yet he did not return, reward, repay
  The deep wild passion which was welling o'er:
  Knew he not well by the sad look she wore
That she was dying with concealed desire?
  Could he not love the impassioned maid who tore
From savage hands the flaming brand of fire,
Cut the embedded thongs, and braved the Indian ire?

There was a white girl whom the Indians stole
  A few days after the white youth was saved
By Fatah's hand. The youth had given his soul
  To this young girl ere either was enslaved:
  Again had Fatah interfered, and braved,
To save the captive girl, her father's wrath;
  Again their thirst for blood the warriors waived
Till they should once more march on the war path,
When they would be avenged — would capture, kill and scath!

Fatah, with love's quick eye, beheld the flame
  That burned so brightly in those hearts so true,
Yet still her own wild love lived on the same,
  All quenchless, hopeless, unrequited, too;
  Yet there was love, or something like it, due;
And tho' the youth did oft to her express
  His love, his homage, he ne'er thought to woo
This dark-haired daughter of the wilderness;
He could not love her more — nor Leanora less.

Young Leanora, tho' divinely fair,
  Was less majestic than the sad Fatah —
In grace and dignity could not compare
  With the wild maid who knew but nature's law
  Now Fatah's wifeless father, when he saw

Amongst his women not a fairer one
  Than Leanora, claimed her as his squaw,
And this time swore his bidding should be done!
And how, alas, was she this worse than death to shun?

Must the huge savage take her to his arms?
  With this gigantic monster must she mate?
Must the white youth resign her love — her charms?
  Would Fatah, if she could, avert her fate?
Alas! had Fatah not good cause to hate
The maid who claimed the love that she desired?
  In exultation would she not await
The ruin of the rival who aspired
To be the wife of him whom Fatah's soul required?

But 'twas their only hope — with streaming eyes,
  Their brave protectress the sad captives sought;
Nor their petition did Fatah despise,
  Nor answer deign, but sat absorbed in thought —
'Twas evening now — to-morrow would be wrought
The dreadful deed the captives dreaded so,
  And the brave Fatah, feeling now that nought
Could make her happier or augment her woe,
Said to the suppliants —"rise! arise, and let us go!"

On fleet steeds mounted, now away, away
  O'er hills and vales the youth and maidens sped,
Ay, madly sped, for well they knew that they
  Were followed fast — still faster than they fled;
Fatah led on, but scarce a word she said
Until they reached a spot that had been cleared;
  Upon this spot was Fatah born and bred —
Here erst her father's wigwam was upreared —
But white men had approached, and red men disappeared!

The sun had risen — it was autumn now —
  The yellow leaves were lying on the ground;
Here mournfully did poor, sad Fatah bow —
  Lost and absorbed in agony profound;
  Her comrades gazed uneasily around —
Beyond the tide they heard their village bell;
  Just then from the deep forest came a sound —
O God! 'twas Fatah's father's well known yell!
"Fly to the river! fly! — once over, all is well!"

Fatah sprang on her steed as quick as thought,
  And led the captives to the Ohio's side,
And here a stray canoe, some drift had caught,
  Saved the fagged steeds from swimming o'er the tide;
  Safe in the light canoe, they soon did ride
Far from the shore, now lined with many a brave;
  Fatah stood up and waved her hand in pride —
Then springing over, sank where none could save!
Her knell, the warriors' wail — her winding sheet, the wave!

NEW YEAR'S EVE, 1874.

HAS Bedlam broke loose! Look away down the streets!
    Every one has gone crazy that every one meets!
Sweet ladies, sweet misses, big men and big boys,
Are striving to see who can make the most noise!
And what is this noise, this confusion about?
'Tis the bummers bumming the Old Year out;
'Tis the revelers making this clatter and din,
For at midnight the happy New Year comes in?
Old '73, with a deal of uproar,
Is gone like one's footprints upon the sea shore;
Swept away by the clamorous and toppling surge,
While receding and roaring its everyday dirge.
And the Old Year is gone! O, the hopes that it brought!
How many were blasted, or ripened to naught!
And the hearts — O, how many lie cold and unstrung,
That were gladsome as ours when the Old Year was young!
And how many of ours will lie cold in the ground
When the next happy New Year is gleefully crowned!
But if ours shall be still there are others will beat,
To mirth as inspiring and music as sweet.
The New Years will come, the glad days reappear;
But the question arises — Who of us will be here?

BRIDE OF THE DANUBE.

BY how many wiles he won her heart,
    Is a mystery that will ever remain unknown;
But the legend says they were ordered apart,
And the maiden fell down as if struck by a dart,
    When she found that her lover was gone.

He was not of the class that could aspire,
    To a maid of her culture and high degree;
But he was full of ambition and pride and fire,
And was always looking and aiming higher,
    And there was no one so gallant as he.

By stealth ran the courtship in secret begun,
    And the father was crazed with wrath when he woke
To the fact that a penniless plebeian had won
The heart he had pledged to a heralded son,
    And dire was the vengeance he spoke.

How the lover lurked near, although banished the clime,
    And lacking in friendship, influence and purse;
How he gained the maid's prison and thought it no crime;
How they sought the old priest and were married meantime;
    It is needless for me to rehearse.

High in the old castle the maid was immured,
    To come forth on the day she would wed with Sir Hugh;
Months passed, when her seeming assent was secured,
And the castle was lighted and the nuptials assured,
    And the news like a prairie fire flew.

The moonbeams were melting at twelve in the night,
　In the river that lay at the foot of the lawn;
The old castle was brilliant with guests and with light,
As Sir Hugh, with the maid in immaculate white,
　Stood forth—then a bound and a shriek—she was gone!

As the curate came forward she glanced at the door—
　There he stood—he was fatally true to his word;
And then there was flight, and pursuit and uproar;
But the pursuers they paused when they came to the shore,
　For no sound of the lovers was heard.

But a quick glimpse was caught by the crowd on the green
　Of two faces as pallid as the pale moon's ray;
And a white robe that shone in the shimmering gleen
Went down with the faces and was never more seen,
　Nor the spot where they vanished away.

Nor yet of this legend is the saddest part told,
　For the father on entering his daughter's late jail,
Found a babe in her bed that was moaning and cold;
It was withered and looked prematurely old,
　And it died with a tremulous wail!

The castle's a ruin, but still, if you seek,
　Old peasants a haunted apartment will show,
Whence, they tremblingly tell you, one night in the week,
The moan of a babe brings a female shriek
　From the river that rolls below.

REGRETFUL MEMORIES.

TO KATE.

WHAT!—Weeping Kate!—Come hither, child—
　My fair one in distress!
How late the stars looked on and smiled,
　And Luna's light did bless
Our rapturous loves!—and thou wert bright
As the sweet stars of yesternight!
　What sorrow doth oppress?
Is there worse penalty in store
For stolen bliss than want of more?

Then, Kate, be pacified!—You see
　Yon flowers—how glad are they;
Yet they gave to the honey bee
　Their sweets but yesterday.
The flowers, like you, in not refusing,
Made sweets the sweeter in the losing,
　And what was stol'n away;
Took leave in such a whirl of rapture
That no one could regret the capture!

Then, Kate, I pray you not to weep:
　The glittering tears repose
In those fair lids like pearls asleep
　At morn in the opening rose.

The morning-glories, weeping dew,
Are not so lovely, Kate, as you,
    As rising tears disclose,
The surging tide in love's deep well
That makes my Kate's aorta swell.

I found you like an April flower,
    That pines for warmth, to bloom;
Till summer's heat, with quickening power,
    Brings forth its sweet perfume:
An embryonic butterfly,
Whose gaudy wings Old Sol must oye,
    And fairies paint whose plume:
Just as love's magic paints the brow
Of the sweet beauty near me now.

When racked with undefined desire,
    She met my impassioned gaze,
One touch of love's galvanic fire
    Set her wild blood ablaze;
Then Cupid glued ripe lip to lip,
And 'twas too late for us to slip
    From love's bewildering maze:
And both were lost in that mad spell —
That seven times heaven! — Well, Katie — we l!

What is there worth possessing here
    Save bliss like we have found?
And why should we be starving, dear,
    For sweets, when sweets abound?
Let not the raven's voice be heard,
But listen to the mocking-bird!
    There's beauty all around;
The gold-fringed hours of life's young day,
Strew roses as they glide away.

Then let me kiss away those tears;
    I must not see thee weep;
Thou'lt not regret in after years
    The secret we must keep;
But in life's riper, somber hours,
Regretful memory's softening powers
    Athwart the past will sweep;
Awakening echoes in the breast,
Of voices long since hushed to rest.

Soft tinklings of the silvery bells
    That chimed in bygone years
Far down in the young heart's deep cells,
    Fall gently on the ears!
And traced upon the youthful brain
Are lines that through all life remain —
    Some tint that reappears
When memory breathes upon the scroll
Where sleep the treasures of the soul.

Rewhisperings in the matron's ear
    From girlhood's early dreams
Of love — these are the sounds most dear,
    However strange it seems;

And the sweet light of love that's past
Away down to the grave will cast
  Its melancholy beams;
Saddening, yet cherished till we die!
Wherefore, there's no one knows, nor why.

CUBA.

FAIR sea-girt isle! forever green,
  And gorgeous with rich fruits and flowers!
How many a black and bloody scene
  Hath marred thy vales and sunny bowers,
Under the fell, red-handed reign
Of the great world's chief cut-throat Spain?

But time will terminate thy woes,
  Fair jewel of the Sunny South! .
The sea shall swallow up thy foes,
  Driven thither at the cannon's mouth.
Then, onward! — Let the watchwords be,
By freemen's hands be Cuba free!

Our starry sisterhood of States
  Have purple robes and cups of wine,
To lure thee from the cruel Fates;
  And garlands woven to entwine
About their weeping sister's brow;
And longing arms await her now!

Our constellation lacks a star —
  Our gentle goddess wants the gem
That sparkles in yon sea afar,
  To enrich her glittering diadem.
Then, onward! — let the watchwords be,
By freemen's hands be Cuba free!

LINES TO INZA.

LET me gaze on thy face once more!
  One last look on thy fair young brow;
Whate'er I may have craved before,
  Is all that I can covet now.
Turn not thy sweet young face away;
  O, do not let those fair lids fall! —
They shut from me the light of day,
  And leave my throbbing heart in thrall!
When those bright orbs refuse their light,
My soul is lost in Egypt's night?
  How long must we be thus estranged,
And hours to come be like the past?
  Should love that never roved nor ranged —
Not meet some slight reward at last?
  Some slight reward — a whispered word,

Like music maddening the young brain,
  Or like the warbling of a bird
In winter by one's window pane —
  A kind word spoken through the eye —
A smile — tho' half suppressed — a smile
  Like a faint rainbow in the sky,
Or apples on a desert isle
  To the wrecked mariner?   But no!
The wild love which I bear for thee,
  Begot by wretchedness and woe,
And nurtured by insanity,
  All quenchless as the fire that lives
Deep hidden in the mountain's breast,
  Receives no light save that it gives —
It blesses none, nor is it blest;
  But rather has it been accursed
Through all its stages from the first.

JEALOUS?

AND dost thou think the homage paid
    To other smiles, to other eyes,
More serious than the glance which played,
  With blossoms, birds and butterflies
That blessed the groves through which I passed
As late I sought thy cottage last?

My heart goes wandering forth for thee
  Like a struck roe in wildwood bowers,
Sipping like the lone honey bee
  The nectar of the wayside flowers,
But urged with sure impulse and strong
To thee with notes of love and song.

Twine me a braid of thy soft hair;
  One ringlet of thy jetty curls
Were dearer to my heart than were
  The costliest gifts from other girls!
O, yes, the merest toy from thee,
Wert thou away, were wealth to me.

A GIFT AND VOW.

TO LIZZIE.

A TRIFLING gift my heart here gives
    To thee, the fairest girl that lives;
But O, 'tis pure as that sweet toy
My mad heart craves to crown its joy.
'Twas by most skillful fingers wrought,
And from my heart to thine is brought;
But it comes with a fearful oath,
And who takes one accepteth both!
Thou tak'st the gift? — then hear the vow—
The pledge, the oath I make thee now.

So here it is, and thus I swear,
By heaven and earth and sea and air,
And by the stars, the moon, the sun;—
By each, by all, by every one:—
By the sad notes of mateless doves;—
By all that man or woman loves;—
· By all that man or woman hates;—
By all the Furies—all the Fates;—
By midnight's gloom—by noonday's cheer;—
Even by that sacred, pearly tear
That stole adown thy damask cheek
When hearts were full and words were weak;—
By every hope on which we've dwelt;—
By all we've feared—by all we've felt;—
By love that glows with such excess
That could I love thee more or less,
That instant would my spirit take
Its flight in space—my heart would break;—
By that white neck on which I've hung—
Those lips to which my own have clung
Till heaven and earth's whole store of bliss
Seemed concentrated in one kiss:—
Yes, by those sweet lips and those eyes
Where all my heaven—my treasure lies—
Those lips—those eyes!—by those—by these—
By all thy winning witcheries;
Those vows thy honied tongue has given,
Writ in my mad heart and in heaven;—
By all of these, O maiden fair,
I swear, I swear, I swear, I swear,
That I do love thee—love thee more
Than ever mortal loved before!

FAREWELL TO WOMAN.

IF I'm not in a funny fix
  The deuce may take my hat—
Accused of certain treacherous tricks,
  (No matter tho' for that,)
When God knows, tho' my will is good,
I *can't* be guilty—wish I could—
  It makes one feel so flat,
(Not having done a thing amiss,)
To bear the blame without the bliss.

'Tis true, my weakness for the women
  Is always cropping out,
And costing me, sometimes a trimmin',
  Or curtain lecture bout;
And I am troubled every hour,
Because I long for every flower
  And rosebud on my route;
And can't content myself with one,
No matter what the law has done.

Yes, yes! I almost grieve to say
　I worship every she;
But then, somehow or other they
　Care not a curse for me;
I seldom get a pleasant look
From Patsy, Peggy, Poll or Suke —
　What can the reason be?
I know some uglier men than I
For whom a score of ladies sigh.

I never had a female friend,
　(I've now not one — how blest!)
Whose love or friendship did extend
　O'er thirty days, at best,
Ere by some freak of my hard fate,
Her friendship was transformed to hate,
　And she, put to the test,
Soon proved that she was worth no more
Than scores who jilted before.

Yet I have praised the softer sex
　In soft and silvery song,
And having woman for my text,
　I ne'er could preach too long —
From her all inspiration flows;
And I care not if friends and foes
　Adjudge it right or wrong,—
But the sweet light her soft eye gives,
Is all for which my spirit lives.

I want no wealth but woman's eyes,
　No power beyond her bounds,
Seek no salvation save her sighs,
　Fear nothing but her frowns;
I ask no nectar but her lip;
Give me but her companionship
　And I'll dread not the wounds,
That want of wealth — that worldly care —
May make me taste, and feel, and bear.

I never see a pretty girl
　But what I want to kneel —
It puts my head in such a whirl —
　I can't tell how I feel;
But still it seems I ought to bow
And praise or worship her somehow;
　Yet I could ne'er reveal
By look or word how I adore —
Love — worship — idolize — ay, more!

Bright woman having thus in me
　So wild a worshiper,
'Tis strange I should forever be
　So deeply damned by her;
I fear the devil cast my lot
Precisely where he should have not;
　But he must be a cur,
Who, without observations ample,
Would buy or sell the sex from sample.

Still, as to woman, I declare,
   The lessons I have had
Teach me that, while her face is fair,
   Her heart may yet be bad;
Her love she sometimes can divide;
Her passions, (jealousy and pride,)
   Run her forever mad —
Keep her forever out of fix,
With hickups, hate, and hysterics!

But after all, with all her sins,
   She's all that's bright below;
With our first breath her love begins,
   And ends with life's last throe;
Apart from her there's nothing pure;
Her love is all that can allure,
   And her most fiendish foe
Must bless the hour that linked his life
With mother, sister, daughter, wife.

But now farewell to womankind!
   With trembling I recall
What I endured, when dumb and blind,
  Ye held my soul in thrall!
Tho' a wild lover heretofore,
I henceforth and forevermore,
   Repudiate ye all!
No glance from woman's winning eye
Shall henceforth cause my soul a sigh.

I'll tear my heart from out my breast
   If it will not be still!
Affection shall not be its guest;
   I'll teach it not to thrill
When woman's glance illumes its throne;
The shock, if felt, shall not be shown —
   I'll meet out ill for ill;
My heart, so deeply cauterized,
Shall henceforth hate — loved or despised.

Thus am I forced to yield — resign
   All that is worth a tear —
That which (altho' 'twas never mine,
   Was all that made life dear,)
Sweet woman and her love — her lip,
Whose dew I never more must sip,
   For now I prize and fear
Alike her lip — her love — her hate —
Pshaw! what the devil do I state!

I really am not well to-night,
   My temples throb with pain;
And like a poor unshriven sprite,
   Wandering 'midst cloud and rain,
My spirit wanders, yet with hope;
So does the hunted antelope,
   When its poor young is slain,
Still hover, heedless of the cost,
Near where its earthly all was lost!

IT WILL LIVE AND ABOUND.

TO KATE.

THE love that's so thrilling,
  The love that's so true,
The love that's so willing,
  When it knows it is you:
The love that takes hold of you
  Ere you can think,
And starves you and keeps you
  From sleeping a wink;
The love that's so gentle,
  Yet fierce, as you know,
That sets the brain whirling,
  And swells the heart so;
That haunts you in dreams;
  That charms you awake;
That softens the beams
  Of the moon in the lake;
That thrills you with rapture;
  That racks you with pain;
That bathes you in sunshine
  And soaks you in rain;
That inspires, now with hope,
  And now whelms in despair;
That makes you too constant,
  Yet fickle as air;
That grinds you with jealousy,
  And rends you with fears;
That hoodwinks the eyesight,
  And deafens the ears;
That makes the tongue fluent,
  Or dead in your mouth,
As the winds chance to blow
  From the North or the South;
That ties the heart's tendrils
  To the girl you adore,
And makes you long for her,
  And two or three more;
O, the love once so selfish,
  The love once so hot,
For the dear maids so elfish,
  Now gone and forgot!
And the love that came after,
  (Like the wind's shifting whirl,)
'Neath the smiles and light laughter
  Of some other sweet girl!
O, this cherish'd love, maiden,
  Though fickle 'twould seem,
Is with life's essence laden,—
  Is the soul of life's dream!
I have felt it for many
  As I feel it for you,
But hardly to any
  Was I ever so true!
O, this love, with its sweets!
  It will live and abound,
While a faithful heart beats
  And a girl can be found!

THE COLOR OF MY LADY'S EYES.

TO KATE.

ONE thing I'm puzzled much about—
   The color of my lady's eyes;
It keeps me in delicious doubt—
   Gives every hour a new surprise!
To-day I worship them as blue,
   Tho' yesterday I thought them brown—
Perhaps a shade betwixt the two;
   But sweet—(let that be written down!)
Yet softly blue as yonder sky,   ·
I will maintain until I die.

But let me take another look—
   Now, by St. George, they're black as jet!
I'd swear to that and kiss the book!
   (Now wait till that is conned and writ!)
They're sweet and black!—now look at you!—
Which are they—black or brown or blue?

I can't say which—I can't decide—
   (Blow me, but now I think them gray!)
They're sweet—(in all but this I've lied!)
   And blue, were I to die to-day!
And yet they charm me so I doubt
Which hue is in and which is out!

No maiden hath such eyes in town,
   They are so fine, I am so smitten!—
You smile!—Now, by my soul, they're brown,
   And still so sweet—(let both be written!)
And yet, upon my Bible oath,
I swear they're blue or brown, or both!

But, lady, lady, I give o'er—
   Your eyes a riddle still will be;
I drink, I analyze, explore
   Their precious light—I see, I see!
Your eyes have Cupids hid behind,
   Shifting the colors of their fire,
On purpose to perplex mankind!—
   (But they are blue, else I'm a liar!)

LAST WISH OF THE MINSTREL.

BRING me, my love, some drops of wine—
   Perfume them with thy dulcet breath,
And press thy dewy lips to mine,
   Ere yet I walk the way of death.
Tho' death is stealing o'er me now,
   A moment would I linger here,
Till thou canst pledge a sacred vow
   That memory will revere.

Perhaps thy lip's delicious dew,
   Perchance the wine's reviving power
May send my life-blood forth anew
   One moment in this dying hour.
Swear by the everlasting sun,
   Swear by God's rainbow, arched on high
That thou wilt change my name for none,
   But wilt my widow die.

"Thou shalt not die, my minstrel dear!
   I swear by every star above —
I swear by every scalding tear —
   By all our past and present love —
By all that's low, and all that's high —
   By every flower, and every tree —
I swear to thee thou shalt not die,
   But shalt remain with me.

"Drink this pure wine — 'twill soothe thy brain;
   Physicians know not thy disease;
They shall not torture thee again
   With nauseous doses such as these;
My love shall cure thine every ill,
   And sweeten every cup of woe,
And thy bright name shall dazzle still
   Wherever love and language go.

"But should the fickle Fates decree
   To take thee hence and leave me here,
Thy widow's only wish would be
   To join thee in a holier sphere.
Thy widow and thy former bride,
   Pure as her charms to thee were given,
Would lay them lifeless by thy side,
   And reunite with thee in heaven.

"The heart that is so truly thine
   Can never feel another flame;
Read in these weeping eyes of mine
   Indelible thy deathless name."
"Enough! — the dying minstrel's wife
   Will still his faithful widow be.
I die in peace — adieu to life,
   To song, to love, to thee!"

OUR HEARTS ARE BROKEN NOW.

TO MAGGIE.

LOVE'S last farewell token,—
   Passion's parting vow,—
Relics of hearts broken—
   Broken, broken now!

Although careless seeming,
   Still the unbidden tear
Finds me dreaming, dreaming,
   Dreaming of my dear.

O, 'tis useless trying —
  Struggling with this love!
I am dying, dying,
  Dying for my dove!

Thoughts of what we've tasted,
  How they mad the brain!
Moments wasted, wasted,
  Not to come again.

And the broken hearted
  Have no hope in store,
When thus parted, parted,
  Never to meet more.

So farewell, sweet star,
  Eclipsed in clouds from me —
Till death, tho' sundered far,
  I'll think — I'll dream of thee!

A PLEDGE THAT WAS BROKEN.

THIS irrevocable and solemn vow
  I pledge the man that's near me now;
No other man shall taste nor touch
These lips which he has pressed so much;
No other man shall find the way
That he has found and ever may;
I will be true as love to him
While waters run and fishes swim;
No other man my love shall know,
While flowers shall bloom and grasses grow.
My soul, my body here I give
To be his own while we shall live,
And no temptation, bribe nor power,
Shall break the pledges made this hour;
I call upon my God above
To witness here my plighted love,
Signed in our blood commingled, writ,
Here read my name in proof of it!
And false if ever I shall be,
May God in death abandon me!

WHEN PASSION DIES.

O LET me die when passion dies,
  When summer birds and summer flowers,
And woman's lip and woman's eyes
  Lose their bewitching powers.

When love's mad raptures lose their taste,
  And skies and suns no more are bright,
And sweetness near me goes to waste
  For want of appetite.

Yes, when my blood shall cease to burn
  With passion that inspires so much,
Or, when love's golden apples turn
  To ashes at my touch;

And when dear woman's dulcet breath
  No more shall wake my slumbering muse,
Then let me go and lie with death,—
  There's nothing more to lose!

TONES THAT LINGER.

TO MISS LULA L——D.

AND it was only yesternight,
    I saw the jeweled fingers play,
Whose movements in their mystic flight,
  Flung sweetness every way.
O lily hands—O taper fingers!
O music that so sweetly lingers!—

So sweetly lingers in the brain,
  Like sunny dreams in summer time,
That ravish yet impinge on pain,
  And perish in their prime!—
Like rose-tipped pleasure's fading fringes,
Or ecstacy's expiring twinges.

O maiden with the regal brow!
  O maiden with the queenly air!
Your music haunts my spirit now,
  I hear it everywhere, ·
As soft and sweet as vesper chimes,
Or loves, or half remembered rhymes!

And is that brief sweet vision o'er?
  Is memory all that may remain?
And may I hear on earth no more
  That love enwoven strain?
Whose echoes come with cadence clear,
And memories sad, yet sweet and dear!

THE OHIO RIVER.

FLOW on—flow on—thou mute and mighty river!
    Flow on in silent and unmurmuring majesty,
Past farms, and towns, and cities, till thou pour'st
All thy accumulated waters in the boiling,
Eddying, heaving, headlong Mississippi.
Thus thou hast rolled unknown, unnumbered ages,
Not deigning in thy vast magnificence
To note by mark intelligible to man,
The fate of nations or the flight of years.
In vain doth man stretch forth his feeble hand
To lift the veil that hides thy history;
In vain doth his weak intellect essay

To fathom the past ages, and to fix
The date of thy proud birth. Tho' he can trace
Thee to thy mountain origin, and note
Down in his vain vocabulary, his names
For thy ten thousand tributaries.
Thou bear'st no mark upon thy silent tide,
Nor on thy bordering bluffs, nor fertile plains,
That gives the numbers, insignificance, or greatness
Of that lost race of men, who, years agone,
Sent forth their shouts o'er thy meandering waves —
What name they gave to thee, or who they were,
Or where they lived, or how, and when they died,
Are all unknown to us. No tree nor stone bears aught
That gives a clew to their identity.
All that we know is that thy bordering plains
Were once inhabited by a race of men,
Unknown alike to history and tradition;
Their crumbling walls, and ruined forts bear proof
That they were used to warfare and to strife.
Hast thou no diadem beneath thy waves?
No sculptured marble, weapon of defense,
Or implement of husbandry or art,
On which is mark'd in hieroglyphics rude —
The rise, the fall, the fate of this lost people?
Didst thou arise and spread thy mighty waves
From hill to hill, and swallow up this race,
With all their works and deeds, and every trace
And clew and vestige of their history,
Bearing them on thy billows to the sea?
If thou wouldst deign to hold converse with man,
How many a tearful tale couldst thou unfold,
Of that lost race of men, whose very name
Is buried in the impenetrable gloom
Of bygone ages! Many a legend lost
Couldst thou bring vividly before the view,
Even of more recent times, and since thy banks
And bordering plains have been explored and claimed
By men professing to be civilized.
Re-echoing o'er thy waves long years ago,
Went the shrill battle-cry, the startling yell
Of the wild savage and untutored Indian;
And from thy shady banks went up to heaven,
The curling smoke of his calm council-fires;
And mirrored in thy waves how oft have been
The frightful forms of furious, fiendish men,
Painted for war, and bent on deeds of blood!
How oft hast thou beheld the horrid din
Of the rude war dance and the hellish glee
Enacted round the broiling, shrieking victim!
Among the giant trees that shade thy banks,
Ofttimes have met fierce foemen face to face,
When strife, and strength, and stratagem were used
By the red warriors and their pale-faced foes.
Like lightning flew the messengers of death
From the unerring rifle, through the brains
And bounding hearts of brave belligerents!
Here dying heroes heeded not the knells
From ringing rifles, as their warm blood flowed

In bubbling jets upon the virgin soil;
While scalps were rudely, fiercely torn alike
From dead, and dying, and disabled men;
But time has changed the scenes upon thy banks;
The trees that shaded them have been cut down;
Luxuriant crops are growing in their stead;
The red man's battle-cry is heard no more;
Thy fertile plains form many a happy home
For the oppressed and poor of every clime.
On either side thy banks do mark the bounds
Of sister states throughout thy tortuous length;
Thy winding current is a broad highway,
A liquid road for men of every nation.
And bustling cities stand upon thy banks,
While thousand towns are ranged on either side,
Whose spires and domes are glittering in the sun,
While countless villages bedeck thy plains;
Ten thousand crafts are floating down thy waves,
Freighted with the rich products of thy soil;
And countless steamers buffet with thy billows,
Making thy banks resound with their shrill voices.

TO MAGGIE.

SWEET Maiden, I have sent thee here,
    Some lines, 'midst hope and doubt and fear;
Forgive this rashness; O forgive;
Let me in thy sweet memory live;
And fancy here, where all is white,
The burning words I dare not write,
A heart that's loved too long in vain;
A heart inured and schooled to pain,
That heart brings here, on love's quick wings,
Its purest, holiest offerings —
On love's quick wings — the electric fire
That fills the soul with mad desire,
More sudden than the lightning's flash,
And makes the pen so wildly rash;
And makes the heart so madly beat
For lashes and for lips so sweet! —
And eyes — O heaven! — where concentrate
The spells that rule so many a fate!

LOVE AT FIRST SIGHT.

TO KATE.

DO you remember how it came? —
    The shot, the flash, the fire, the flame —
The thrilling, killing, quivering dart,
That made my blood stand still, then start,
With crushing, welling, swelling whirl,
Straight through my heart? — one glance, my girl —

One accidental loving look,
Like shock of Galvanism, shook
And stirred emotions broad and deep,
Which till that moment lay asleep! —
A flash of most delicious flame
With thy first glance unbidden came;
A sudden flash of soul-lit fire,
Like God's quick breath upon the wire,
Swept o'er my pulses and heart-strings
With new and novel ravishings;
I was transformed — I saw new moons,
And clustering stars in rich festoons;
About thy brows wild roses clung,
Enchantment from thine eye-lids sprung.
The groves were full of gaudy birds,
And vocal with their wooing words;
Nude Cupids capered in mid air,
I heard new music everywhere:
The world was suddenly, strangely bright;
And this was love — "Love at First Sight!"

LINES TO A ROMPING MISS.

GO to now, let me twine my arm
    About thy neck of snow!
I swear it will not do thee harm
    To grant a kiss or so.
Nay, nay; start not — I would not wrong
    One jetty curl of thine;
I rob but to enrich my song;
    The melody is thine.

Bewitching tease, it is not right
    To flirt in fun so much,
And then to look as black as night
    At every earnest touch.
Nay, nay, sweet lady, frown not thus
    At my rude, humble suit;
Young Love is smiling now on us,
    And how can I be mute?

And still I feel, on further thought,
    Thou'lt yield the point to me —
Canst thou be wedded, won, or bought? —
    Or wilt elope with me?
The words of caution which grandmas
    Force down the maiden's throat,
Teach her to swerve from Nature's laws;
    Then fling them all afloat,

And listen to the tales of love
    I fain would teach thee now —
Eve's daughter art thou not, my dove?
    There's none more fair than thou;
But Eve was frail — all girls are frail —
    It is of heavenly birth:
If female frailty were to fail,
    Where were the joys of earth?

There! there!—'twas but a stolen kiss —
Thou wilt not miss it much —
'Twas fraught—like this, and this, and this —
With Love's electric touch.
Enough — we'll feast not on thy shame,
Thou sweet, ungenerous wench,
Who fan'st with roguish feats the flame
Thou com'st with ice to quench.

AN EDITOR WHO WANTED OFFICE.

A TRAGEDY IN THREE ACTS.

ACT I.

SCENE.— *A bed-chamber. Time, noon.* FRYSINGER *in bed. Enter* FRAU, *who takes him by the heels.*

Frau. Time long ago. Up, sluggard, up and at 'em!
The candidates do scour the country round:
The spooks and sprites, and goblins of the damned,
Do scurry o'er the knobs — and Uncle Jim
Hath written forty yards of thin hog-wash
To circumvent and blast you in convention.

Fry. My God! has the convention day arrived,
And found me unsupported? Stand you aside;
I'll dress and join the rabble on the square,
And urge my Yankee birth and German accent
As reasons for promotion; while the Hoosiers,
The natives, born in cribs and open fields,
Who sigh for office, must give way and yield
To me the nomination.

ACT II.

SCENE.—*The same room and bed.* FRAU *feeding* FRYSINGER *cabbage soup with a teaspoon.*

Fry. O, feed me freely! I am faint — is't true
That the convention's over, and I defeat?

Frau. It is too true! Not only art defeat,
But the slim vote did couple aggravation
To downright injury and direct insult!

Fry. Put on my pants, give me my pen! I will
Write thirty·columns now. I'll no more Democrat.
Now, bolters, I am with you.

ACT III.

A SPIRITUAL SEANCE.

SCENE.— *A room in Brownstown.* MRS. KIEGWIN *seated at a table. Enter* BARR, GEORGE MURPHY *and* PUGGAWAUGAN.*

Pugg. Is the spirit of William Frysinger present?
Spirit of Fry. Yaw.
Pugg. Are you happy?
Spirit of Fry. Nicht.
Geo. M. You died so sudden that 'tis thought, dear Fry,
You suicided — tell us, is it so?

* Spiritualists.

Spirit of Fry. Nicht.

Barr. Speak, noble Fry, and tell me, if you can,
If foul means were employed to cut you off,
In the proud hour when your vast intellect
Had beaten down the foes of spirit-rappers;
Was't ratsbane in your beer? or cursed leaves
Of henbenon or hemlock in your pipe?

Pugg. O, speak; give us a sign.

Spirit of Fry. I did ask office and I was refused —
I was consumed with longing to be auditor,
When the malignant *Times*, with ridicule
Did so besmirch me that the Democrats
Did shout with laughter at my near approach;
And I became a buffoon, and the butt
For every idiot's jest; and the small dogs
Did hoist the leg and use me for a post.

Pugg. Alas, poor Fry!

Spirit of Fry. Then I withdrew and asked if I might keep
The office of trustee another term;
For I had made a good thing from that office,
By indirections and great stringing out
Of legal ads, but more by slipping in
Superfluous ones and charging up the score,
And I did promise, should I be elect,
To keep the schools six months in every year,
To make a bridge o'er every running stream,
And put the highways in first-class condition;
With many other flowery promises,
To win and soften the rough Democrats;
But all was useless; the fell Abe McCormick
And hellish Adam Heller did conspire,
And raise the devil and the Dutch against me;
And I did fall so hard that my great heart
Burst ope and here I am.

Barr. Art in the bad place, Fry?

Spirit of Fry. Yaw, yaw; but Democrats are plenty here
Who are a credit to the cursed crew
That run the late convention.

THE GIRL THAT TOOK MY HEART AWAY.

TO MISS H. O.

THE heart should have its sentries out
  Or it may perish by surprise,
When lovely woman is about,
  Of fatal glances from her eyes;
And even if those orbs are closed
  There's danger, and at any hour
The heart may fall that is exposed
  To any form of female power!

And thus my heart, unguarded, late
  Was tak'n almost without attack,
And she who took it did not wait
  To see if I would beg it back!

I was beset by cruel curls,
    And charms no pencil can portray,
Owned by the sweetest of sweet girls —
    The girl that took my heart away!

O'er my quick nerves her glances sped
    As lightning speeds o'er webs of wire,
Lighting the soul whence light had fled
    With gleams of love's galvanic fire.
And now, like some poor captive bird,
    My soul is fluttering to be gone
Away, away to her whose word
    And smile it fain would feed upon.

O, there is language in those lids,
    And soft words trembling in those eyes,
And witchcraft in that smile that bids
    A thousand fond emotions rise!
And as I love the stars that shine,
    Or sweet flowers in another's vase,
So may I thee, nor claim as mine
    The treasures of that angel face!

O COME TO ME IN DREAMS!

TO MAGGIE.

"O COME to me again in dreams!"
        Sighed she for whom I'm pining, weeping;
"Last night while slumbering (the moonbeams
    Were on my pillow sweetly sleeping)
Your worshiped form stood by my bed,
    The soft light on your pale brow shone,
And soon I thought you lay your head
    Upon the pillow with my own.

"I felt your warm breath on my brow,
    Your burning kisses on my lips,
While rapture's sigh and passion's vow
    Hid reason in love's charmed eclipse.
I felt your heart against my side,
    And I could count each wild, mad beat
As mine tumultuously replied
    In unison divinely sweet.

"Your fingers strayed among the tresses
    Upon my shoulders unconfin'd,
And though half dreading your caresses,
    My arms about your neck were twin'd.
I could not speak — what could I say? —
    You stifled every thought that sprung,
And kissed each murmured word away
    While yet 'twas trembling on my tongue.

"Thus, without power to speak or move,
    My blood fired with celestial flame,
I lay entranc'd, while rapturous love
    Thrilled every fibre of my frame.

O, such caresses — such wild kisses! —
　They were too much for womankind!
And racked with maddening, burning blisses
　I woke! — but, heaven, what did I find?"

Thus sighed my dear, voluptuous maid,
　Quivering with passion as she spoke —
Convulsed with joy, yet half afraid —
　For I was with her when she woke!

TO LULIE.

THOU radiant sunbeam of the home
　　Too dark without thy cheery light,—
Thou treasure guarded as the gnome
　Guards treasures hidden from the sight,—
Now vanished like a sun-lit cloud —
Wherefore one aching brow is bowed.

A gushing, bubbling fount whereof
　A soul was drinking to excess,
Until, unknowingly a gnoff,
　It woke to rayless wretchedness —
Finding its treasure a bright gem
Set in another's diadem.

True copy of thy father's self,
　Perfected in a woman's form —
A brilliant, cheery, airy elf—
　With heart so true — with love so warm —
Impassioned, gentle, serious, wild —
Pride of thy papa's heart, fair child.

Fair reproduction of thy pa,
　In feeling, feature and in fire,—
With more than his good parts — each flaw
　And imperfection of thy sire,
Softened with woman's sanctity,
Becomes a special grace in thee.

LINES WRITTEN IN A STRAY ALBUM.

TO-DAY, while on thy merry rounds
　　Amongst the gay, the fair, the free,
My lonely sanctum thou hast found,
　And what wouldst thou, fair book, of me?

Wert thou by thy fair owner sent?
　Or without leave art thou astray?
Is it design or accident
　That brings thee to me here to-day?

Thou mute thrice-welcome messenger,
　Bringst thou not hope to sweeten grief,
Traced here in burning words by her,
　All viewless on some snowy leaf?

O, such I've fancied is the fact,
  And as I've turned thy pages o'er,
My eager vision have I racked
  Some hidden sentence to explore.

But all in vain — I have not found
  One word to tell my wounded heart
That she who doth inflict the wound
  Will give one balm to sooth its smart.

So, book, begone! — go home to her
  Whom no one sees but to adore,
And leave her silent worshiper
  Still wretched as he was before.

NOT IN THE LIGHT.

NOT in the light
  Of life's bright morn,
But in death's night
  Doth Fame adorn
The minstrel's brow:
  In life scarce named,
  In death how famed!
Thus, ever thus — somehow
  The sunshine men
  Prize only when
Earth lies eclipsed in cloud:
  Thus without thought
  Men pass for naught
Whom Genius hath endowed:
  And immortality is brought
To Genius in its shroud.
  The heart grows old,
  And fervor cold;
Youth's — manhood's vigor wasted
  In vain pursuit
  Of tempting fruit
Never, never to be tasted!

AN INVOCATION.

APPEAR, appear, appear, appear,
  If there be a spirit near;
Goblin, grimalkin, and sprite,
I am here alone to-night;
Spirits of the damned or blest
Come and do your worst or best.
If you have existence now
Indicate the fact somehow;
If you hear this voice of mine
Give, O give a sound or sign,
YOU who did impoverish thought
To enrich the works you wrought,

Leaving to the after bard
Only what you did discard,
Have you status still in space?
Then come to me face to face,
Spirit of Shakespeare! and in fire
Sweep one chime upon my lyre·
Come in lightning or in cloud,
As in life or in thy shroud.
If there be a soul that's fled
Can come to us from the dead,
Bard of Avon, it is thine,
Then appear, appear to mine —
To some sense of mine — to sight;
Come in blessing or in blight;
Or if not so manifest,
Grant, O grant me this request:
If thou canst impart the flame,
Such as at thy bidding came
To thy giant intellect,
Flashing from the gods direct,
O, return it to the earth,
That poesy may have new birth.

SHED NOT A TEAR.

LET not a tear of grief be shed
  When I lay in my winding sheet;
But let my coffin be of lead,
  And filled with every perfume sweet.

Exclude from me the atmosphere,
  And water, that still wooes decay;
I would not perish! — O, I fear
  The worm that eats the flesh away!

I dread the worm! — its loathsome trail! —
  I fear the putrefactive force;
I fear preserving means will fail
  Without dismemberment — divorce

Of watery organs from their seats —
  Evisceration! — dreadful word!
As frightful as the worm that eats! —
  Yet to fear either is absurd.

My heart to her who loves me best,
  My brain to him most like to me;
And to forgetfulness the rest.—
  (The soul? — to immortality?)

I do not fear to be forgot,
  I thirst not for posthumous fame;
But curse the world that lets me rot,
  Even tho' it eternize my name.

Therefore let me be mummified;
   If air and water are withdrawn,
And membranes, flesh and sinews dried,
   Decay has naught to feed upon.

But O, for all your souls are worth,
   I charge you bury not my corse!
If I am covered — clogged with earth,
   I'll haunt you if I can — or worse!

But pack me in preserving salt,
   And let me rest above the ground,
Walled in a strong, cemented vault,
   Upon some lofty mount or mound,

Where children and the village maids
   May climb to me amidst green trees
And where the fairies, gnomes and naiads
   May hold their moonlight revelries.

MEMORY.

MY MOTHER.

IS it with joy or grief that we remember
   The sunny spring-time of our childish glee? —
The pangs, the tears of boyhood's bleak December?
   For children have their woes as well as we.
O Mother dear, the first and earliest ember
   That love lit in my bosom glowed for thee —
Glows on through life, and the last vale I cross
   I'll load with lamentations o'er thy loss.

My mother's love! gone ere it was regarded:
   O memory of her care and her caresses
And watchfulness! — I wonder if rewarded?
   Unconscious carelessness my heart confesses.
O youth! short-sighted — selfish, and how sordid!
   Regret! — it dampens, deepens, and depresses.
Erst doting much, *now* if I had thee here
   How would I dote upon thee, Mother dear!

Spoke harshly to thee? — O. I may have done it!
   Put burthens on thee thou shouldst not have borne?
Embraced some error when thou bad'st me shun it?
   Was willful, thou being wearied, weak and worn?
Lost thy approval when I might have won it? —
   O Mother, did I much to make thee mourn?
Not much, perhaps, but conscience will recall
The ghosts of childish errors, grimed in gall.

O Memory, come, may'st thou not be a curse?
   Bring'st thou not more of blight, of gloom, than gladness?
Deprived of thee, were our condition worse?
   Dost thou not seem the single source of sadness?
To the racked brain dost thou not oft rehearse
   Tales of the past till it is forced to madness?

Was't thy weird work that the old man beguiled
Till he became the second time a child?

No cutting conscience were it not for thee;
    No harrowing hell pent up within the breast;
The past a blank — the present — future free
    From the remorse that wrings with its unrest:
Nor the unreal made reality
    By making yesterday's to-morrow's test:
To-day's enjoyment — rapture — O, how great
Could we forget, and not anticipate!

O Memory! mousing miser! — crack, O brain!
    And heart, heave with emotions till you break!
Weep eyes! — well up, O tears, until you drain
    The fount of sorrow! — sleep, your farewell take!
O earth, drape you in mourning! — there remain
    Naught but remembrance! — brain and bosom ache! —
The echoes of my mother's voice still ringing,
Surcharged with sadness and but sorrow bringing!

THE LITTLE ONE THAT DIED.

TO ARABELLA.

THERE was a little trembling vine,
    In early life, that threw
Its tendrils round this heart of mine,
    For from my heart it grew.

It put its little petals forth:
    My world was in its sphere:
To me more than my life 'twas worth,
    And every treasure here.

But it was struck with early blight,
    Its blossoms ceased to blow:
It shrunk, it withered from my sight,
    So many years ago!

And still for it my spirit pines,
    And vainly I have tried
To write some tender little lines
    To the little one that died.

WHERE IS THE STAR?

'TIS true I came upon thee late,
    I have no reason to repine;
Another's by decree of fate,
    By fortune mine, or partly mine:

Mine only when he is away,
    And then in rapture's very height
I weep that blisses mine to-day
    Were his, perhaps, but yesternight.

The charms now mine are his as much;
  The beauties that so craze my brain,
Are subject to his loathsome touch —
  Have been so oft — will be again.

O wormwood! — bitterness! — O gall!
  O cursed ties that shackle thee!
With less than half, yet wanting all,
  My soul is wrung with agony.

Damnation! — if there be a hell,
  With half of heaven, I have it here;
Where is the star whose influence fell
  Disruptures thus my atmosphere?